The Hit
and
The Marksman

The Hit
and
The Marksman

Brian Garfield

Five Star • Waterville, Maine

First Edition
First Printing: November 2003

Published in 2003 in conjunction with Tekno Books and Ed Gorman.

Set in 11 pt. Plantin.

Printed in the United States on permanent paper.

Library of Congress Cataloging-in-Publication Data

Garfield, Brian, 1939–
    The hit ; and, The marksman / Brian Garfield.—1st ed.
        p. cm.
    ISBN 0-7862-4322-8 (hc : alk. paper)
    1. Mafia—Fiction. I. Garfield, Brian, 1939–
Marksman. II. Title: Marksman. III. Title.
PS3557.A715H58 2003
    813'.54—dc22
                                            2003049308

Table of Contents

The Hit

Chapter One

The noon sun beat down on the road, on me, on the dry desert foothills. The road was narrow blacktop, snaking down by switchbacks toward the plain and the city. In the Jeep I was doing only twenty-five but the wind had a searing, abrasive edge against my face.

I was half stunned with fear: I had just left a meeting at which sentence had been passed on me. You're not wearing our silks, Crane. Nobody cares what happens to you and the woman. Forty-eight hours to deliver or die.

My numb brain was making images of Joanne when I looked in the rear-view mirror and saw the chrome teeth of a big station wagon bearing down on me from behind. I had been too preoccupied with my own impending execution to notice it before; no telling how long it had been there. He was riding my tail with reckless arrogance; the dusty grille of the car seemed ready to take a bite out of the Jeep. He was a tailgating imbecile, driving with suicidal aggressiveness, not more than ten feet behind my bumper. All the rage and frustration of the past bouts climaxed in my gut; out of sheer malice, I hit the brakes—hard.

The station wagon swerved; I heard the indignant panic-stricken yelp of horn and then the big car wobbled past, just clearing me, with an arch swish of skidding rubber.

Instead of thundering away, the station wagon pulled to the curb. His brake lights dashed angry red and the wagon's tail went up in the air. It stopped short, the door swung open, and the driver got out.

The road was too narrow to get by him. I pitched to a stop. Suddenly I wanted this stupid, meaningless fight with a total stranger; I felt like a fight, I wanted to kill the son of a bitch.

He was a good-sized man about my age, fair hair and a round boyish face. He looked scared: he wore the expression of a man who was about to burst into tears.

I climbed down from the Jeep. That was when I saw the .32 automatic in his fist, hanging at arm's length. I stopped, bolt still.

He said, "You're Simon Crane."

It wasn't till then that I recognized him. He might as well have said, You're the bastard that's been banging my wife.

He lifted the gun. I had an impulse to burst out in hysterical laughter.

I said, "Okay, Mike."

Mike Farrell's mouth worked; his eyes weren't tracking well. He was as close to the thin borderline of madness as I was. He stood there, jaw working, no sound coming out.

I said, "You must have been staked out back there. This couldn't be coincidence—you followed me down from up there."

"Sure." He got it out between his teeth.

"What for? To shoot me?"

He shook his head. "The gun's just insurance." He talked without moving his lips. Ex-cons are easy to spot. They talk in monotones; their body movements are slow and careful, their gestures muffled, expressions immobile, eye movements restricted. Mike had all the earmarks. His face, rig-

idly composed now, was betrayed by the restless, terrified
eyes.

I said, "Insurance for what?"

"Turn around and lean on your hands."

I glanced at his gun and obeyed, flattening my palms
against the hot hood of the Jeep; I had frisked enough of
them myself to know how it was done. I was wearing Levi's
and a yellow shirt; there weren't many places I could conceal a gun. He went over me nervously and stepped back
when he was satisfied I wasn't armed. It was the second
time today I'd been frisked.

"You can turn around."

I straightened and turned. Sweat dripped from my forehead into my eyes. Mike Farrell said, "I got to talk to you.
Will you listen?"

Will a dollar buy ten dimes? Mike was the only chance I
had to get out from under the guillotine.

What I said was, "You're holding the gun."

He kept it pointed straight at me while he backed up to
the open door of the station wagon. He took out a handkerchief and wiped the steering wheel, controls, door handles,
ashtray; swung the door shut with his hip and came back to
me. He walked around to the passenger side of the Jeep and
got in.

"Come on. You drive."

"What about your car?"

"I can't use it any more—they can trace it to me. Come
on, Crane, I need to get under cover."

I got in. "Where to?"

"Just drive. I'll tell you where to turn."

We drove down the narrow snake of a road into the sub-
urbs, hit an avenue and turned toward the city. He refused
to talk except to bark directions at me now and then. He

had the gun down at his side where outsiders couldn't see it, but the hammer was back and I had no chance to jump him. Driving under the blistering sun, I was remembering the things Joanne had told me about Mike—that he was terrified but harmless. I wasn't sure she was right. Prison changed a man's attitudes toward a lot of things: I had seen enough of them, after they came out. For the weaker ones things had narrowed down to a habitual fight for survival— just staying alive in that cage of hardened cons, making sure nobody stuck a knife between your ribs. It could be like that with Mike: the residue of paranoia, hanging on like prison pallor. Or it could be guilt and the fear of discovery, if he'd done the hit.

Somebody had done the hit, that was clear enough. I had forty-eight hours to find out who. If I didn't produce I was dead, and so was Joanne—and Mike was the only lead we had.

He told me where to turn. I went through adobe gateposts into a district known as Las Palmas, a onetime high priced residential neighborhood built in the late twenties by market speculators and bootleggers. At the time it had been a suburb, five miles outside the city; by now urban cancer had pushed the city limits ten miles beyond, and Las Palmas squatted forlorn in a sea of cheap stucco development shacks. The wealthy types had moved far up into the foothills, whence Mike and I had just come; half the huge white elephants in Las Palmas were deserted, boarded up— nobody had a use for houses with servants' quarters any more. It was a good place to hide out.

It was a little cooler under the heavy trees that lined the curved roads. We bumped across potholes in the narrow lanes and went past one abandoned mansion being used as a pad by a troop of hippies; a dozen of them sprawled on the weedy lawn with guitars and joy sticks. Mike pointed out turnings and we picked a clumsy route through places hardly wide enough for the Jeep, swung past a forbidding oleander hedge nine feet high and opaque as a brick wall, and suddenly Mike said, "Hold it."

I braked to a stop.

"Back up and turn in there."

I did so, driving into a chuckholed gravel path that cut through the oleanders.

"Park it here."

We were hidden from the street. He showed his gun and waved me up the narrow broken-flagstone walk toward the house. Once it had been magnificent. The roof was shingled with red half-pipe tiles, chipped and busted. The veranda had a gallery of Moorish arches, overgrown with brush and cactus. An empty oval swimming pool in the yard, rimmed with Mexican porcelains, was full of dead leaves and sand.

An Air Force jet went over with a sound like a long piece of canvas being ripped. Mike walked by me and gestured with his gun. I stepped over the broken glass on the porch and followed him inside, noticing that the warped chipped-paint door scraped across the floor when he pushed, leaving part-circle scratches where it dragged sharp bits of sand and glass across the concrete.

He backed in, holding the gun on me, looked around quickly and beckoned. The airless room was hot, thick with heavy body sweat. Mike, or somebody else, had spent some time in the place recently.

I said, "What happened to Aiello, Mike?"

"I think I'll ask the questions. Come in here."

I walked in. He made the mistake of letting me get too close, and I went for him.

I grabbed his wrist, got the left hand when he shot it up,

and bore down hard. The gun was pointed at the ground and I held his right hand that way; I twisted, grinding the grip on both his wrists, forcing him to his knees. He wouldn't let go. He made no sound; his breathing was quick and shallow, his eyes very large, his teeth grinding.

Abruptly I let go his left hand and batted across to the gun, wrenching it away. Curiously, he had removed his finger from the trigger, so it didn't go off when I yanked. It wouldn't have hit anything but the floor anyway; maybe he preferred to take a chance on me rather than run the risk of attracting attention with the noise.

He was on his knees, twisted down. I put my shoe in his chest and shoved. He went backward onto the stone floor. His head hit back with a blunt noise.

I reversed the gun in my grasp. The crack on the head hadn't completely knocked him out but he was dazed, stunned; he would be limp and useless for a while. I peeled back one eyelid to make sure there was no concussion. He made little grunting noises with each breath.

There wasn't much furniture—an old couch, a broken table, a lawn chair. An ancient refrigerator stood by one wall, its door crumpled and bent open on the hinges. I got him up and carried him over to the couch and put him down. There wouldn't be any water in the place anyway; all I could do was make sure the skin wasn't broken. Then I went back toward the door, where the air was better. I kept his gun in my fist.

From the open door I could hear only cactus wrens and robins and an occasional airplane; none of the city sounds reached this backwater neighborhood. For a moment faint voices reached me and I tensed before I realized what it was—the hippies we had passed, coming to me on the wind. I listened to their voices and guitars, soft-singing their *cris de coeur* of alienation in the heat, and turned to have another look at Mike. His eyes were closed; he breathed evenly. Haggard and sallow, he looked like a weak youth grown prematurely old. He was thirty, perhaps a bit older, but he appeared both younger and more ancient than that.

He would come around but it would take time. Jumpy and irritable, I felt his forehead and then settled down to wait in the lawn chair. Until I talked with him I wouldn't know how this nightmare was going to end. It was possible all of us would be dead soon—Mike and Joanne and me. I sat watching him, remembering how this had begun, this morning, just a few hours ago.

The phone had rung. It had lifted me from a wallowing sleep; it rang three times before I shook off the fragments of a paranoid dream and groped for the receiver.

"Simon? Were you asleep?"

Shock of recognition: it was Joanne. Her voice, which I hadn't heard in months, made me instantly defensive: "I still am."

She spoke before I could get the phone away from my ear. "Please don't hang up." She sounded taut—agitated, close to the edge.

"What is it?"

I heard her breathing; after a moment, during which she seemed to pull herself together with an effort of will, she said, "No. You're too groggy to listen. Wake yourself up— I'll hold on."

I grunted, put the receiver on the bed, got up and padded to the window. Slits of white light chiseled past the edges of the doubled Army blanket I used for a drape. I pulled it aside and blinked away the morning blaze that came in hard off the desert hills.

It took time before I could keep my eyes open without squinting. The blaze of lemon sunlight struck the window obliquely. Particles of mica and pyrites in the earth made the hills shimmer where they fell away toward the city, eight miles and two thousand feet below. The mountain-ringed city sprawled wide and flat, a pale checkerboard of shopping centers, cardboard houses, Laundromats, drive-in movies. The old quarter, Mexican adobe, was distinguished by heavy trees, green-gray in the distance. River and railroad sliced through on a bias, one pouring down from piney mountains to the northeast, the other rolling through from Texas to California.

It was a big town, dusty and low to the ground, and very, very hot. Two hundred thousand predigested people in three hundred square miles of standardized houses, cars, supermarkets and bowling alleys.

I blinked and stood grinding knuckles into my eye sockets, wishing I had never had a phone installed. The image through the window undulated in hazy waves, heat-smog over the city. Beyond, toward Texas and Mexico, the foothills were studded with dots of creosote, cactus, creek-bank cottonwoods; farther away the high ranges loomed, dark timber peaks slashed by faces of white rock that reflected the sun like fields of snow. The sky, dusty at the horizon, deepened into cobalt clarity overhead.

By the time I could look that high without squinting, I was awake. I turned back from the window.

The bed was rumpled from alcoholic sleep. I picked up the phone and glanced at the clock—it was almost nine. "Okay. Good morning."

"That's better. Are you all right, Simon?"

"Hung over some."

Joanne said in her husky, practical voice, "I'd be flat-

16

tered if I thought you were still tying one on because of me."

Six months ago, I thought, she would have added a comma and "darling." Now it was just a polite question, edged with remote concern and crowded by her obvious agitation. I had an image of her face, framed tight by short dark hair. Acidly resentful, I said, "I'm surprised they let you get near a phone. Where are you?"

"In a phone booth on Corral Drive. Simon, I have to see you—but now I think it would be better not to talk about it on the phone. Something's happened at—at the place where I work."

"I'm not having any, Joanne—I'm keeping out of it."

"I don't know if you can." She did sound terribly subdued. "You may already be involved. Look, if it was just something personal—do you honestly think after what we went through last winter that I'd come running to you to hold my hand? Simon, if I could think of another soul on earth—God knows I don't want to impose on you, but there just isn't anyone else. I'm in trouble, I need help."

"What is it, then?"

She said, almost in a whisper, "I'm shaking like a leaf."

"Trouble with the organization?" I said stupidly.

"Trouble isn't the word for it. Simon, you used to be a policeman, you'd know what to—"

"I told you," I said dully, "I don't intend to get within a mile of the cops or your boy friends, either one."

"I can't talk on the phone," she said, sounding drained. "Please, Simon."

I closed my eyes. "Suit yourself. I'll be here."

When she hung up I sat on the side of the bed with my eyes shut, pinching the bridge of my nose. After a stretch of time I batted into the bathroom to shower and shave and scrape thickness off my teeth. The face in the mirror was weathered more square than long, not remarkable. A textured face that took a dark tan and kept it; scarred and busted here and there because I was once a cop, subscribing to the idea of justice before realities had canceled my subscription.

They had retired me compulsorily on half pension "due to 20 percent incapacitation from bullet injury incurred in line of duty." Encysted in my right thigh, under the crowfoot scars, were the fragments of two .357 bullets, special homemade softnoses that had splintered on impact. Now and then a twinge of sciatica lanced through the leg, but I was hardly among the walking wounded; the disability was more like .02 percent than 20—a hardly perceptible limp on damp days. It had been an excuse, not a reason, for them to get me off the force.

The slugs had been put in me by a cop named Joe Cutter, by mistake—he said—one night when we had split up to come at a team of burglars from opposite ends of a hardware store. Cutter had a zealot's pride in his .357 Magnum hand cannon. He had paid for it himself. He spent evenings in his soldier-tidy antiseptic apartment devising sophisticated recipes for homebrewed ammunition.

My retirement, which I had not fought, had been a separation without sorrow. They probably still had a dossier on me in the Inactive file: Simon Crane, 30, ht 6 ft 2 in, wt 185, eyes gray, hair black, unmarried, parents deceased. City grade and high schools, state university—bachelor's in History, minor in Journalism, letters in tennis and in baseball the two years we'd gone to the College World Series at Omaha. University ROTC, two years an Army Intelligence lieutenant. Then three years a newspaper reporter while I decided what I really wanted to do with my life, to justify my existence. Finally, with zeal to the police force. Rookie to patrolman to detective 2/G—and back to patrolman. I had bucked too many bagmen.

There were a few others like me. Cops who cared about one or two other things besides grease and the pension you got after twenty years on the force. Cops who believed in the notion that the law was a fine precision mechanism designed to right wrongs. They learned. Some stuck it out, trying to reform from the inside; some quit, joined the FBI, became juvenile probation officers or set up their own private detective agencies; some, like me, forsook the rat race. They all quit for the same reason: they ran up against the organization. You got evidence on a hood and it looked ironclad and then the hood's protectors stepped in: the organization's battery of attorneys marched into the courtroom, the organization's bagmen got to the judge. One honest cop's testimony against the paid perjury of half a dozen hired witnesses—where could you find legitimate citizens to testify in Mafia cases? Good citizens didn't know anything about the organization's operations; how could they testify? If you had a corroborative witness, he was likely to be another hood, and the organization's attorneys didn't mind ruining his reputation to get the client off. Then it went to the jury—what Darrow called "twelve men of average ignorance"—and even if you got past that obstacle, got past all the obstacles of appeals and delays, achieved the nirvana of a conviction—even then you ended up with a judge who passed a sentence of fifteen weekends in the House of Detention on the hood, who laughed at you when he walked out of the courtroom. The public bought the mockery with the "It's God's will" sophistry of small minds; the legal system had been satisfied because the system thinks a lot about the rules of the game but never asks whether the game itself has any meaning.

In the end it became just another entry in a file some-place. You brought them in and they went right out again through the revolving door. You came to loathe the organization, and that kind of deep hate was a fervor that got stronger with time and frustration; there was nothing to do, in the end, except quit. To preserve whatever was left of sanity.

When I left the force, feeling as if I had lived through it merely because I happened not to have died from Cutter's .357 fusillade, I considered going to work as a private oper-ative—one of those eyes who investigate husbands who play golf when it rains. I couldn't work up any enthusiasm for the idea, or for going back to newspapering, a jungle of scrambled copy in which every edition ought to have eight-column banners on the front page: "ENTIRE CONTENTS FICTION."

When I tried to explain it all to Joanne, she had told me my point of view was sophomoric and misanthropic. Maybe so. For six months I edited a slick regional monthly that sandwiched gorgeous color photos of southwestern scenery between articles that tried to justify the Paleolithic right-wing notions of the rich ranchers who owned the magazine. The views weren't mine but the salary was high. I thought, at first, money would make a difference.

But after a while I sickened of the idea of spending money I didn't have to buy things I didn't need to impress people I didn't like. That was when I gave up the job, and job-hunting, and took my indefinite sabbatical. I moved out of my downtown, semi-detached, split-level, modern, air-conditioned bungalow garden court apartment (with pool privileges), and bought the old rock fort in the hills with the last of my severance pay.

It came cheap; nobody wanted an ugly stone house so far off the main-traveled roads. No one seemed to know who had built it, or when. It was old, squatting sunblasted and craggy on the desert hill, with its own well and its six rooms, or seven depending on your method of counting, and its sizable population of centipedes and black widows which congregated in the seams between the rocks. The lights, refrigerator and noisy rooftop swamp cooler were powered by electricity from a small Koehler diesel generator bolted on a wooden platform in a lean-to against the back wall. The enclosure looked like the cover on a coal chute; the little two-cylinder engine sat two feet off the ground on its platform to keep dust out of the works. It thumped and clattered incessantly; it was an intolerable gnashing of pistons and valves, pulsing out unsteady direct current.

The nearest neighbor was three miles away; the hills were all rocks and dust and cactus. A hundred feet behind the house was a square stone shed that had once been a carriage barn. Inside it, I kept the rock equipment—tumblers, grinders, barrels, diamond saws, drills.

I supplemented my pension by rockhounding. As a business it was pointless—an individual with secondhand, backroom machinery couldn't make much of a living . . . But its pointlessness was part of its beauty. Out of the tumblers came brilliant gems—for rings, pendants, earrings, rockbolo desert neckties, all the gimcracks tourists picked up in curio shops. The rocks didn't bring in much money but they made me a time and a place: time to wander the desert and mountains in search of the garnet and agate and countless other semiprecious stones that littered the canyons in uncut, unpolished disguise.

It was a land of heroic proportions. It was dangerous if you took it for granted; you shook out your boots in the morning before you put them on, to avoid scorpion stings, and you kept the legs of the bed in half-full cans of kerosene to dissuade the bugs from crawling in with you. The sun burned wherever it struck. But when you took a breath, it tasted clean and you knew nobody had ever breathed that lungful of air before you.

I poured a glass of milk—I have never liked coffee—and took it outside. The dry heat made my cheeks sting with shaving rash. I brooded on the rose bushes Joanne had planted along the gravel walk. She had left herself all over the place. The roses were starting to bloom again; in the desert you could get five or six blooms in a year if you kept them watered. I turned on the faucet and watched the water make mud, flowing along the shallow trenches from bush to bush. I had spent a month self-disciplining myself into the conviction that it hadn't been important enough for me to bother tearing out all the reminders of her by the roots. But her phone call brought it all back, very whole, very sharp and vivid.

It was going to be a scorching hot day. In the shade on the front step I drained the milk and thought about what we had said six months ago. It had been one of those miserable conversations where neither of us could meet the other's eyes. "Darling," she had said, "I wish we could have kept it casual, the way you wanted it, but I'm not made that way. It's my fault—I know you didn't want it to get too intense."

I had tried to persuade her to change her mind. She had lashed out (afterward I understood why): "Simon, you're hiding away up here, you just can't commit yourself to anything or anyone. You tried to fight city hall and you lost, so you quit. You haven't got room left in you for me or anything else outside yourself. I've already had that with Mike, more than I could take. I haven't the strength left."

The Jeep had been packed with my rock chisels and canteen. I had acted tougher than I felt, because I couldn't fathom my own contradictory feelings. I had climbed into the Jeep and she had walked over to me and said, "I won't be here when you get back." I had driven on down the hill without looking back to see if she was watching. It turned into a rotten day—I wanted to call her but wasn't sure whether she wanted me to. Sometimes it was hard to be sure of Joanne's meanings; she was changeable: sometimes she told you only part of the truth because she thought the whole truth would hurt.

I had seen her only once after that—a week later, an accidental meeting. She had let it slip; I never knew whether it was deliberate or an honest slip—She'd said something that had given me a foothold and I had pried the rest out of her, questioning her roughly like an interrogating cop, and finally there it was: Aiello. I was an ex-cop—an ex-honest cop—and Aiello had told her to stay away from me. She hadn't told me before because she knew my temper; she didn't want me to go gunning for Aiello because I wouldn't have a chance against the organization.

I knew better than to ask her to quit working for Aiello. I had never even asked her how she'd got mixed up with the organization in the first place. Those were questions you just didn't ask. It went without saying they had some hold over her. They always do.

I had told myself, angrily, it was her choice and I had to honor it. We had to avoid each other for however long it might take to blunt the edges of dangerous emotions. I had to acquiesce because I could not compromise her with the organization; Aiello was not an understanding or forgiving type and his organization played rough.

★ ★ ★ ★ ★

Now I saw the dust of her car coming up the dirt-road from the county highway. I felt ill at ease, betrayed; I had steeled myself against her absence but now she was coming back, not for the reason I would have wanted.

It was impossible to ignore my anticipation—I wanted to see her.

I waited in the shade until she drove the beige convertible into the yard and parked beside my Jeep. She had the top down; she turned and watched through her sunglasses as I walked out of the shade to open the car door. She didn't smile. "Thanks for letting me come."

Very gravely, I said, "Is it bad?"

"As bad as it can get." She swung her legs out, stood and smoothed down the tight skirt—it was white poplin; she wore a green sleeveless blouse that clung to the curved undersides of her breasts and showed off her smooth brown arms. She had a dancer's hard little body, superb legs; her face was small, heart-shaped and lovely.

The wind had roughed up her hair; there was a thread of moisture on her upper lip. She looked heat-flushed and scared. I couldn't really make out her eyes through the big sunglasses. She looked faint. "I feel like such a fool. Nothing can happen on a beautiful day like this, can it?" Her smile was quick and nervous. She kept looking down the road, as if somebody were chasing her. "Can't we talk inside?"

"Sure."

She had a curious detached fortitude; I had seen it before: the world could be falling down around her and she would still have to set the stage, get everybody in position before telling them about the disaster. We walked toward the house. I was sharply aware of the quick rat-tat of her heels on the gravel and the nylon whispers of her thighs. Her head hardly came up to my shoulder; the skirt was tight, but she moved along quickly with crisp lithe strides.

I went inside after her and let the screen door slam behind me with a weatherbeaten, slapping sound. It made her jump; she smiled apologetically and slumped against the doorjamb, leaning against it with her shoulder propped up. She said, "I'm in a state of absolute utter panic," and shoved herself toward the kitchen. She marched in and disappeared around the corner. I followed scowling, and when I reached the kitchen door she was filling the percolator.

"I don't even know how to begin. I suppose that's why I'm puttering around like a madwoman." She put the sunglasses away in a pocket sewn in her skirt. Her big violet eyes were provocative, more from habit than design. She measured the coffee and put it on to boil.

I said, "Why don't you sit down and get a grip on yourself. I'll do that."

"You've got no talent with coffee," she said. "I've got to have something strong and hot or I swear I'll collapse right here." She shook out a cigarette and found a match by the stove. Her hands trembled violently. I took the match away from her; she clamped the cigarette in her teeth while I lighted it.

She shook her head in violent angry defiance, as if to clear it. She took a deep drag on the cigarette and let it out slowly; she gave the coffee a waspish glance, because it hadn't already come to a boil, and when she had exhaled the lungful of smoke she said in a half-hysterical airily light way, "Aiello is gone."

"What?"

"Gone. Just . . . gone. The house is empty and the safe's wide open. Empty."

She tipped her head far over to one side like a little girl and gave me a peculiar, savage grin. "Isn't it lovely?"

My pulse thudded. "Great," I agreed. "You'd better tell me about it."

She waved a hand in an arch gesture and turned to face the stove; over her shoulder she said vaguely, "They'll think I did it, naturally. Got rid of Aiello somehow and robbed the safe."

"Naturally?" I echoed dryly. "Sure. Naturally they'll pick you first—I mean, you being an expert safecracker and all—"

"Don't make jokes," she snapped.

I scraped a hand across my mouth. She lifted the coffee off the stove. I couldn't see her face, but the line of her back was taut, tense, brittle, like a cornered animal.

The coffee smoked as it poured out of the pot; it was black and oil-thick. She carried the mug into my small living room.

I followed, stopping in the doorway. The roof cooler pushed a slow damp breeze across the room. I waited until she sat down on the couch and then I said, "All right. Go over it again—try to make some sense. What happened?"

She tucked her feet under her and held the coffee in both hands and blew on it. "I got to the house at seven-thirty, as usual. Aiello likes to work before ten and after four—he hates the heat, he spends the middle of the day in the indoor pool with the air conditioners blowing on his vodka collinses."

"Only this morning he wasn't there."

"It isn't that so much; he often spends the night out, but when he does, he always leaves somebody in the house on guard. This time there was nobody. And the safe, wide open and empty. Papers scattered around the office. The place has been ransacked."

"Maybe he cleared it out himself and took the stuff somewhere else for safekeeping. Maybe he got word there was going to be a raid."

"I don't think so," she said.

"Why not?"

"I just don't." She looked up momentarily. "I know him—you don't."

"Uh. What was in the safe?"

"You'd be better off not knowing."

I shook my head. "If it's what you think it is, the mob will react. The kind of reaction will depend on what was inside the safe."

She took a suicidal drag on her cigarette and stabbed it out in the ash tray. With smoke trailing from her mouth she said, "Let's just say there was enough to make it worth their while to kill half the population of this town to get it back."

"Cash?"

"A lot of cash. And files—the kind they couldn't afford to see in print."

"How much cash?"

"I never counted it," she said, snappish. "It was a hell a lot, millions I suppose, but I don't know. I'm supposed to be Sal Aiello's secretary but there are a lot of things I don't get to see."

"Go on."

"Look, Simon, I'm only part of the front. All the big shots try to look like legitimate businessmen, and part of the act is having a pretty secretary who doesn't look as if she came out of a reform school typing course. Aiello has his finger in quite a few legitimate businesses, enough to keep me busy with correspondence and phone calls and filing. I know it's all a front and he knows I know it, but it's the kind of thing you never say out loud. I don't get to see the books and I've never even been in the same room when he had the safe open. The safe isn't in the office, you know—it's in the library. But I've absorbed enough loose talk to know they keep dynamite in that safe. Aiello isn't the only one who uses it. Vincent Madonna has things in it. So does Pete DeAngelo and any number of others. It's like a central clearing station for all of them—it's an old vault they bought from a California bank that went out of business."

"How old?"

She blinked. "How should I know?"

"It's not a silly question. If it's old enough, it's easy to crack—and they wouldn't keep top-secret dynamite in a cracker box."

"Of course they would," she snapped. "My God, Simon, sometimes Aiello keeps a hundred thousand dollars in cash lying around the office in unlocked drawers. Nobody has the nerve to rob the Mafia."

"Apparently," I remarked, "somebody did." It occurred to me this was the first time I'd ever heard her use the word "Mafia." I said, "Who else knows about this?"

"I don't know. Maybe they haven't discovered it yet. What time is it?"

"Nine-thirty."

"He didn't have any appointments for today. But Madonna and DeAngelo drop around when they feel like it. So do a lot of other people; it's like a clubhouse up there. I know I haven't got much time—God, Simon, when I saw the mess I knew all of it, right in that split second, I knew I was in terrible trouble. I don't know what to do."

I watched her for a moment, then headed for the bedroom. "Stay put a minute," I told her, and went to the phone by the bed. I dialed Nancy Lansford, my neighbor down the road, a two-hundred-pound spinster who lived on a small inheritance and spent the winters taking tourists and school children on nature walks in the desert. She owed me a few favors—her house was full of polished rocks I'd given her. She was a relaxing old windbag, tart and practical as only a fanatically conservationist old maid could be.

She answered breathlessly on the fifth ring; I identified myself.

"Oh, Simon, good morning, isn't it a beautiful day?" She had a reedy, chirping voice. "I was outside watching a buzzard with my field glasses. Aren't they remarkable birds? Why, only last week I—"

I cut her off: "Nancy, I need a little help."

She answered immediately: "Name it."

I grinned into the phone. "I may have some visitors this morning and I'd like to have a little advance warning if they decide to come. Would you let me know if any cars start up the road toward my place?"

"Of course. But why—"

"I haven't got time to explain," I said. "If anybody drives by your house, just dial my number, let the phone ring twice, and hang up. Don't wait for me to answer, just hang up after two rings. Got it?"

"I've got it. I must say you sound very mysterious."

"I'll tell you about it later," I said, thanked her and hung up.

When I looked around, Joanne was standing in the doorway, her eyes wide. She narrowed them and said, "I was eavesdropping."

I nodded. "If they want to find you, this is one of the first places they'll think of looking. I'll feel better with a few

29

minutes' warning." Nancy lived three miles away, at the foot of my road.

She said, "I'm glad—because I'm sure they'll be after me." She went back into the living room. When I got there she was back on the couch with her coffee, lighting another cigarette. She was addicted to menthol cigarettes and strong coffee.

She said, "You never asked me any questions, but I suppose you must have figured out that they had something on me, to keep me—loyal."

"Yeah," I said, without inflection.

"It was in that safe."

"What was it?"

"I don't want to tell you. What difference does it make? Papers, tape recordings, pictures, movie films. It was there. Now whoever took it has it, and I'm scared of what they may do with it."

There wasn't much for me to say. I waited. Presently she resumed: "Naturally they know I knew it was there. They'll assume I wanted to get my hands on it so they wouldn't have a hold over me any longer. And they'll assume I told you about it, and you and I cracked the safe, to get it, and got rid of Aiello somewhere. They'll assume that," she added with a shudder, "because if fantasies came true, it's exactly what I would have done."

"You mean you were planning to burgle the safe?"

"Don't be silly, I wouldn't know how. But I wanted to— a silly dream, I guess, but it was the only hope I had. I even thought of conning you into helping me do it." She slanted a smile at me, twisted and nervous. "The irony is, I didn't do it, but they'll blame it on me, anyway."

She made a face, drew her shoulders together, and sat hunched forward with her elbows between her knees.

"Simon, I'm scared to death they'll kill me for something I didn't do."

I sat down by her and squeezed her arm. She pulled away, out of my reach. "Don't—please. Don't try to comfort me, I didn't come here for that."

"What do you want me to do, Joanne?"

She shook her head violently. "God knows. I'm just running blind. I ran to you because I thought you could protect me. Just another stupid dream—what can you do? Nothing. But here I am. Simon, I haven't healed over—I'm still in love with you, if it has to be said—but I don't want this madness to be an excuse for us to start things up again. I meant what I said last winter and I want to leave the air clear, not have that hanging between us, because I just don't have the strength. That empty safe has nothing to do with the way you and I feel about each other, or did feel or will feel. I know we gave each other something we both needed—anyway, something I needed—to feel alive again and persuade myself there was some little bit of hope left somewhere."

Her voice trailed off; she was tense, expecting an argument. I wanted desperately to give her one. But I had my own injuries. I looked down at her: she sat hunched, brooding, ready to jump, hating the dismal trap she was in. She couldn't accept it with the bleak resignation of a tough alley broad because that wasn't her style; she had never belonged in the world they had trapped her in, which was one reason, I supposed, why she was valuable to the mob. She was animated, tidy and alive, slightly vain, often careless with risks, ruthlessly amorous yet amazingly—even after all of it—innocent of malice. She drove too fast and drank too much; she ran a headlong race with life, graceful in spite of the daily bitterness she must have felt, chained to them; and incredibly, all of it had left few marks on her. I hadn't seen her in months before this morning; she hadn't changed at all, except for the tight lines around her mouth and eyes that were evidence of the strain of the moment. She was still, as always, girlish, lively, saucy, defiant. "Remember me?" she had said once—"I'm the girl with the cauliflower heart."

I stood up. "All right," I said. "Neutral corners—I'll keep my hands to myself. Let's get this figured out."

She gave me a quick grateful look, and became smaller and heavier with relief, strain flowing out. She was looking with preoccupied anger into the coffee dregs and she was arrestingly beautiful in profile. I looked away and said, "If you want me to do you any good you'll have to lay everything out on the table. You're holding a lot back."

"What is there to hold back? I've told you what happened. You always have to make things so damned complicated."

"There's got to be more than you've told me. Nothing you've said so far convinces me you're in too much trouble. If the house is empty and the safe's open, why not assume Aiello just skipped? Took the money himself?"

"Aiello? You couldn't get him outdoors in this heat."

"He disappeared in the cool of the night. Maybe he's holed up with a nice cuddly air conditioner—or on a plane to South America."

"He'd never get all that stuff through customs," she said. "Believe me, he didn't do it himself. He had no reason to. He'd have been stealing from himself, and from his friends. Vincent Madonna had things in that safe—Aiello wouldn't have the guts to steal a ten-cent stamp from Madonna."

I recalled the front-page stories of automobile death traps wired with bombs. The rubouts and hits, attributed to the Madonna mob but, of course, never proved. Madonna was the head of the local Family: the don *vin done*. Salvatore Aiello was his *caporegime*—one of his field commanders in the Cosa Nostra pseudo-military setup. I had heard rumors about rumors—that there was bad blood between them, for no known reason other than the fact that Madonna was Sicilian while Aiello was Neapolitan. But she was probably right: no hood like Aiello would risk the wrath of the entire international organization by absconding with his boss's money. But what the devil could I do about it? Joanne couldn't hide from them any more than Aiello could. What chance did we have?

I turned toward her, opening my mouth to speak, and that was when the phone jangled in the bedroom.

She shot off the couch. I froze. The phone rang a second time. I turned my face toward the bedroom.

After a minute I realized I was holding my breath. The phone had not rung again. Two rings, and silence.

I strode across the room. "It could be anybody at all," I said, "but let's not take a chance."

"I'll get out of here."

"No. They'd see your dust."

"Then I'll hide."

"Can't hide your car," I said. I had gone into the bedroom; I opened the footlocker. Cops have to buy their own side arms; I still had my .38 Police Special. I checked to make sure it was loaded, put it in the hip pocket of my Levi's and went back into the living room. She was chewing her lip. I said, "We may as well face it now," and opened the front door. "Stay behind me."

I held the screen open for her and then walked down past the rose bushes and stood watching the dark blue Ford come snarling up the dusty grade toward us.

Chapter Two

Watching the car come up, I was counting on the mob's need to keep things quiet. Ours was a city in which the Cosa Nostra overlords still maintained impunity, with bought-and-paid-for cops and politicians, and a degree of anonymity: the southwestern Families hadn't hit *Life* magazine, local newspapers hadn't started any crusades, and PR men for Madonna's modernized mob gave enthusiastic support to the Anti-Defamation Committee when it insisted there was no such thing as "Organized Crime"; if the town had any crooks with Sicilian names that was just coincidence.

Maintaining good public relations and a peaceful surface of quiet was particularly vital to the mob right now: through his political mouthpieces, Madonna was exerting pressure to introduce legalized gambling into the state. It was sensitive; he couldn't afford untoward publicity. Sal Aiello's disappearance would be bad enough; the mob wouldn't want to have to explain Joanne's disappearance—and mine—along with it. So I didn't really expect them to use too much muscle—unless they knew things I didn't know. I glanced at Joanne in the shadows by the screen door; she was holding out on me, I knew that. I didn't have time to press it out of her.

There were two of them in the car—Cosa Nostra soldiers modestly masquerading in Hawaiian sport shirts. I knew them by sight: Ed Baker and Tony Senna. Baker was a bookie and numbers runner, not long on brains; he was driving the car but I knew he would let Tony Senna do the talking—Senna, who must have been a carney barker in some prior incarnation, was one of the mob's running dogs, an enforcer with a glib tongue and a cruel sense of humor.

The Ford rolled to a genteel halt ten feet from me and both men got out, not hurrying, not showing weapons, though it could be assumed they had guns under the flapping shirttails.

Tony Senna walked around the car with both hands in his pockets and glanced at Joanne before he formed a smile with his teeth and said to me, "Hello, flatfoot. Hot enough for you? I hear the burglars are only breaking into air-conditioned houses." It elicited a bark of laughter from Ed Baker, a big-nosed brute with shoulders like a Percheron, who looked as if he belonged behind a butcher's counter. Baker, a onetime prelim fighter, was a grade-B Hollywood gangster with the personality of a closed door.

Senna, sizing me up through his accidental smile, was another breed—a small, thin hood full of conspiratorial mannerisms; a sharpie. He had waxy Latin skin but you got the feeling you could have lit a match on his jaw.

He said casually, "How're they hangin', Crane?" and shot a shrewd glance past me at Joanne. "Pete thought we might find her here. Pete's pretty smart sometimes." He meant Pete DeAngelo, Madonna's *consigliore*, the number two man in the Family.

Senna smiled again. "You ain't talking much."

"What kind of talk did you have in mind?" I said.

Ed Baker talked without moving his lips: "He's got some heat in his back pocket, Tony."

Senna chuckled. "See how long it took him to spot that,

35

Crane? I swear, Baker's the dumbest guy I've ever met. He can't even remember what comes after Walla." He chuckled and drew a circle in the sand with his toe, and looked up abruptly, as if trying to catch me off guard.

He said in a different voice, "You mind if we have a look around the place?"

"I mind," I said, "but if it'll clear things up, go ahead and search. Just put things back where you find them."

Without turning his head, Senna spoke over his shoulder to Baker: "Look around, Ed."

Baker went toward the house. I stood back and kept an eye on him while he went past Joanne. She was stiff but composed; she met his glance without flinching. Baker went into the house.

Senna was smiling again: "I'm glad you didn't argue, Crane."

"I never argue with a criminal type," I said.

His smile disappeared instantly. "Save the cute answers," he barked. "You wasn't surprised to see us and you seem to know what Ed's looking for in there, which makes it a good bet it ain't here, and a better bet you know exactly what's going on. Which puts you in a hard place. Now you want to say something funny?"

He whipped his small-eyed glance toward Joanne and said, "Dolly, you take some pretty dumb chances. It wasn't smart for you to come here."

"All right," Joanne said coolly, "I'm not smart. Is that a crime?"

"I wouldn't know," Senna said. "I ain't read up on the law." He was, obviously, just talking to pass the time—he would make up his mind what to do with us after Baker finished his search. He probably had his orders from DeAngelo, and whatever they were, nothing we could say would change his mind; I intended to save my arguments for the higher-ups, if it got to that stage. But I backed up three paces to stand where I could watch both Senna and the front of the house; I didn't want Ed Baker coming around behind us.

Ed Baker came out of the house after a while and shook his head. "Nothing."

"You sure you looked everyplace?"

"Yeah, I'm sure."

"You're a goddamned genius," Senna said with vicious irony. "Can you think up anything else you ought to do now?"

"Naw. It's clean."

"Well, then, just to make sure, you might haul your ass over to that shack with the rock machinery in it."

"Uh," Baker said, and swallowed. Senna said, "And after that take a walk around the place and see if you spot any fresh-turned earth."

Baker scowled and moved away toward the rock-tumbling shack. I made a half-turn to keep him in sight. I hadn't seen any gun-bulge against his shirt but Baker was the type who could squeeze a tennis ball flat in one fist.

I said to Senna, "He won't find anything. We haven't got what you're looking for."

"We'll see." He turned again to Joanne: "One or two people ain't going to like it much that you came runnin' up here instead of going to your real friends right away and telling them what happened. You gave your solemn word you was going to stay away from this cop, and your friends respected your word. It ain't likely to sit well."

Joanne said, "If I knew what had happened I'd have told them. I don't know."

Senna's look of sarcastic disbelief prompted me; I said,

"Look, she didn't know anything and she got scared. She thought she'd be blamed for it."

"For what?" Senna breathed, and to Joanne: "How much you told the cop?"

"He's not a cop."

"Yeah. Ex-cop. He's still got the odor from here."

I gave him a cool smile, wanting to give him no satisfaction. He said to her, "One more time. How much you told him?"

She spread both hands. "How much do I know? Nobody lets me in on any secrets, you know that."

I said, "She went to Aiello's house at seven-thirty and found it empty. The place had been torn apart. She got scared and came here. That's all there is."

Senna considered it. "Maybe," he said. "Maybe." He turned and watched the shack, waiting, until Baker came out and shook his head and began to prowl the grounds, head down like a sniffing bulldog. Senna said abruptly, "Dolly, I'll want your car keys a minute."

"They're in the car," she said shortly.

Senna grinned "Don't never leave your keys in the car," he said. "Some crook might steal it. You know eighty percent of stolen cars had their keys left in them? Dumb." He walked over to the convertible, glanced inside, reached in to get the keys, and walked back to the trunk. He opened it, looked, and shut it; put the keys back in the ignition and spent a moment bent over the car with his back to us, pulling up the seats and looking underneath and shoving them back in place. Then he lifted the hood and looked under it—an automatic gesture, I suppose, though I couldn't conceive of anybody hiding valuable flammable papers in the engine compartment of a car. He slammed it shut and sauntered back toward us, smiling vaguely. "Ain't no blood in the trunk, which could be a good sign." He walked to my Jeep and gave it a cursory glance—there is no place to hide anything in an open Jeep—and came back.

He watched Baker for a few minutes and finally, evidently satisfied himself that Baker wasn't going to find anything; he turned to me and said, "Aiello will turn up."

"I guess he will," I agreed judiciously.

"He'll turn up dead, or he'll turn up alive. I kind of suspect he'll turn up dead."

"Uh-huh."

"If he does," Senna said in the same regular tone, "you and the girl friend are the number-one suspects. Naturally me and my friends don't fly off the handle, we don't jump to conclusions, and maybe Aiello'll turn up in Tijuana with a blonde on each arm havin' a fine time. But it don't look likely, does it?"

It wasn't a question that required an answer. He went on:

"He had some goodies that belonged to some of us. Me and my friends, I mean. You know, like Pete? We're kind of anxious to get it back. Now, if you two got it; it might be a good idea for you to give it back. You could pack it up and ship it to Pete anonymous, so we wouldn't have any way to prove who sent it, but you'd be in the clear because the heat would be off—unless, of course, we happened to find out you killed Aiello and ditched him someplace. I'm just making suggestions, you understand. We're all civilized people; we don't give orders or make threats. But just as a suggestion I might mention it wouldn't be considered friendly for either one of you to try to leave town before we find out what's happened to Aiello and the stuff that disappeared from his house."

Baker was still on the prowl; Senna called him over.

They got into the car and Senna was smiling amiably when they turned the car around and drove away.

Joanne hadn't moved an inch. Now her shoulders lifted defensively and she put the back of her hand to her mouth. I walked over to her and put an arm around her shoulders and walked her inside; this time she didn't argue. I sat her down on the couch and said, "I think you could use a drink."

"Make it a double," she said in a small voice.

I made a drink for her and stood nearby while she gulped half of it down. I said, "Aiello will probably turn up soon, trying to get out of the country with the loot."

"Don't try to calm me down with lies." Her hands dug out a mangled cigarette like an addict snatching an overdue fix. "They can't let it lie, Simon. The things in that safe were too hot. They've got to find them."

"They won't find anything by killing people. They know that." I turned half away from her, hardening my gut consciously before I said, "Senna said we were the prime suspects but he was just making talk. If they didn't have a line on somebody else, they'd have been a lot rougher on us. If they really thought you knew where the stuff was, they'd have put the snatch on both of us and you'd be sweating it out right now."

I wheeled toward her and said flatly, "Who is it, Joanne?"

Her eyes flashed. "You're babbling."

"You've been holding something back."

She put the drink down, jammed the cigarette pack into her purse and snapped it shut; got up and headed for the door, icy and stiff. I let her get as far as the door and then I said, "It's Mike, isn't it?"

It stopped her in her tracks.

Her teeth were white against the tan face. "What—what gives you—"

"He's back," I said, making it a statement.

She took a breath. "How did you find out? How long have you known?"

"I didn't," I said, "until you just said that."

The menace in her eyes came and went quickly, and was replaced by self-disgust. "I never was a good liar."

"I'm a hard man to lie to," I said, not softening it. "Now sit down and finish your drink and tell me about Mike."

She moved back to the couch like a mechanism, sat by reflex and leaned back; her eyes never left my face. I stared at her until she blushed. When she finally spoke it was without apologia or preamble:

"They let him out of prison yesterday. He came back to town last night. I honestly don't think he meant to get in touch with me at all—he only wanted to see Aiello and try to straighten things out so they wouldn't get after him all over again. But Mike always did have a talent for trying to soothe troubled flames by throwing oil on them. Simon, I swear to you he had nothing to do with Aiello disappearing."

"Can you prove that?"

"No, but he—"

"Don't swear to things you don't know," I said. "Christ, of all the asinine things to do. All this rigmarole just to protect Mike Farrell—why? You're not even married to him any more?"

"He didn't do it," she said adamantly.

"Did you see him?"

"Only for a few minutes."

"When?"

"Last night. He'd had a big argument with Aiello and he

wanted a shoulder to cry on. My God, Simon, I wouldn't even let him come in the house. He stood on the porch and bleated at me through the door—I had it on the chain—and when I wouldn't let him come in he stormed back to his station wagon and went away with his tires squealing. I expect by now he's halfway to the Mississippi River."

"Yeah. Maybe carrying the loot from Aiello's safe."

"No."

"Why for Christ's sake didn't you tell me all this in the first place?" I demanded.

Her answer was quiet and level: "Because I knew you'd jump to conclusions, just the way you have. I knew you wouldn't understand. I knew you'd get stupid and blind jealous—it's a weakness you've got."

I didn't have time to stop and ponder whether that was true or not; I swung around the room, wheeled to face her, and said with desperate rage, "Didn't it matter at all to you that you might have got both of us killed? It may still happen! We're talking about an organization that lives and breathes distrust—nobody believes anything. If they find out you held out on them about Mike being here, they won't give you another chance to change your story."

She said flatly, "Mike had nothing to do with it. If I told them about him they'd waste a lot of time hunting him down and they'd probably kill him, and it wouldn't get them anywhere; they'd still need to find Aiello and the loot. And believe me, Simon, we'd be in much worse danger then than we are now."

"You keep saying you know he didn't have anything to do with it. Can you back that up with anything besides intuition and conceit?"

"Certainly."

"Name it."

"He couldn't have done it, that's all. I don't mean he didn't have the chance. I have no idea whether he has an alibi that will stand up. But I do know he's terrified of the Mafia; the only thing he's ever wanted was to keep them happy with him. He'd grovel and crawl if he had to—he'd be a sniveling yes-man, he'd polish Aiello's shoes. He'd do anything in his power to avoid getting them mad at him again. Mike would be the last man in the world to try anything like this."

"He's been in prison. He could have changed."

Her only answer was, "I saw him last night. You didn't. Simon, you've got to understand Mike. You've never known him."

That much was true: I had only seen Mike Farrell at a distance. Before he'd gone to the penitentiary he'd had a nightclub combo at the Moulin Rouge; he'd been a fair saxophone player.

She said, "He's one of those nervous men who are forever lonely. Even when he wants to he can't share himself. I guess I must have married him because I could see he wanted to break out of that frightened shell, but he never has. I was like a lot of girls who mistake long silences in young men for maturity, but I was wrong, he wasn't mature at all—you have to remember I was only nineteen then, it was a long time ago."

I sat hipshot against the windowsill and watched her. She wasn't looking at me. She said, "People like Mike are—parasites, Simon. He'd never kill a man or rob a safe—it takes too much initiative. Mike never does anything on his own. He's one of those people who feed on everyone they touch. It's compulsive, they can't help it—they hurt the people who love them until the love dies. I don't know, maybe a psychiatrist would blame it on his parents—he

43

took me back to Cincinnati to meet them once. His father's a shopkeeper, a nice little man, about as ineffectual as wallpaper. Mike's mother was one of those big loud clubwomen who remind you of express trains. A martinet. She only wanted to use Mike to feed her own vanity—he was just something for her to be proud of when he played solos with the school band. The rest of the time she didn't want him around."

She picked up her drink and drained it quickly. "He's an insecure man—full of anxieties. He's never had nerve enough to steal anything, let alone a gangster's money. It took me a long time to find out what half the wives in the world can tell you—a woman can never change a man. I tried to give him some backbone because I thought I loved him, but it just didn't work. He hated being a musician and he hated everything about his life, and finally he got involved with Aiello and the organization."

"Aiello," I said, "or Vincent Madonna?"

She gave me a sharp look. "Yes, him too." The name made her uncomfortable; she hurried on, as if to fill the gap of silence:

"I was young and wild—that was six years ago, we'd been married two or three years. It was exciting to me, all those fast characters. I won't pretend I didn't enjoy it in a way, but then it started to get dirty. I got trapped in—something I don't want to talk about, something that got Mike scared of them."

"Scared of who?"

She flapped a hand; her face was averted. "Aiello, Pete DeAngelo, you know. The organization. Mafia, Family, Cosa Nostra, whatever they're calling it now."

I said, "You've never told me much about Mike."

"I wanted to forget it."

"You'd better go on, now that you've started."

When she glanced across the room at me I saw that her lip corners were turned down. She said, "I suppose so. I told you Mike got scared. He started drinking too much and making risky remarks about the mob—the kind of talk they didn't want to get around. It was only bravado; he had no idea he was offending anybody. But he suffered for it— they threw him to the wolves. He went to prison."

"It was a narcotics charge, wasn't it?"

She nodded. "Of course he was framed."

"Are you sure?"

"I'm sure," she said wearily. "He'd gotten involved in some shady things but none of them had anything to do with dope."

"Go on."

"Well, he went to prison, and at first I enjoyed playing the role of waiting for an absent husband—it gave me a kind of untouchable immunity, but at the same time I didn't have to put up with Mike. I know that sounds strange, but Mike did a good job of turning me sour on men. Even after he went up he kept browbeating me, accusing me of selling him into Egypt. By the time he relented and apologized, I was past caring any more. Imprisonment for more than two years is grounds for divorce here and I divorced him. But he kept writing letters, pleading with me to come on visiting days, and once in a while I did, until about a year ago. Then I met you, and I stopped going to see him. After that I didn't get any more letters from him. The last time he wrote he said he was sorry for all the trouble he'd caused me and he wouldn't bother me any more, wouldn't even come to see me after he got out."

She stopped long enough to light a new cigarette; then she said, "Simon, he's a poor, twisted, frightened man.

He's bitter and neurotic and a fool, and far too much of a coward to have anything to do with a thing like this. I just felt I owed him this much, to keep from getting him involved if I could help it."

Her hand still trembled, the cigarette wedged between two fingers. She seemed to have run down. I said, "You said you did something that got Mike scared before they railroaded him into prison."

She composed herself. "It's ancient history. I've forgotten it."

"Sure you have."

"It's something you don't need to know about, believe me."

"Mike knows?"

"Of course."

I just scowled at her. Finally, avoiding my glance, she made a gesture. "All right, hell, I was young and everything was exciting, the more thrilling the better. The company was fast and there was a sense of—well, violence in the air, and I liked it. And I admit I was getting damn tired of Mike and his whining."

"And?"

She looked at me and her face changed. It became a self-conscious smile, crooked and wry and helplessly apologetic. "Aiello."

"For Christ's sake!"

"It wasn't really an affair with him. We were both drunk and Mike was away somewhere running an errand for him."

"Of all the wretched—"

"I was barely old enough to vote," she said in a taut little voice. "I told you, it doesn't do any good to go into these things."

"Goddamn it, didn't you know who he was?"

"I knew he was big. I guess I didn't know how big. Look, Simon, at the time I was like a modern-day flapper and they were like harmless bootleggers with their big cars and parties and flunkies all over the place. I didn't know about the sordid part then, the hard dope and the strongarm and the killings. They didn't let you see that part of it. It was only after Mike was arrested that I found out—"

"Found out what?"

"Nothing. Let it drop—please."

"You told me you didn't know anything about Aiello's operations outside of his legitimate fronts—was the whole story a tissue of lies?"

"Of course not," she said wearily. "I told you the truth. Think, Simon—would they let me know anything else?"

I made a face. "So you don't want to talk about it."

"That's right."

"You've got that stupid, stubborn look on your face. I suppose wild horses couldn't drag any more out of you."

She gave me a mock-sweet smile, and remained mute.

With a sickening suspicion of what it might be, I didn't press that line of questions. I dipped the toggle of the ancient Pilot radio and walked across the room. "Want another drink?"

"No."

I poured half a glass of ginger ale, laced it with nothing stronger than ice cubes, and glanced at my watch: time for the ten-thirty news, which was why I had switched on the radio. The forty-year-old Pilot was my only concession to the electronic age; television, with all its implications, terrified me. My whole trouble, I thought, is I'm a hopelessly old-fashioned obsolete sumbitch. The radio took its time to warm up and finally said, ". . . in Paris this morning. The new French government disclaimed any connection with

47

the pro-Viet Cong demonstration. Meanwhile, in Saigon . . ."

I quit listening; stirring ice-cubes with one finger, I was making my brain work. Assuming Joanne was right and her ex-husband was in the clear, what was left? I thought of a couple of long-shot possibilities. One, a quarrel inside the mob—a split between Aiello and the don, Madonna. It happened once in a while; and I recalled the rumors about bad blood between them. Perhaps Aiello had gone to the mattresses—taken cover in a prepared lair while he set up an ambush to trap Madonna, summoned the members loyal to him, and got ready to go to war for control of the Family.

It was possible, but I doubted that was the way it was. Joanne knew Aiello pretty well, and she had described him as a man who liked his comforts. He was rich—why should he take the chance?

There was another possibility. The structure of a Cosa Nostra Family was complex—rigid and codified. The top man passed instructions down the ladder of rank until finally they were delivered to the button who had to carry them out. There were a good many intermediaries between the don and the man who actually committed the crime. Sometimes the button didn't even know why he was doing it; he almost never knew, for an absolute fact, where his orders initially came from.

It was simple insurance. If the button was picked up and decided to turn informer, he couldn't identify anybody except the minor-league middleman who actually gave him his orders. Once in a while, when the heat became too intense, it was necessary to protect the top man. To do that, the mob only had to break off one step of the ladder, at any point at all, to guarantee the top man would never get involved—a middleman had to disappear. For example: the law might have traced some marked payoff money as far as

Aiello. Aiello then would have to disappear, for Madonna's protection.

The law. Most of the cops and judges sold themselves as casually and regularly as streetwalking whores. But the mob couldn't always get to the federal bureau cops or the grand jury special investigators from upstate. Sometimes the organization just had to cover its tracks, hunker down and wait it out like a jackrabbit in a hailstorm. Of course, if that was the reason behind Aiello's disappearance, then Madonna knew all about it, and the visit we'd just had from Senna and Baker was just camouflage. I was an ex-cop; perhaps Madonna thought I would get word of the visit back to the cops. It could help throw the cops off the track.

There were a great many ifs in that. As a hypothesis it didn't work very well. If Aiello's disappearance had been engineered by the mob, it would have been done in a neater way. There were too many loose ends. The mob would have set up a cover: Aiello was on vacation, or had gone to Grand Bahama on casino business, or had gone back to the Bronx to sit with a sick uncle, or was fishing in the Gulf of California. It would have been so easy to explain his absence that the lack of explanation was a pretty sure sign Aiello's disappearance had taken the mob completely by surprise. Certainly if they'd planned the disappearance in advance, they'd have found some pretext to keep Joanne away from the house long enough to get things tidied up.

The more I went around in mental circles, getting nowhere, the more I resented getting implicated in the mess. I wanted to shout out, I'm me, I'm Simon Crane—I'm not your everyday skid-row patsy. I was working up a good angry steam when the radio announcer intruded his voice into my consciousness:

". . . and on the local scene, this just in. The body of a

man tentatively identified as Salvatore Aiello has been found by construction workers on the site of the new interstate highway in Mexican Hat Canyon. A construction company spokesman said a grader operator discovered the corpse buried in fresh-graded earth where the crew was about to lay down fresh pavement. According to the spokesman, in another few hours the body would have been permanently concealed under a new concrete highway.

"According to police reports, Aiello has been linked frequently with several alleged racketeers throughout the Southwest since he moved here from New York in the early nineteen-fifties. Police say a preliminary examination indicates the cause of death was two bullets, possibly thirty-eight caliber or nine millimeter, lodged in the brain after entering the skull above the left ear. The police will not confirm or deny the possibility of gangland execution, but if that is the case, it would be the first confirmed underworld slaying here in the last nineteen months. We have not yet been able to reach Aiello's secretary or business associates for comment. Stay tuned to this station for further developments and all late fast-breaking news items. The gasoline price war continues unabated, and spokesmen for . . ."

I strode across to the radio and turned it off. Joanne was staring at it; her hands and body had become still. She hardly seemed to be breathing.

I went from the radio to the couch, picked up her cigarettes and matches and stuffed them in her handbag, pushed it into her hands and said, "Come on."

"What? Where?" She seemed stunned.

"I want to get you to a safer place than this. Then I've got one or two things to do."

She was not the kind of girl who had to reply to everything that was said to her; she trusted me enough to get up

50

and walk through the door when I held it for her. Outside, I squinted in the sunlight and said, "We'll take both cars. You go out first and I'll follow you. Drive down to the Executive Lodge and wait for me in the parking lot—I'll be right behind you."

"Why both cars?"

"I'll be going places from there and you may need yours." I didn't add that I wanted to hang back on the way down and make sure she wasn't followed.

I didn't bother to lock the house; I went over and climbed into the Jeep. She started her car up and gave me a long look through the windshield before she put it in gear and swung around past me and headed down the hill. Feeling the dig of the .38 in my hip pocket, I backed out and turned to follow her.

Chapter Three

I kept the Jeep in second gear and lay well back to avoid Joanne's dust cloud. She slewed around the bends faster than I liked to take them; by the time I reached the bottom of the dirt road she was a quarter of a mile down the county highway, roaring toward the city.

I was watching to see if any cars pulled out to follow her; watching my own rear-view mirror as well. If there was a tail, he was an invisible one. Joanne squealed under the freeway overpass and led me across the north side of the city on the six-lane boulevard known as the Strip, which was a raw, neon five-mile stretch of gas stations, hamburger joints, car lots, discount barns, loan offices, artsy-craftsy galleries and gaudy supper clubs. It was peopled by gaily-costumed sun-worshipers, small-time crooks and kids in riot-hued cars with bald tires. A block away to either side were the tract developments—sleazy cracker box houses with gravelly little desert yards, erected by speculators who put ten percent down, financed the rest, and made huge after-tax profits by deducting heavy depreciation. Future slums.

The Strip was notorious for its spectacular teenage murders and for the fact that Vincent Madonna's stooges owned most of the car lots and all the supper clubs. Everybody knew it, but of course nobody could prove it. Brightly sunlit, brand new, and never more than one story, the Strip's clean, modern buildings seemed incongruous to outsiders who felt underworld characters inhabited only shadowy alleys in tall concrete-and-brick slums. You had to travel the Strip at night to get the full effect—motorcycle punks circling with deafening roar, hippies wandering the beer joints, herds of fat Cadillacs browsing in front of the supper clubs, slick-haired hoods and very thin divorcées cruising the bars in search of kicks.

Thirty years ago it had been a cow town, 25,000 people. Now the population was swollen tenfold by the retired, the drifting, the failed, the health-seeking, the opportunistic, the escapist. Every year the number of retail bankruptcies was staggering. It had the fragile aura of impermanence— no yesterdays and no tomorrows; eat, drink and gather ye rosebuds. It was a slick, chromium imitation of Los Angeles in the desert.

Ahead of me, Joanne's convertible turned past a gas station that had its pennants flapping, went around a divider and headed south through the housing tracts. The sun baked my head and shoulders—at 127 degrees, asphalt becomes muddy in the streets, and it was already tacky and soft. An Air Force jet whistled past at low altitude, climbing and shrieking, cracking eardrums and plaster and glass as it zoomed upward to clear the mountains. If you called the base and complained, you got the non sequitur of the decade: "Be glad they're ours." The boys were up there rigorously defending our country against air attack from Mexico. A few months ago one of them had crashed into a supermarket and killed eleven people.

The Executive Lodge sprawled near the south freeway cloverleaf. It was a big new motel with all the efficiency of an electronic computer, and all the warmth. I had picked it because I was fairly certain it didn't belong to one of Vincent Madonna's dummies.

An intense layer of heat lay along the parking lot. I pulled in beside Joanne's convertible and spoke:

"I'll be out in a minute."

She gave me a startled-fawn look and glanced toward the street. She was thinking about the fact that she was in full view of the road. I pointed to the narrow covered paveway that shaded the ice and coke machines and said, "Try the shade," and got out of the Jeep. I watched her walk into the passage, swing of hips and clip of calves; she didn't ask any questions. The sun was miserably hot.

I folded the Jeep cushion down to keep the sun off the seat, and went up the sidewalk under the concrete eaves. The heat sizzled through the soles of my desert boots.

The lobby was sterile and cool, almost deserted. There was a coffee shop with a counter and a round rack of paperbacks at the cashier's desk. The echoing imitation marble door and soft-lullabying Muzak gave the place a mausoleum air. The walls were fake rough-stucco ornamented with phony Mexican artifacts. There were the obligatory plastic flowers and potted plants.

The desk clerk had a crew cut, vest and tie, and an earnest chamber-of-commerce face. Groomed and tanned, he was probably the terror of the swimming pool. He gave me the subliminal leer which desk clerks practice for use on men without wedding rings who check in for a double before noon. Without making an issue of it I let it drop that my wife and I had driven overnight from Los Angeles, to avoid the day-driving heat, and wanted a quiet room—preferably in back—to get a few hours' rest before an evening appointment. I didn't care whether he bought the story. The important thing to sell was the Los Angeles idea; I signed in as Mr. and Mrs. Chittenden of Sherman Oaks, filled in a fictitious make and model of car with a California license plate number, and paid cash in advance. If the room clerk filed us in mind as two adulterous Californians having an affair, so much the better. The fact I paid cash instead of using a credit card would reinforce that idea.

Dangling the room key, I headed for the front exit, then made a detour toward one of the open acoustic phone cubicles along the front wall. I had picked up the receiver before I noticed that the phone had no dial; obviously it went through the motel switchboard. I was about to replace it on the hook when a girl's voice chirped on the line and I thought, To hell with it, the risk was negligible; I gave her the number of police headquarters.

"Are you registered here, sir?"

I thought. "No. I'll leave a dime at the desk when I finish the call."

"Twenty cents, sir."

"Yeah." They must make a bloody fortune on phone calls.

I heard the girl chortle. "Ordinarily we don't let outside people use the house phones, sir, but since this is the police number it must be all right."

"Yes, ma'am," I drawled. I could hang up, but it hardly seemed worth the trouble . . .

"Police headquarters, Patrolman Garcia. Hello?"

I said, "Lieutenant Behn, please."

"Sure. You happen to know what division that'd be?"

"Homicide," I said.

"Okay. I'll get you Homicide, they'll put you through to him."

It took two more relays but finally I heard his voice: "Behn here."

"Larry, this is Simon Crane."

"Well, well."

55

"Can I talk to you?"

"It's your dime."

Twenty cents, I thought. I said, "What have you got on the Aiello case?"

"Why do you want to know?"

Larry Behn was one of the handful who had decided to stick it out and fight from the inside. A long time ago I had decided to trust him. I said, "I used to be pretty close to Aiello's secretary and it looks like they think she was involved in it."

"And if she was involved, you were too, hey? All right—where is she?"

"She doesn't know anything," I said. "I can't help you, anyway—I'm not with her now. I assume you've got it down as murder. I only heard the radio flash."

"Murder, yeah. Two slugs in the head, no powder burns, and he sure didn't bury himself."

"Have you got anything? Not for broadcast."

I heard him breathe. He was thinking. Finally he said, "Right now we haven't got much worth talking about. They're running the slugs through the lab for comparison photos. In a day or two we may find out something from the FBI central files. But if it's a mob execution, I doubt it—they'd use a clean gun. Otherwise, what can I tell you? No tire tracks worth talking about, no footprints, no fingers. A little rubber from an automobile floor mat stuck on his belt, but it would take us twenty years to find the right car to match it. Nothing under the fingernails. Postmortem lividity shows he was killed someplace else and taken out there for burial. No sign of the murder weapon. We figured it for a mob hit at first but we've checked out people like Pete DeAngelo and Tony Senna and Ed Baker, and I think they're all clean. They've all got alibis of one kind or another but they're not the kind of alibis they'd cook up if they'd known they were going to need alibis, if you get what I mean. I even checked out Vince Madonna—he's clean on it, too."

"How do you know?"

"No comment," he said, which told me the answer: Behn must have had surveillance on Madonna last night, for one reason or another, and the tail must have reported that Madonna hadn't had any contact with Aiello.

"Any ideas, Larry?"

"Nothing worth the waste of breath. Maybe it was some sorehead that got muscled by the mob."

"Maybe," I agreed, thinking of Joanne's ex-husband, Mike Farrell. Maybe.

"Time of death?"

"The medical examiner says between two and five this morning. Look, Simon, you haven't talked to me and I haven't told you a thing, all right?"

"Sure," I said, frowning and thinking.

After a minute Behn said, "Look, I realize it's your dime but I've got a few things to do besides sit here with a dead phone on my ear."

"Sorry," I said. "What was he wearing?"

"Aiello? Sport shirt, trousers and belt, slippers. No socks. Deceased had a handkerchief and some loose change in his pockets. No wallet, no keys. If it means anything, he usually wore a toupee and he didn't have it on."

"Dentures?"

"He had his own teeth." I heard Behn hawk and spit—I could picture him aiming into the green metal wastebasket beside the cluttered desk. He would sit back now, phone hooked between shoulder and tilted head, going through papers and tossing them on various piles as he spoke to me.

Behn was a freckled bony redhead with an undershot chin and a huge Adam's apple.

I said carefully, "You've been over his house by now."

"Yeah. Nothing out of the ordinary. The place is empty, nobody home, but no sign it was messed up any."

So, I thought, somebody cleaned it up before the cops arrived. I said, "Was the bed slept in?"

"Can't tell. It was made up, but not with clean sheets. We got to the housekeeper an hour ago and she said she always makes the bed with hospital corners. Whoever made it up this time didn't use them. So maybe he spent part of the night in bed and got up and somebody made the bed after he left."

"Any bloodstains in the house?"

"Not so far. We've still got the crew out there."

I said, "Okay, thanks. I'll—"

"Not so fast. I've been patient and polite—now it's your turn. How much do you know about this?"

"Less than you do, evidently."

He grunted. "No. Won't wash. You said the Farrell girl may be involved, and we've got a flyer here that says her ex-husband got sprang from the state penitentiary yesterday. Too many coincidences, Simon."

"It sure looks that way," I said agreeably. "Any line on Mike Farrell?"

"Half the force is looking for him. So far, nothing. We checked the girl's house but she hasn't turned up." And no doubt he had a stakeout on Joanne's place now. Behn's voice went on: "Farrell got off the bus yesterday afternoon at five and we lose him right there."

I said, "I talked to somebody who saw him last night. He was driving a station wagon."

He pounced: "How'd you get that? Who told you?

Simon, where are you right now? Maybe you'd better come in and we'll have a little talk—"

"Maybe later," I said. "Right now I haven't got anything that could possibly help. We'd waste each other's dime. I'll be in touch."

I hung up before he could protest; crossed the lobby, dropped two dimes on the desk, pointed a thumb at the phones, got the cashier's nod and went outside into the broil.

Joanne was still in the roofed passageway, wearing her dark glasses and a scowl. I handed her the motel key and told her where to find the room, then went out to her car and drove it around back to meet her.

A weedy lot stretched to the back fence, beyond which half a mile of empty land separated the place from the near boundary of the Air Force base. The flayed, sunbeaten, baking pan of the desert reflected a shimmering heat mist into the air.

There was no one in sight. She unlocked the door and we went in. It was one of those interchangeable rooms, furnished in cheap modern pine with plastic tops and vinyl upholstery, watercolor prints on the walls. The full blast air conditioning had chilled the room to an inhospitable temperature; it had a vaguely antiseptic smell. Everything was very new: you could live forty years in a room like that and it would never be home. The aura of loneliness held ghosts of solitary salesmen, teenage assignations, conventioneering drunks, yapping vacationing kids.

Joanne sat on the bed, kicked her shoes off and crossed her fine long legs. Then she fished for a cigarette. During all this stage business she didn't once look at me. She was, I realized, terrified. She nudged a discarded shoe with her toe and said absently, "I'm always cranky when my feet hurt."

"Sure," I said. "Look, there's no such thing as a perfectly safe place for anybody. Nobody's immune—there's always random chance to mock you. But this ought to be as safe as anyplace for a few hours or even a few days. I'm pretty sure nobody followed us, and it would be a blind million-to-one shot if anybody saw us who'd recognize us and know what to do with the information."

"All right," she declared, "I'm safe. Until tonight or next week or whenever they find me. What happens in the meantime?"

"I'm going to try to take the heat off."

"How?"

"There are a few things I can try," I said, and let it ride like that; she didn't press it. I said, "We're Mr. and Mrs. Chittenden from Sherman Oaks if anybody asks. Do you know how to use a gun?"

I tugged the .38 out of my hip pocket and she looked at it without feeling. "I suppose so," she said. "But if you're thinking of bearding Madonna in his den, you'll need it a lot more than I will."

I put the gun on the bed beside her. "If that was what I had in mind," I said with a little grin, "I wouldn't get within a mile of him with a gun."

She didn't smile. "You're a sweet, generous son of a bitch, Simon. I wish—"

Whatever she had meant to say, she didn't finish it. I tried to dismiss it with an airy gesture and a casual voice: "The one born every minute, I'm him." I bent down and gave her a quick brushing kiss, without force; she didn't draw back, and I straightened quickly and went to the door. "Stay put until I call you. They've got a lunch counter in the lobby—room service might be better. Watch TV and don't think about things, all right?"

"Sure," she muttered. "Sure. I'll be all right. Simon . . . be careful." She sounded miserable.

I made a face and went. Got in the Jeep and pointed it out of the lot. As I stopped at the stop sign, I heard a car rushing forward from the left and turned in time to see a green sedan speed by—glimpse of a thick, red-nosed man, squinting and hard-jawed behind the wheel—then it was gone beyond the freeway overpass, the wind rush and dopplering-down engine roar fading. Nobody I knew. I chastised myself with profanity for being a jumpy fool and chugged onto the road, headed for the foothills east of the city.

As the Jeep surged along the eastbound boulevards I reviewed what I knew about Vincent Madonna.

Madonna, at fifty-five or thereabouts, had arrived in the States at the age of six or seven, grown up in East Harlem and the Bronx and graduated from hoodlum to crook to gangster. At various times he had been named publicly by the FBI and other agencies as a wartime gasoline ration-coupon racketeer (arrested in 1944; released when witnesses failed to turn up), as a labor union and slot machine boss, and—in the early fifties—as the top enforcer of the Mosto Family, which went west to Las Vegas in 1949 and moved into the Southwest. When Don Frank Mosto had died of natural causes a few years ago, the resulting gangland earthquake had settled with Madonna firmly established; even since then, he had stood on his empire like a crowing cock on a dunghill. He was big and powerful and had tried to polish himself with a surface of respectability, but he hadn't succeeded; Madonna had come a long way up from the gutter but he never managed to wash off the smell. He lived in a world inhabited by dinosaurs and circumscribed by the law of *omerta*—the Cosa Nostra code of silence. He paid a New York outfit $20,000 a year to keep his name out of the papers; he put a price on everything, and a value on nothing. A nice cozy chap to deal with. I had never met him, but there wasn't a cop south of Boise who didn't know him by sight.

The foothill suburban ghetto which Madonna inhabited was singularly free of crime—a fact that had puzzled me when I was a cop, because it was the kind of rich folks' neighborhood that normally makes fine pickings for cat thieves and night-crawling burglars. I soon learned the warnings had gone out: independent crooks were to stay out of the area and avoid giving it a bad name. Any lone wolf crook who ignored the warnings was likely to disappear permanently. Madonna didn't want to give the cops any excuse to prowl the neighborhood, because he didn't have all the cops in his pocket. It would have been not only expensive but impossible: there were certain cops he couldn't get to. Not all cops were actively corrupt, although virtually all of them were passively corrupt: they couldn't help knowing their buddies were on the take, but they did nothing about it. Corruption was not open, it was never admitted; a bribed cop stood on tenuous footing, and wasn't likely to confess his corruption, not even to another cop he was sure was equally guilty. And no honest cop could feel safe in blowing the whistle; he couldn't be sure of the superior officer to whom he had to blow the whistle. The power of graft-producing organizations like Madonna's lay in that twilight dubiousness: no official could trust a fellow official enough to spell out what he knew.

Vincent Madonna's command fortress was a sprawling foothill mansion perched on a cactus-studded knell with a view of the entire city. It was an architectural bastard—part Spanish adobe-mission, part Texas ranch style, part Sunday

Times house-beautiful feature page. All on one story, it had several wings and outbuildings, spidering out with the shambling graceless opulence of a Las Vegas motel. There were sprinklers on the lawn, ticking loudly, and four or five cars cooling their wheels in the circular gravel drive, including Madonna's 1941 Lincoln Continental, a painstakingly restored classic. Everybody's got to have a hobby. The smell of the watered grass was a warm spice that registered keenly in my nostrils when I parked the Jeep behind the Continental and stepped out.

I had taken for granted that the place would be festooned with alarm systems and bodyguards; the latter assumption proved accurate enough—the door swung open before I got to it and a rum-looking Neanderthal gave me a sizing up which I associated in my mind with the look a hungry piranha would direct toward a raw hunk of bleeding flesh. He wore a sport jacket which he had obviously only put on in order to open the door so that his shoulder-holstered gun wouldn't show.

"Yeah?"

"I'd like to see the Don. I'm not armed."

"What name?"

"Simon Crane."

"Mr. Madonna expecting you?"

"It'll come as no surprise," I declared.

The bodyguard looked uncertain; then, abruptly, he turned to look over his shoulder at someone who had come up behind him. It was hard to see inside against the blinding light of the exterior sun, but then I heard that wheeze of a voice and recognized it immediately: an old injury to the larynx had reduced Pete DeAngelo's voice to a harsh whisper.

"Who's all this?"

The bodyguard took a step backward to explain to DeAngelo who I was and what I wanted, but DeAngelo brushed him aside and came forward. His tall frame filled the opening. "Hello, Crane."

DeAngelo was a sleek, cold man, hard and handsome and poison-cruel. He was a dandy: he was wearing white tapered slacks, white loafers with pointed toes, an ascot under a high custom shirt collar. His polished nails glinted. If MGM ever decided to make the *Pete DeAngelo Story*, the role might have gone to Robert Wagner. He had a deep suntan and opaque eyes; he revealed all the feelings of a marble slab.

I gave him plenty of time to look me over. We had met before a few times—twice at the station house when he'd come to bail out a couple of the boys. Among his other accomplishments DeAngelo was a bar-admitted lawyer. He was also Madonna's *consigliore*—councilor and right-hand man. His reputation was for ambition, brains and smooth if ruthless efficiency.

I said, "I'd like a minute with the Don."

"What for?"

"To save me trouble and save you people time and effort wasted on wild goose chases," I said, watching his face. If there was any reaction inside him, he made no sign of it.

He glanced back at the bodyguard, who was tugging at his cuffs and scowling. The bodyguard had a disturbing way of leaning so far forward his feet seemed nailed to the door. Buster Keaton used to do that, I thought. DeAngelo said in his grating whisper, "Keep him company, Freddie," and went back into the house without another glance at me. DeAngelo's shoes had heels that clicked like dice.

Freddie propped himself in the doorway with his arms

folded, keeping me out under the sun. I said, "You're from Chicago."

He shook his head and grinned. He looked like the type who was chronically on the lam. I said, "Hot, isn't it?"

"Bet your ass," said Freddie.

Presently DeAngelo clicked back into sight, an intense hungry panther, and nodded to Freddie. DeAngelo's smile, pointed at me, was without menace; but I felt a chill. He rasped, "Okay, he wants to find out what you've got to say. Come on." He turned without further remarks and walked to the center of the sepulchral living room. I went inside and heard the door click shut behind me. By then DeAngelo had turned and lifted one palm toward me to stop me. He said, "Mind a frisk?"

"No."

"Go ahead, Freddie."

I let Freddie paw me for guns and when he was finished I followed DeAngelo through an arched corridor to the back of the house. He opened a sliding glass door and led the way out onto a flagstone walk that ran along to the tiled apron around the swimming pool. It was a big blue pool shaped like a bell, with ladders and diving board. Heat bounced off everything—the water, the walls of the house, wings which enclosed the pool area in a U, the flagstones and gravel, and the barbed wire-topped brick wall that sealed off the far end of the patio. The place was an oven.

Vincent Madonna, the sun worshiper; lay fully clothed on a chaise lounge, shaded by a huge beach umbrella-table. As I approached he had the poolside telephone propped against his ear. The phone was doing most of the talking; Madonna listened. He gave me one glance with eyes hard as glass, nodded, waved a hand and turned his profile to me, listening to the phone.

Madonna was stout, his features fleshy, his chin dark with heavy stubble halfheartedly covered with talc. He was beginning to look jowly and fold-cheeked. His hair, black and thick and glossy, was combed carefully back over the small ears. The backs of his hands were hairy. He wore a suit with no tie; his wardrobe, rumpled and creased, represented an obvious outlay of about $800. He looked as if his life's ambition—to be pictured in a full-color, full-page magazine advertisement for whisky—had been frustrated by the desert heat.

Madonna had closed his eyes in distaste; now and then he interrupted the telephone's monologue with a baritone grunt. Agony and patience chased each other across his face. The phone complained lugubriously. Finally Madonna's face assumed an expression of total tormented revulsion; he spoke briefly, and returned the receiver to the cradle before opening his eyes.

He looked up and beamed at me.

DeAngelo said, "He's clean."

"I'm immaculate," I said.

"We'll see," said Madonna. He glanced past me—a skinny dark-complexioned sycophant scuttled out of the house with a document in one hand and a fountain pen in another. Madonna said, "Can't that wait?"

"No, sir," said the sycophant. He put the document down on the beach-umbrella table and held his hand on it while Madonna took the pen and signed at the tip of the sycophant's finger. Madonna glanced at it and lay back on the chaise; the sycophant put the pen together, picked up the document, blew on the signature, folded it in thirds and went.

Not until that one was gone did any of us speak. Then it was Madonna, fingering a Frank Paradise billiard cue, who directed his affable avuncular voice at me: "How clean are you, Crane?"

"That's what I came to see you about."

Pete DeAngelo husked, "Now tell us something we didn't already know."

Madonna lifted a hairy hand to still him; he said to me, "Mentioning no names, let's just say at the moment you and your little friend are alive on a rain check. I state that as a fact, not a threat."

"I understand," I said. "Look, this is all off the record. I'm not carrying a tape recorder around. I'm not interested in meddling in things that are none of my business. I'm sure Tony Senna reported on the visit he paid me this morning—he looked around and he didn't find whatever he was looking for. All I want to do is put this to you: if Joanne Farrell and I had taken anything important out of Aiello's safe, we wouldn't be stupid enough to wait around afterwards—and I wouldn't be stupid enough to come up here and argue about it. She had nothing to do with it, I had nothing to do with it, and I'd like the chance to prove that to your satisfaction."

Madonna fixed me with his intent hard eyes; Pete DeAngelo moved forward, heels clacking, and said in his raspy whisper, "If that's your best artillery, Crane, forget it, it's a dud. You couldn't sell that story to a hayseed who's in the market for the Brooklyn Bridge. Listen—you're in trouble with us, and you don't slide out of it just by coming up here and bleeding on Mr. Madonna's patio."

Madonna shushed him again with a hand. "Let me have him for a few minutes, Pete." He smiled amiably.

DeAngelo's mouth pinched together, looking like a surgeon's wound, but finally, giving no acknowledgment that he had heard the dismissal, he turned on his heel and left us. Madonna, for a brief moment, scowled toward the pool, and I knew why: DeAngelo had committed a *faux pas*. It was against the rules for the Cosa Nostra to let an outsider know about any division of opinion within the organization; that kind of knowledge could be dangerous—it could give outsiders a chance to set member against member.

The glass door slid shut. I figured at least one bodyguard was watching us but it was hardly worth staring to find out. I returned my attention to Madonna and said, "Look, if you really think I'm it, then you've not only picked the wrong horse, you've got the wrong track. Concentrating on Joanne Farrell and Simon Crane will never get your belongings back for you."

"What is it you want me to do?" he inquired with his friendly businessman's smile.

"Lift the heat," I replied promptly. "You've got that girl scared to death."

"Well, now," he said, steepling his hands together and tipping his head back to look at me, "for the sake of argument we'll assume we both know what you're talking about. Understand, I admit nothing. But let's you and me set up what the lawyers call a hypothetical case. Assume I've got some interest in some items that might be missing from somebody's safe. Assume there's been a lot of sensational publicity about somebody's murder, and there's going to be more publicity, and I don't enjoy that at all—in fact you can assume somebody's busy right now, planting news items about how the deceased must have had personal enemies from back east or something. Assume, in other words, I don't want any more rumbles. You follow?"

"Sure."

"Okay. So we're prepared to be nice and quiet and civilized about it. If you turn in the missing items within twenty-four hours, or prove you and Mrs. Farrell couldn't possibly have taken it, then you can assume I'd be willing to forget the whole beef."

He smiled. I suppose he meant it to be an engaging smile.

I felt dismal but not surprised; it had never been anything better than a long shot.

He looked at his watch, shot his cuff, and said pleasantly, "It's pushing noon. I'd be willing to go the few extra minutes—call it noon tomorrow, your deadline."

"And if I can't produce?"

He shrugged his meaty shoulders and picked at a hairy ear. "I don't throw raw meat on the floor, Crane, it's not my style. I leave it to your imagination. I only mention there are friends of mine who don't mind putting the screws on people, hard, to find out what they know and what they did with stolen property."

He didn't have to spell that out. I said, in a lower voice, "You can't get blood from stones. She doesn't know anything—I don't know anything."

"Then all you've got to do is prove it."

"How many people do you know who can prove where they were between two and five in the morning?"

"Too bad you're not married," he answered, smiling slightly. Then he tipped himself up on one elbow and said, "If some of the fellows decide they have to put the screws to you two, they wouldn't leave you around alive afterward to testify about it. You understand that?"

"I understand it," I said, "but I can't buy it. You haven't got enough evidence to justify it with the organization. You haven't got any evidence at all, period. I know it wouldn't have to stand up in court, but you'd have to show something."

"Maybe if you two were members of my organization. But you're not. You're not wearing our silks, Crane. Nobody cares what happens to you and the woman." He shook his head and said sadly, "The minute I laid eyes on you I knew you'd be one of those guys who had to do everything the hard way. I wish you wouldn't keep arguing—you made your pitch, I didn't buy it. That's all there is to it. You came to the wrong store to sell your kind of merchandise."

I took a breath. "Twenty-four hours isn't enough time for a scavenger hunt. At least give us a couple of weeks."

"To get out of the country with the stuff?"

"You know better than that. We—"

"Nuts. You two are the number one suspects. If you want it spelled out, it goes like this. Mrs. Farrell had the motive—things in the safe she wanted to get her hands on. She had the opportunity—she was one of only four people who had keys to the house and the alarm system, and the other three people are accounted for. I'm one of them, the housekeeper makes two, and then of course the deceased, he had keys, it was his house. You see, it's those keys that narrow it down, Crane. The alarm system down there is wired on a direct circuit that sets off an alarm here in my house if anybody busts into Aiello's place. Whoever went in there last night had to have a whole set of keys, not just something to pick the door locks with. There was no sign the place was jimmied or the wires cut. Aiello turned up dead wearing bare feet in slippers, which means he was in bed. If he'd had an appointment with anybody he'd have put socks on, he was the type; he didn't go around in his bare feet when he had company."

"It could have been anybody he knew," I said. "Somebody gets him out of bed and he goes to the door and sees it's a friend, so he switches off the alarm and opens the door and lets them in."

Madonna shook his head. "No. There's only a small number of people he'd have trusted enough to let them in the house alone with him at that hour of the night, and they've all been checked out. You see?"

I opened my mouth, but the phone beside him rang. Madonna picked it up and talked and listened. When he hung up his smile was fixed. He looked up at me and said, "Room Seventy-Two, Executive Lodge. Mean anything to you?"

I tried hard to keep it off my face. Madonna shook his head, making the kind of face he would use chastising an errant small boy. "A poor try, Crane—and maybe it'll give you some idea how far you'd get if you tried to hustle Mrs. Farrell out of town. It wouldn't be discreet." Watching my face, he added gently, "You're not a very good loser, are you?"

"I'm not playing a game," I snapped. "Look, I'll beg if I have to. At least give us the two weeks. Maybe the cops will turn up something by then."

"Why should I bargain when I've got a corner on the market? No deals, Crane—no gentlemen's agreement."

I said bleakly, "What the hell do you expect to win by this?"

"It's what I don't expect to lose," he said. Then he swung his legs over the edge of the chaise and stood up. He was a surprisingly tall man. He kept his voice friendly: "You made a mistake, Crane. You probably figured us for a pack of brainless thugs, and you should have known better—nobody gets where I am without brains. You made an error, you and the Farrell woman, trying to play cute and fast with us. Who do you think you're dealing with? I started peddling the streets of Harlem when I was nine years of age. So let's not insult each other. Where's the stuff you took out of Aiello's safe?"

"I don't know." I lifted both hands. "One week—at least give us that."

"Like you said, the cops might turn something up if I let it go too long. And putting your same hypothetical case, we could assume I can't afford to have the wrong people get their hands on the missing items. A week's too long. But I'll tell you what I'll do, Crane, to prove we're all civilized. I'll double your time. Call it forty-eight hours." Still smiling, Madonna put his thick arm over my shoulders and walked me to the sliding glass door.

Chapter Four

When I stepped up into the ancient Jeep, flipped the key and punched the starter, all the while watching Freddie who stood leaning impossibly forward in the doorway like an ugly immutable gargoyle, I was reviewing in my mind the confrontation with Madonna and regarding myself, my performance, with dazed wonder. Here I was with forty-eight hours between us (Joanne and me) and our joint funeral, yet I seemed to be behaving with cool aplomb. I had faced Madonna not with ravings, and not with begging desperation, but with some kind of detached calm which had sealed itself around me like a plastic bubble.

It was, of course, the kind of deadpan repression that masked absolute hysteria.

I lifted one hand and flapped it nastily at Freddie, whose Neanderthal face made no acknowledgment but watched with bovine intensity while I backed the Jeep out of the drive.

I turned down the narrow curvy asphalt lane; my mind had gone into neutral, I wasn't even attempting to lay plans. Paralysis; I suppose I had consigned myself to execution. I formed the vague idea of buying a half-gallon of tequila, taking it to Joanne's room, and getting splendidly drunk. I thought of a rock patch back in the Peloncillos which I had always meant to explore but had never gotten around to; it welled up in me an almost nostalgic yearning for all the planned things I had never done and, now, never would do. Books I meant to read, places I meant to see, old friends I wanted to see again. Joanne's image blossomed in my mind, vivid and sharp—the warmth of her body, the lusty bark of her laughter, flash of eyes, toss of head. Riding the Jeep through a low dip in the road, I had the sudden feeling she was sitting just behind my shoulder, and all I needed do was turn around and look into her smiling violet eyes, encircle her with my arms, fold her close against me, hearing her husky laugh, scenting the fragrance of her hair.

It came to me that the sharp sense of loss was stronger in me than my own private fear of danger. That lonely sense of imminent loss stunned me: I hadn't let myself believe she had come to mean so much to me.

The feeling of having her just behind my shoulder became so strong that my eyes shifted involuntarily to the rear-view mirror. Of course there was nobody in the bed of the Jeep. What I did see in the mirror was the shark-toothed chrome snout of the big dusty station wagon, bearing down on me from behind.

Mike Farrell got out of the car and took me at gunpoint in the Jeep to the boarded-up old house in Las Palmas, and a few minutes later I was sitting there in a lawn chair holding Mike's gun and waiting for Mike to struggle back to consciousness.

Mike sat up with a pained grimace. "Jesus."

"How do you feel?"

He cringed when I spoke; his eyes dipped toward me, bloodshot. "I got a headache right down to my toenails."

"You hit the door with your head."

"You knocked me down and got my gun, huh? Trust me to do that right." He gave a nervous, braying cackle.

The heat was close and oppressive. When he looked at the gun I had, he flinched.

I let him have a good look at it. Then I said, "What happened to Aiello, Mike?"

"I swear to God I don't know."

"What happened to the stuff in his safe?"

"How the hell should I know?"

"Then why are you shaking like a jackhammer?"

"Because my head hurts, goddamn it." He looked away from me. The room was enormous, with baroque arches and domed ceiling. Mike sat like a taut-wound watch spring, his face down, heavy with thought. When he looked up again, he studied me with skittish caution and an apologetic, cowardly half-smile. His face was sweat-drenched and greenish; his baggy trousers, unpressed and too big for him, gave him the pathetic look of a diminutive circus clown. He must have lost weight in prison.

Suddenly he said, "What he had in that safe, Crane, it was enough cash to make a fast down payment on an aircraft carrier. They think I've got it, don't they?"

I said quietly, "How do you know what was in the safe?"

There was soft insinuation in my voice but he didn't react. He said, "Aiello showed it to me," in a morose offhand tone. I went over to the window near him and perched on the sill—Mike's head turned on bulging neck tendons to keep me in sight. I dangled the automatic over one knee. As a cop I had learned to sit above a man when questioning him.

I said, "How much?"

"What?"

"How much does it take to make a down payment on an aircraft carrier?"

"Someplace between two million and three million.

Closer to three." Seeing my look of disbelief he added quickly, "I swear it's the truth—look, that's why I wanted to talk to you."

"Why me?"

"Because you and me and Joanne, we're all in the same fix. We got to get together on this. Maybe we can work it out if we put our heads together."

"You seem to know an awful lot about what's going on," I observed.

"Look, Crane, I didn't make the hit on Aiello and I ain't got the money."

I said, "Let's hear the whole thing."

"Okay—but first you got to tell me what you were doing up at Madonna's. You working for him now?"

"No."

"And I just take your word for that?"

"Suit yourself. Here's one for you: what makes you think they've fingered you for it?"

"How else can they add it up? It's what I'd think if I was in their shoes."

"Why?"

"It's a long story."

"If I get bored," I said, "I'll yawn."

He swallowed and squeezed his hands. When he rubbed them together the sound was scratchy and dry. He kept staring abysmally at the gun in my hand; finally he said, "Look, all I want is off the hook and unless things have changed a lot in a couple hours, you're in the same boat. Can we help each other, Crane?"

"How do I know unless you tell me what you've got in mind?"

"I hope to hell you can help," he muttered. "I got nobody else."

"You've got yourself."

"Yeah," he said, off-key. "I been having myself for years."

I didn't say anything. He tried to glare at me but he couldn't hold my eyes. He lifted his shoulders and let them drop; juices seemed to run out of him and he said in a weary voice, "Let me tell it my own way. I got to start way back at the beginning or you won't understand it. I been rehearsing this for two hours this morning. How much you need to know."

When I made no answer he gave me a spasmodic shrug. "Look, I was a sax man, a pretty good sax man, and I used to be clean. I had this four-man combo and we booked around town, little toy wages but I had talent and I figured I'd make it. More talent than a lot of Charley the Stars ever had, but they eat. I didn't know that then.

"I figured if you could blow good and hit all the notes that move, all you had to do was wait for some A-and-R scout from Columbia to sign you up.

"Things were going okay. We moved into the better clubs and cut a few sides and the money got good. I was young. I married Joanne about then—everything felt groovy. Jesus God how innocent we were! Did you know she was a virgin when I married her? She was nineteen years old.

"But then I lost two good men, the bass player got drafted and the piano man went to the Coast, and I had to break in a couple idiots that didn't know their brass from their oboes. So okay, so we keep working, but all the time I keep seeing forty-year-old horn men dying from malnutrition and TB and alcoholism. Good bands are a dime a dozen. All of a sudden I could see I don't want to spend twenty years playing crumb joints and have nothing to show for it except a mountain of debts and creases in my neck and maybe a habit for booze or hard dope. I had to do better than that for Joanne. You get what I mean? Or am I trying to describe a color to a blind man?"

He had warmed up; he was enjoying the sound of his own voice, but I had to let him go on at his own pace. I nodded at him and said, "I understand."

"Okay. So I got sick and tired of the life we were leading, that's all. Jesus, I was in love with Jo. But the way we lived, Sweet God. I figured she deserved better."

His voice ran down and he sat scowling. I didn't prompt him. After a while he said sourly, "You know, you really ought to pay extra for the story of my life."

He looked up with a twisted smile and resumed:

"Then they went ape for rock. They brought in all these stupid long-haired kids where the drummer plays the melody in the band and all they know how to do is jiggle a lot and make enough noise to make you stone deaf. Now I'm too old to get in that bag, see? I'm a musician for Christ's sake. It's the last goddamn straw.

"Right then we were working the Moulin Rouge, which was the only room left on the Strip that wasn't using rock. I could see it wouldn't last—I learned about squeeze plays the first time I got jumped in an alley by five kids bigger than me. Man, I figured here I was making only a hundred a week but next month I could be starving to death." He uttered a B-flat grunt of sour laughter and threw up his arms, gesturing. His arms fell to his sides and he said gloomily, "So one night Sal Aiello, he owns the Moulin Rouge, he comes to my door selling Mafia cookies."

He looked at me to see what effect that had. "I'm not dense," he said defiantly. "Look, Aiello offered me a chance to write my own ticket, and if I turned it down where was I supposed to go? I wasn't about to go back to the bottom—I been there, it's too crowded. So I gave my boys their closing notice. That's one thing you learn in that business—how to get off."

I said, "So then Aiello gave you a job. Doing what?"

"Bagman," he said without hesitation. "I was clean, no criminal record. I was ideal—the cops wouldn't shake down a guy like me at embarrassing times like when I'm carrying a satchel full of payoff money for the monthly sheet of pot-belly politicians."

"Who'd the money go to?"

He looked at me from under his thin eyebrows. "I don't think that's included in the price of your ticket."

"All right," I said, saving it for later. "Go ahead."

"Okay, I'm on the payroll and then something happens that gets me sore at Aiello." He squinted at me as if to divine how much I knew about that.

I decided it would help to tell him. "I know about Aiello and Joanne."

"Christ. Everybody alive and his idiot half-brother seems to know about that. Hell, I guess I should have kept it to myself, but she was my wife. The bastard didn't think I'd lift a finger. He thought I was too scared. He was right. Christ, that crazy Jo goes and shacks up with him just for kicks I guess because she didn't know any better, and what do I do about it? Nothing. Oh, I belted Jo a few good ones, but I didn't go near Aiello. If I had, I'd have ended up part of the pavement on a road-construction job. Like he did. But the trouble with me is, I didn't know enough to keep my mouth shut. I got pissed off—hell, who wouldn't?—and I loaded up with too much to drink one night and I started beefing in a bar about that bastard Aiello. I didn't spell anything out, just called him some names, but Pete DeAngelo hears the tail end of it. That's my luck. So Pete hears me beefing and he walks me outside and taps me around a little. Maybe I had that coming. It taught me my lesson. But right after that I find a couple cops waiting at my house with a warrant and a half a kilo of uncut heroin they claim they found taped inside my toilet tank. It was a railroad— you never saw anything that raw. I was clean, man, I never in my life messed with narcotics."

"Who planted it? The cops?"

"No. Aiello or DeAngelo, one of them had it done. Then they phoned in an anonymous tip to the cops. They made sure Joanne was out of town that week so it wouldn't get pinned on her—they wanted her around here handy where they could keep pins stuck in her."

He turned palms up and looked at me. "And you ask me why I think they're after me. I can't pretend I didn't have a beef against Aiello—it gives me a nice neat motive to go after him the minute I get out of jail, right? Good old Aiello. When I got arrested he was as nice and fatherly as you could ask. Comes to the visiting room and tells me it's all for my own good, the organization likes to keep the hired help in line and once in a while it calls for teaching a little lesson. I'm the student. He gets me an organization mouthpiece and the guy pleads me guilty, which I was in no position to argue. I walk into Superior Court and the judge hands me seven to ten years, and then Aiello tells me the boys don't hold any hard feelings, it's just this is the way things get handled when you step out of line. He promises me there'll be a good job waiting for me when I get out, and he gives me his word on his mother's grave nobody's going to touch Joanne while I'm away. Of course that's to keep me from getting so unhappy I might decide to sing to the cops. Joanne's their hostage to make sure I don't talk right?

But I figured Aiello meant what he said about treating me square when I got out—which is why I went up there last night."

Maybe he thought he detected ironic disbelief in my face; he said angrily, "Hell, what else could I do?"

"You tell me."

"If I'd turned state's evidence they might have gone for Joanne or they might have gone for me—they can find a way to slip a hit man into a prison cell if they want to. Either one of us could've ended up with our heads in a basket. Okay, so I built up a reputation for keeping my mouth shut, but what choice did I have? It didn't mean I was happy, I admit—if I was happy I wouldn't be here talking to you like this. But goddamn it, I've seen them put the fix on when they wanted to. Tony Senna got arrested a few years ago and he's got a record as long as your arm, but they bribed the Records Division to supply the court with a clean record sheet for the trial, and he got off with a suspended sentence as a first offender. First offender my ass. Then there was a bookie they caught chiseling on the receipts a few years back, so two torpedoes beat his head in with tire irons. Some cop caught them both red-handed, but the fix goes in and when the cop gets on the stand he testifies he saw the bookie fall on his head. They could have bought me the same kind of fix, but hell, they framed me in the first place, why should they?"

He was lying back now, sprawling, staring at the high sepulchral ceiling. "Five years is a long time when you break it up into hours, Crane. The only thing that keeps you going is knowing you're going to get out. But I'm out twenty-four hours and already they're writing up a contract on me. Look, I don't want to go out in a blaze of glory—I don't want to go out at all. That's why I had to talk to you."

"All right," I said. "You're talking. Where does it get us?"

"I ain't finished," he said. "I got us up to yesterday so let's finish it."

I nodded patiently.

"A guy owes me some bucks, see? Sal Aiello. He promised me a job and some bucks to get started again when I got out, and like I told you, I believed him. Why should he lie to me? So I been a good boy, I got my parole and I took the bus back here and I cruised around downtown yesterday afternoon looking for somebody that could give me a ride out to Aiello's house. They don't use buses in his neighborhood.

"Okay, I ran into Tony Senna, he's cruising the taco district picking up shylock money and numbers payoffs. Right out in bare-ass daylight—man, you know the fix is in with the cops down there."

"And?"

"I chased around with Tony, said hello to some of the guys, and finally he finished his rounds and DeAngelo picks us up in his Mercedes. Every time DeAngelo whispers at me I get the feeling he's trying to sell me a used car, but I needed the ride out to Aiello's and that was where they were headed. There was some small talk like how did I like stir and who'd I get to know up there. DeAngelo's put on a little weight and wearing a fancy Sy Devore-type suit looking like a goddamn movie star and I could see everybody was doing fine while I was away. There's a lot of talk about getting ready to legalize gambling. Finally we get out to Aiello's place—big house, pool, panoramic vista, the works. About a mile north of Madonna's place. It was dark by the time we got out there. DeAngelo goes right out to the pool and strips down and starts splashing around,

striking poses for a chick Aiello's got decorating the pool—
you know Aiello, he's always had a harem problem."

He paused to marshal his memories, probably wondering
how much I really knew about Aiello and Joanne. Aiello had
been a relentless womanizer with a broken-down libido who
used women and discarded them; sometimes I wondered
how much satisfaction such men got from their compulsive
conquests.

Mike muttered, "Aiello was kind of tilted about dames."
He sounded strangely wistful, but he didn't follow it up.

He changed the subject harshly: "Anyhow, when I got
there Aiello was as per usual, all jovial and friendly, wall-to-
wall booze and this nice piece of fluff, Judy Dodson's her
name, pouring his drinks and lighting his cigars for him. A
hot pillow dame with a topless neck—you know the type."

When he looked at me, I gave him a nod.

He said, "Aiello gave me a drink and bragged about how
the business has expanded since I went up. He's built a new
wing on the Moulin Rouge, where I used to work, so they
can turn it into a casino soon as they buy enough legislators
to push the gambling bill through the state house.

"DeAngelo and Tony Senna keep drifting in and out
with phone messages. After a while it gets cool by the pool
so we go inside, which is when Aiello goes over to the safe.

"It's a great big bank vault, in the library. Covers pretty
near the whole damn interior wall. Aiello signals DeAngelo
and me and the Dodson chick to come look inside. Like I
told you, enough cash to choke a whale. I counted the
stacks, and if each stack was full of bills of the same denom-
ination they had showing on top, then my estimate has got
to be pretty close—somewhere around three million dollars,
like I said. Most of it out in the open. There were a few
lockboxes too, on shelves inside. I didn't see what was in

them. Aiello likes to show off stuff like that—liked, I mean, he's dead. Anyhow he told me he knew I took a bad fall, the judge was too tough, and he says the organization wants to make it up to me now that I've showed how true-blue I can be. I kept my mouth shut, you see. So he takes a wad out of the sack and hands it to me."

Mike reached into his baggy pockets and took out a thick sheaf of bills tight-bound with a rubber band. "Close to five grand in twenties and fifties," he explained, and put it back where he got it.

"After that Aiello told me to keep my shirt on, they'd find me a good job shortly and in the meantime I should have a good time. Then DeAngelo starts to pump me—he seemed to think I'd spread all kinds of loose talk in stir. I told him I'd kept quiet—would I be that dense? DeAngelo and Aiello were like a pair of cops where one puts a cigarette in your mouth and the other slaps it out of your face. Right then I got a funny feeling down the back of my neck, you know?

"It took a while to convince them. Finally DeAngelo seemed to buy my story, and he left. Tony Senna was someplace around the house and he left with DeAngelo, in the Mercedes. Aiello takes me outside to see them off. Then he hands me the key to that station wagon and tells me I can use it as long as I like. So I get in the car and drive out. The girl was still there with Aiello. I came into town and stopped at a bar and had a few, and all the time I couldn't get rid of the idea they were setting me up for a patsy. They don't need me, see? I started thinking about how much sense it might make for them to kiss me off a mountain cliff one night. Maybe I was wrong but Joanne can tell you I was rattled as hell. I couldn't think of what to do so I went to her place, but she wouldn't let me in, I guess I don't blame her. I made a bitch of her life."

"Where did you go when you left Joanne's?"

"Back to the Moulin Rouge."

"They close at one," I said. "Where'd you spend the rest of the night?"

He hesitated. "Look, I got to tell you the truth—hang me with it if you want to. When the Moulin Rouge closed I bought a bottle and took it with me. I drove up the Strip clear to the foothills and parked and had a little consultation with the bottle. I don't remember how much of it I killed but I was pretty damn drunk by the time I decided to get it over with. Whisky courage. I drove up to Aiello's house again."

He let it hang in the air, watching me while I watched him. Finally he closed his lids down and said, "Crane, you've got to believe me. It was about four this morning. There was a car coming out of Aiello's drive just before I turned in. I didn't get much of a look at it—a Cadillac, I think; all I'm sure of is it was pink. My headlights picked it up and it was pink. I didn't pay any attention to it just then because why was I supposed to suspect anything? I drove on in and got out of the car and the front door was wide open, the lights were on. I went inside. The place was a mess. Aiello wasn't there, the safe was open, all that cabbage was gone, even the lockboxes—the safe was absolutely empty. I smelled sulfur, like powder-smoke after a gun goes off, you know? Man, I didn't stick around—I went back to the station wagon and got the hell out of there. I went to Ed Baker's place—he's got a little house over by the university. Tony Senna and a couple others were there, playing cards— they'd been at it for hours. I grabbed a sandwich but I was too drunk and too bushed and too scared to sit down and play cards, so I went in the back room and went to sleep.

"When I woke up Senna and Baker were crawling all over my station wagon, tearing the damn thing apart. I guess they didn't find anything—you got to figure there'd be bloodstains in the car if I'd carried Aiello's corpse out to that roadbed and buried it. Of course I didn't know what they were looking for at first, but then later I heard the radio news about the body and I knew that's what they'd been looking for in the station wagon. All right, they didn't find any stains, and that slowed them down. But the way Senna looked at me I knew I was a long way from being off the hook. I went in the john and I could hear them out in the kitchen. There was a phone call, probably DeAngelo, and after Senna hung up he told Baker to get his gun because they were going out to your place to pump you and Joanne and see if you had the money. So they went, and as soon as they were gone I got in the station wagon and came over here. I had to think."

"Why here?"

"It used to be a drop. I'd pick up satchels here once in a while. I think a long time ago they used the place to pass dope from dealers to pushers."

His voice ran down. He sat sweating in a dark pool of shadow. I said, "Three million dollars is a lot of cash. What was it doing in Aiello's safe in the first place?"

"They used the vault for a collection point for everything this side of El Paso and Salt Lake."

"They wouldn't just let all that cash lie idle in the safe. What was supposed to happen to it?"

He looked at me; he was deciding whether to answer. He said, "Jesus, why not? Look, the way they worked it, Aiello would hold the stuff they collected from various enterprises all over the district. They kept it in cash because they didn't want any records for the tax boys to dig in. This was the raw take, you understand. All sizes of bills, unmarked. The mob's got its own legit banks back east, Long Island and New Jersey, but out here they don't, so it was handy to have that big old bank vault in Aiello's house. They'd let the cash pile up until there was enough for a shipment—maybe four million. Then they'd satchel it into a small van with two or three torpedoes and armor plate and more locks and electric guard systems than you ever saw, and Aiello and DeAngelo would ride with it over to Los Angeles. Over there they'd work through a dozen banks, change the money into cashiers' checks and bank letters under phony names. They'd take a week, ten days to get it done, all in small batches so they wouldn't attract attention. Then somebody flies it over to Switzerland—they've got dozens of numbered bank accounts in Zurich. It used to be Madonna who called the turns but he never touched the stuff with his own hands. Usually Aiello and DeAngelo would fly over to Switzerland."

"And the safe was almost full last night?" I asked.

"Close. Like I said."

"It all belonged to the mob?"

"Mostly. A lot of people had pieces of it. And Aiello used to keep money in the safe for people who didn't want to report it for taxes—private money."

"Who else?"

"I don't know names. Outsiders, but I don't know which ones."

He got up and wobbled toward the door to get air. I stayed close with the gun. He said, "God, I feel like I just got out of the hospital after six months and fell down in the lobby on my way out and broke both legs. Only this time there's no cure. Jesus H. Christ. I belong to the running dead, you know that?"

All this had been preamble; suddenly he wheeled to face me. He said in a sharper tone of voice, "Crane, I've leveled with you. When I heard Senna and Baker talking this morning, I knew the mob was trying to decide whether it was me that took the money, or you and Joanne. Or maybe all three of us. They want to play marbles with our eyeballs. Okay, listen, I played straight with those guys, I said I was sorry, but I'm not going to die for it and I'm not about to write it a hundred times on the blackboard. I want out. If you've got any brains, you do too."

"Go on—spell it out, Mike."

He nodded. "I talk a lot, I know. Reflex habit. But I've been sizing you up. I'm not as dumb as I look. You're one of the mob's prime suspects. I know that because I heard the boys talking this morning. This morning you went up to Madonna's. What for? I asked myself. The answer was easy. You went up there for the same reason I did. When you drove in, I was parked up the road trying to work up the guts to go in and talk to Madonna, beg on my knees if I had to, just persuade them I didn't do it. I didn't have the nerve, but you did. Now, if you'd taken the loot you'd have been long gone by now, I figure. Besides, you're tied up with Jo, and I know her well enough to know she'd never do a thing like this. So let's lay it on the line. You didn't do it and I didn't do it and Joanne didn't do it. What else is there? Madonna himself? I doubt it. Soldiers been drifting in and out of Madonna's place all day, there's a big flap, and I just don't think it's a mob operation. Some independent party is out there someplace with all that loot. But the mob doesn't look at it that way—not yet, anyway. Too many coincidences for them. They know Joanne had keys to Aiello's house and the alarm system—that was why Senna and Baker made a beeline for your place this morning. They know I just got out of the pen and went directly to Aiello's last night and saw what was in the safe. Probably they figure all three of us were in it together, we pulled the caper, right? Just think about that, Crane."

I had; I was. I said, "Go on, Mike."

"Okay, the reason I opened up to you, I want to make a deal."

"What kind of a deal?"

Now there was cunning in his eyes—anxious and fearful, but sly. "Together maybe we can find that loot," he said. "If either one of us finds it and turns it over to the mob, do you think that'll keep them from killing all three of us anyway, just to keep our mouths shut?"

"Keep going."

"Okay. We find it, we split it down the middle, and we go our separate ways."

I said, "What about the mob?"

He tried to smile. "Crane, forty thousand men disappear every year in this country, and a lot of them don't ever get found unless they want to. If it helps you make up your mind, I got a good contact—not through the mob—with a plastic surgeon. You follow?" He dragged a crumpled piece of paper out of his pocket, glanced at it, and handed it to me. I looked at it—the name and address of a doctor in Studio City.

He said, "Keep it, I got another copy. Hell, tie it all up in nice neat ribbons—leave a suicide note if you want to and make it look like you took a Brodie off the Golden Gate Bridge."

He was staring at me without blinking, almost holding his breath.

I said, "What about Joanne?"

"Joanne and me are quits. I won't make waves. You cut

your half with her or do it however you want."

"I notice you didn't offer to split it in thirds."

"I didn't think I had to. I thought you and Joanne were an item together. Making woo, all that crap."

I didn't press it; what I said was, "Suppose we look but we don't find the money?"

"Then we get dead. I don't know about you but I'm dead anyway. What have we got to lose?" He had a point.

I said, "You've leveled with me as far as I can tell. I'll give you this much. Madonna gave me forty-eight hours to produce the money."

"Or else what?"

"He didn't specify. They'll bring Joanne in and then bring me in and they'll work us over to find out what we know."

"And when they're satisfied you don't know anything, they'll rub you out anyway because they can't afford to let you go and blab what they did to you. A sweet pot, Crane. Look, the only chance we've got is to throw in together. We can't go to the cops—they might help us find the stuff but we'd end up dead anyway, and most of the cops I know would keep the money and pretend they never found it."

Which was, I thought, exactly what Mike himself was proposing to do. I didn't point out the irony of his indignation. I said, "Where do you figure to start looking?"

"Have we got a deal?"

"Let's put it like this. We'll work together. If and when we find the money we can decide what's to be done with it. If it looks like we can guarantee our own safety by turning the money over to Madonna, then I'd suggest it's better to be alive and broke than dead and rich."

"That'd have to be a hell of a guarantee."

"If we can work it out that way, will you go for it?"

He scowled. "If it's the only way, hell yes. Have I got a choice?"

"All right. We've got a deal."

He nodded. "Okay. Then the first thing you do is check out the Judy Dodson bird. She was still with Aiello when I left last night. Look, the reason I can't do it myself, I got to stay out of sight. They might take a notion to haul me in any time. You've at least got forty-eight hours and they'll probably keep their hands off you that long, just to see if you can come up with something."

"Any other ideas if the girl doesn't pan out?"

"One or two," he said. "For instance, Frank Colclough and Stanley Raiford."

I looked at him. He had uttered two prominent political names. Frank Colclough, the county supervisor, was a political kingmaker who bossed the county machine. Stanley Raiford, the ex-governor, had been in the news lately, making hard-knuckled speeches that sounded very much like the noises made by a man running for office. It was rumored he was about to throw his hat in the ring and run for the Senate against the aging incumbent.

Mike said, "There were money packages in the safe with their names on them."

"Packages for what?"

"You'd have to find that out yourself. I don't know. The money wasn't payoffs, I know that much. The bag money doesn't get listed like that in the safe. So it was something else, not bribe cash. But it had Colclough's and Raiford's names on it. Private money, probably, that Aiello was keeping as a favor to them. There were some others, but those are the only two names I remember."

I scowled. They were leads but they didn't sound very good. But at least it was a place to start.

Mike said, "I'm going to have to stay under cover. If it wasn't for Jo I wouldn't trust you, but I figure she'll look out for my rights if you get any fancy ideas."

It was a strange thing for him to say. I had no way of disproving the idea that he and Joanne had set the whole thing up, using me as their patsy; no way except the knowledge that it didn't fit with Joanne's character for a minute.

"All right," I said. "You sit tight." I turned to go.

He stopped me. "How about my gun?"

I studied him, then handed the gun to him. He stuck it in his waistband. He said, "I may not stay here, but I'll get in touch."

I said, "If I need to find you, where do I look?"

"Here. Then the Mariache Bar on South Tenth. An old buddy of mine owns it, he's not in the mob. I'll leave word for you with him if I have to move. His name's Maldonado."

I nodded and went.

Chapter Five

Mike Farrell, I thought as I drove away, was a vexing character. If I'd still been a cop, and if I'd had time and facilities, I'd have taken him downtown, booked him as a material witness and sweated him a while to find out how much of his story was true.

I took back streets to get out of Las Palmas, found a phone booth in a shopping center and called the Executive Lodge. I asked for Mrs. Chittenden and when I heard Joanne's voice I said, "Me. Are you all right?"

"I'm fine, but I think our secret is out. Just after you left, I went to get some newspapers and a paperback, and a man saw me in the lobby."

So that was how Madonna had found her—pure blind luck, and all of it bad. I said, "You recognized him?"

"I think so. What's more important, I think he recognized me."

"Is he hanging around?"

"He may be. If he is, he's being discreet—I haven't been pestered since I came back to the room."

"Okay," I said. "You've got my gun, you may as well just stay put a little while."

"Simon, how is—"

"It going? We're in trouble up to the hairline. Sit tight and I'll see you in a little while. Have room service send you a sandwich."

"I'm not hungry."

"Then get loaded," I said. "Keep the door locked and keep the gun handy, right?"

She said dismally, "All right, Simon," and I hung up with a vivid tactile image of the rich warm tone of her flesh, the flash of her eyes.

Either way, I had to take a risk. If I tried to spirit her away and hide her someplace else, I'd probably have to ditch a tail and that would make Madonna angry. This way, leaving her where she was, he might get the idea we weren't ducking out on him. It might persuade him to keep his word and give me free rein at least for a little while.

I looked up Dodson, Judy, in the phone book, found a number listed under Dodson, Judith, and let it ring eleven times. No answer. After a minute's thought I looked up the Atomic Bar and when the bartender answered I said, "Is Phoebe there?"

"Who wants to know?"

"A friend. Tell her Simon says."

"Tell her what?"

"Simon says."

"Christ," he said, and then: "Hang on, I'll see if she's here."

There was some background noise and then Phoebe Willits' whisky baritone voice roared out of the receiver at me:

"Simon, you bastard."

"Yeah," I said. "You'd have to check that with Dad and Mom and they're not here right now. Phoebe, I'm looking for a girl."

"Isn't everybody? Listen, you son of a bitch, if I wasn't old and fat and ugly, somebody'd be looking for me, too."

"Nonsense. You know you're beautiful." In the eyes of,

say, a bull moose; I didn't state that part out loud but she got the inference. I said, "The girl's name is Judy Dodson and she was seen now and then with Sal Aiello. I tried her listed phone but nobody's home."

"She doesn't work for me," Phoebe said. "You working on the Aiello murder, Simon? I thought you quit the flatfeet."

"I did. It's personal."

"Personal, sure. Hang on a minute, Simon, I've got a couple of my girls here, I'll ask them." I waited three minutes. Phoebe was the prototype for all the whisky-madam movies ever made; she was a lusty type, more character actress than madam. She worked a string of girls out of the Atomic Bar, which was a joint barely one step up from the pavement; she was devoted to espionage—a fact known not only to the police, who used her as an informant, but also to all the crooks, who played the game with her by allowing her to overhear harmless bits of information. She adored the game—maybe it gave her a sense of importance.

She barked into the phone in her parade-ground voice: "Big fluffy blonde girl?"

"I guess so. I haven't seen her."

"I'm told a girl like that works at the Moulin Rouge, Judy something. That help?"

"I hope so."

"Simon?"

"Unh."

"You sound like you're in trouble. Anything I can do?"

"No," I said, "but I love you. Thanks much. So long, Phoebe." I hung up and went to the Jeep and drove north through a Mexican slum. It was a littered adobe neighborhood where the kids on the streets watched you go by with big blank eyes and studied contempt; they grew up quickly down here. Anything and everything was for sale, you only had to know where to go and what name to ask for. I'd driven a prowl car beat here for six months and now, driving through, I saw familiar faces. One or two nodded with reserve; the others pretended I was a stranger.

I reached the Strip and turned east, and drove a chromium-neon mile to the Moulin Rouge. It was a long flat building set back a hundred feet behind a wraparound parking lot. The huge sign at the curb was fifty feet tall and shaped like a neon-outlined champagne glass, with the name of the place spelled across it in script. A row of palm trees broke up the austere roofline, running across the front.

There was a thin scattering of cars on the lot. I parked by the side entrance and went in that way; otherwise I would have had to walk through the dining room to get to the bar, and my lack of tie and jacket might have provoked an argument with the major-general at the front door.

Just inside the door I stopped to give my eyes time to dilate. The place was dim; after the hot brilliance outside, it seemed pitch dark. The side door gave entrance through a dirty narrow corridor with doors on either side; the smell, essence of men's room, told you where you were even if you couldn't read the signs.

When I could see through the gloom I went along the short hallway into the bar room. The place was bathed in an unpleasant sea-green light, muted and indirect. The gaudy juke box played bedroom music with heavy bass thumping; loners sat on bar stools drinking steadily, staring straight ahead with drowned faces, and at a round corner table three floor-show ponies sat in the leather booth nursing pink drinks with their smiles glazed on, waiting to be picked up by men from the bar. The three fastened the smiles on me when I appeared.

The barkeep was a minor hoodlum I knew from the old days. If he was all broken up by the proprietor's death he made no show of it. When I slipped in between two empty bar stools and hooked an elbow on the bar, he came down to me and gave me a mildly inquisitive look. I said, "Too bad about the boss."

"Yeah." He wasn't giving away a thing, that bird, so I decided to change my tactics. Instead of asking him any questions I went straight back to the corner booth and said to the three girls, "Any of you know how I might find Judy Dodson?"

They got busy looking at each other. Two blondes and a redhead, none natural. One of the blondes was over-stuffed and ripe, barely tucked into a spare, tight dress which lifted and bunched her abundant soft breasts. She said, "Who are you?"

"Name of Simon Crane."

"Do I know you from somewhere?"

"No. Are you Judy Dodson?"

"What of it?"

I gave her a closer inspection. When she looked up, the light caught the surfaces of her eyes—the most startling pale blue, as if she had gem crystals in the irises. It was easy to see why Aiello had picked her: she was a big, splendid animal, brimming with glandular equipment that suggested—by nature or design—that her sucking needs had made of her a container that had to be filled.

I said, "I'd like to talk to you."

One of the other girls said, "Are you a cop?"

"No."

Judy Dodson said, "What do you want to talk about?"

"In private."

She looked at her companions, shrugged, and got up. She had a swollen hairdo and a pouty face. When she walked away her swelling buttocks writhed. I followed her to a little table opposite the bar and held her chair for her. She grinned. "Man, you are real uptown." She sat; her breasts bubbled over the scooped neckline.

I pulled up the opposite chair and Judy Dodson said, "Pleased to make your acquaintance. Suppose you order me a drink before we start the dialogue. I like Scotch mists."

I ordered from the barkeep and sat back, giving her a friendly scrutiny. Her body was too lush, the kind of figure that wouldn't last, but right now it was ample and stunning.

Making it friendly, I said, "Nice dress."

"Sure. I only shoplift at the best stores."

Her smile seemed a bit cruel until I discovered that she was slightly, almost undetectably, drunk. The result of Aiello's death? I wasn't sure how to approach her with it. The bartender came; his arm dashed in twice between us. We sat jammed against the wall at a table hardly big enough for four elbows and two glasses. When the bartender straightened up, Judy Dodson said, "Gimme a quarter for the juke box," and he handed her a quarter marked with red nail polish—a gimmick barkeeps use to separate shill coins from customers' money when the juke box collections are made.

When he went, I said, "Sit still a minute and let me talk. Two or three people are the favorites for Sal Aiello's murder but if they turn up with alibis you're going to the head of the class. Understand? You were the last one to see him alive."

She didn't seem to react at all. She only brooded down at the tall misted glass. Her lips were parted, moist and heavy in repose. Abruptly she got up. I started to rise but then sat back down. She walked toward the juke box. I watched her buttocks as she walked. I could tell by the way she bent down and squinted at the juke box labels that she was nearsighted. By the time she came back to the table, the big speakers were thumping out a striding jazz waltz. She sat and spoke:

"I hate men. First they soften you up and then they belt you one."

I took a drink of my vodka on the rocks; it was a mistake—the alcohol thundered through me. I said, "I didn't mean to sound tough. I said it all at once so you wouldn't get up and leave before I could ask you a few questions."

"What questions? Who are you?"

"I'm a fellow who needs to find out what happened at Aiello's house last night."

"But you're not a cop."

"No."

She made a face and tasted her drink and pushed her chair back. "Maybe I'll call you in a day or two."

"Call me now, Judy. You heard what I told you. All I need to do is make one phone call. Say to Pete DeAngelo."

"Pete knows I was there."

"Maybe he doesn't know you were still there after Mike Farrell left."

She sucked in her breath and drew the chair close to the table. "Okay. You win. What do you want?"

"Did Aiello have an argument with Mike Farrell?"

"I—yes, what the hell. Yes." She opened her little sequined handbag and took out a pair of glasses with frames that pointed upward at the edges, put them on and studied me through them. "You're physical, you know?"

I said, "What was the beef about?"

"Between Sal and Farrell? I don't know, I didn't pay

much attention. Farrell just got out of jail and he didn't seem to think Sal was treating him generously enough, you know? After the rap he took."

"I thought Aiello handed him five thousand dollars and the key to a car."

"That's right, he did. How'd you know all this? You weren't there." Her powdered face scowled past the glasses. She added, "Pete told you, didn't he? You're working for Pete."

I let her go on thinking that; I said, "What kind of mood was Farrell in when he left?"

"What do you mean?"

"Angry and shouting? Or was he resigned and disgusted?"

"You mean, did he look like he was about to come back and kill Sal? I really don't know, mister. I never saw Farrell but once, and that was last night. I don't know him well enough to tell. He wasn't yelling threats or anything like that. He looked scared, I guess."

"Scared enough to lose his head?"

"I don't know. I don't think so. He just didn't seem the type, you know? He looked like the type who'd go some place and get drunk and cry a lot."

I nodded. "All right. What happened after he left?"

"Nothing."

"You can do better than that," I said, making it harsh.

She grinned. "You're a doll," she said. "Real physical." She was as nasty and sarcastic as she could be. "Look, Pete DeAngelo knows me well enough to ask his own questions, and he sure as hell knows where to find me if he wants to spend a dime's worth of gas. You tell him if he wants me he can come himself—the bastard pawned me off on Sal Aiello like an old pair of shoes when he got tired of me. Who does he think he is? He's a doll, too, just like you—you seem to run in packs, don't you?"

I said calmly, "What time did you leave Aiello's last night?"

Her eyes went to the bartender. He was too far away to hear anything we'd said. She came back to me and said, "I left at maybe nine-thirty. I got to work here before ten. You can ask the bartender if you don't believe me."

I shook my head. "I don't care what kind of phony alibi you set up with the bartender and your girlfriends. I want the truth. Do you think DeAngelo can't sweat the truth out of the bartender if he decides he wants to?"

She picked up the glass and took a swallow and sat for a moment chewing crushed ice. Finally she said, "You bastard."

"What time?"

"Look, I was there till one o'clock or so. Aiello was feeling his oats, you know? He called the club and told them I wouldn't be coming in to work, they should get somebody to cover for me in the show. He had some kind of big deal set up and he always felt horny at times like that."

"What kind of big deal?"

"How the hell should I know? Look, I'm a round-heeled pushover, and they all know I'm anybody's girl. What kind of secrets are they going to let me in on?"

"Was it a deal he'd already made, or a deal he was about to make?"

"Something he was about to do, I guess. Something that was going to happen soon."

"Like getting killed."

She winced. "Look, don't talk like that. I wasn't in love with him but he wasn't a bad guy."

No, I thought. Gangsters are all great guys. I said, "Why did you go to all the trouble to set up a phony alibi for four hours last night?"

She shrugged. "He was killed, wasn't he? How does it look if I admit I spent half the night there? Look, I didn't see anything, I didn't see anybody. I don't know who killed him."

"Nobody was coming in when you left?"

"No."

"Then he was alone in the place. Wasn't that unusual? Didn't he usually have one or two hired hands around?"

"Usually. Not always."

"When you left, did he lock the door and set the burglar alarm behind you?"

"I guess so. He always did. I didn't particularly notice last night."

"Did you leave because you wanted to, or did he tell you to go home?"

She gave me a look. "Well, he told me to go. You know, usually he liked to spend the whole night when he was feeling like that. He was really a cozy, cuddly kind of guy; he liked to sleep all wrapped up together. But at one o'clock last night he told me to get my clothes on and go. He kissed me and told me he'd see me tomorrow—I mean today, now. He was very up, you know, expecting something big."

"Expecting visitors last night, then?"

"How should I know? He didn't tell me anything. I didn't ask."

I settled back and had the last slug of vodka. There was one more line of questioning but I didn't want to open it. Didn't want to, but had to.

I said, "How long have you known Pete DeAngelo?"

"Ask him," she snapped.

"All right, let's do it another way. You must know Joanne Farrell."

"Sal's secretary? Sure."

"How long have you known her?"

Her eyebrows went up. "A couple years, I guess. Why?"

"How did Aiello feel about her?"

"I don't know."

"You saw them together."

"Sure. Far as I could tell it was strictly business. She seems like a cold bitch to me, if you want to know."

A lot she knew. I said, "Then she wasn't there last night?"

"Last night? Look, you tell Pete he sent a pretty dumb guy to talk to me. Pete knows Mrs. Farrell never stayed at the house past business hours. She always leaves around six. I didn't get there till seven last night. She wasn't there. I haven't seen her in weeks. Look, what's this all about? Did Pete send you or not?"

"In a way he did," I said. It looked like a dead end from here on; I stood up, dropped money on the table, and said, "Thanks for the talk. I'll be seeing you."

"I'd just as soon Pete came himself next time. Tell him that for me."

I went outside and had to close my eyes against the glare. The heat was a tangible force, like walking into a foam-rubber wall, after coming out of the icy air conditioning of the Moulin Rouge.

Maybe Mike Farrell, after he'd had half a bottle of whisky, had worked himself up into a state. Maybe he had gone back to Aiello's, persuaded Aiello to let him in, and forced Aiello at gunpoint to open the safe. Maybe. But I doubted it. With all the alarm systems around the place, it was doubtful anybody could have forced Aiello to open the

safe without giving him a chance to trip an alarm somewhere—an alarm that would have alerted Vincent Madonna.

If I believed Judy Dodson, I had a few facts. Aiello had
been anticipating a big deal. He had been expecting visitors
late at night—otherwise why evict Judy?—and a visit at that
hour suggested the visitors were people who couldn't afford
to be seen meeting Aiello in daylight. I recalled the two politicians whose names Mike had mentioned. Ex-Governor
Stanley Raiford, and County Supervisor Frank Colclough.

On the way I wolfed a takeout sandwich from a drive-in.
I found Raiford's house in the old part of town, just past a
mobile home park where rusty steel trailers were propped in
rows on concrete building-blocks, sprouting TV antennae
like weeds, baking aridly in the sun glitter. Raiford's street
had been widened until the thin ribbons of sidewalk were
pinched against the old houses; fences and front yards were
long gone. It was a big two-story house shaded by cottonwoods on both sides; it looked worn and comfortable.

There was nobody home. He had no office listed. Rather
than chase around asking questions, which might take too
much time, I headed for Colclough's place—it wasn't far.

Not far in space, but a thousand miles far in time.
Colclough lived in a rich folks' slum. Blooming plastic
flowers had been stuck into the yard, dyed to match the
swimming pool, and the lawn had been faked on the theory
that the grass is greener after it has been painted. The
house was big enough to have been expensive; it probably
had all the modern accoutrements—tile shower with sliding
glass door, electric kitchen, four bedrooms, dish and clothes
washers and dryer in the utility room, electric panel heat,
central air-conditioning. There wasn't a decent-sized tree

for a mile in any direction; the cretins who built these $75,000 shacks just bulldozed everything away and rolled out the houses the way you would roll out linoleum flooring with repetitive patterns. Doubtless Colclough had obtained the house cheap, or free, from some fast-buck operator friend of his who slapped houses together by the hundreds, just squeaking past the building code by bribing inspectors. Long before most of the mortgages were paid up the houses would be crumbling, warped, leaking. By that time the Colcloughs would have moved on.

There were no cars in the two-car garage, no answer to my knock at the door. But when I turned back down the cracking concrete walkway the next-door neighbor turned off his gardening hose and said amiably, "Looking for the mister or the missus?"

I went across the green, dead lawn. He was a sunburned old man with several chins and an office paunch in paisley Bermuda shorts and a loud shirt. I said, "I was looking for the county supervisor. He's not at his office."

He nodded "He's out of town, you see. Asked me to look after the swimming pool. It's a nice pool isn't it? We often sit around after the sun goes down, watching the bugs on the pool. Nice and quiet and peaceful. Not like the pious rat race back east, not a bit, no sir. Boy, you couldn't get me to go back, not me. Never, not for all the money in Wall Street."

"You're a broker?"

"Retired customer's man," he said, and beamed at me, wishing with all his might he was back in the pious rat race with something to do besides watch bugs skim the surface of a rectangular swimming pool.

The senior citizen said, "If you need him in a hurry, I'm afraid you're out of luck. He'll be gone a couple of weeks."

"How long ago did he leave?"

"Frank and Edith went upstate three days ago with Governor Raiford to organize the election campaign." He was name dropping, of course, but I couldn't complain; at least he was talkative.

"He didn't come back to town last night by any chance? Just for a brief business appointment?"

"If he did he didn't stop by here. My wife and I were home all night. Look, I'll tell you what you do, you can call him at the Stone Mountain Hotel up at the capital, that's where he's staying. We're forwarding the important mail. I'm assuming you want to talk to him about something important—otherwise you wouldn't have come to his home?"

He made it a question but I didn't let him draw me into conversation; I thanked him kindly and strode back to the Jeep. When I got to a phone booth I called Joanne to check on her.

Her voice sounded strange. "Oh—Simon."

"What's wrong?"

"Why, nothing, I only—"

"Is somebody there with you?"

"Yes," she said, eager.

"With a gun?"

"Yes, exactly. Simon, can you come right away? There's something I have to talk about and I'd rather not do it on the phone."

"It's a set-up—he's waiting to trap me?"

"Yes, fine, I'll see you in a few minutes, then?"

"Hang on, darling," I said. "Do you think he'll use the gun? Should I send cops?"

"No, it's all right, I've already had lunch. But thank you for thinking of it. You're sweet."

"Is it anybody I know?"

"No, really, I promise you I'm not hungry, and besides, it would take too long to stop and pick up a sandwich for me. I've got to see you right away—it's important."

"Is this guy alone, no help outside?"

"That's right."

"What does he want? Just talk, not a fight?"

"I think so."

"Okay, I'll be right there. It'll take me twenty minutes."

"Bye, darling."

"Take care," I murmured, and hung up. My hand was trembling on the receiver. I made it to the Jeep and pulled away from the curb and almost collided with a bus that roared by with a swish of pollutant exhaust.

Chapter Six

The Venetian blinds were drawn; I couldn't case the motel room. I stood outside the door and listened. The voices were muffled but I could distinguish Joanne's husky tone and a man's deep round one.

I closed one eye entirely and slitted the other, and stood silent for several minutes, letting the pupils dilate so I wouldn't be sun-blinded when I went in. There didn't seem any alternative. I didn't have a gun and hadn't wanted to take the time to find one. Of course I had one advantage—the knowledge that the man was an amateur. If he'd been a pro he wouldn't have let Joanne do all that talking on the phone. He'd have grabbed it from her and told me to come on in or he'd shoot Joanne.

It was only a surmise, based on experience, but if I'd had any lingering doubts they were dispelled when I stood close against the door and knocked, and he answered by opening the door himself. A professional would have brought Joanne to the door, held his gun in her back and had her open it.

He had a round, soft florid face like a baby's buttocks. He smelled of expensive after-shave. Handmade cordovan shoes, tailored slacks, linen shirt and a bow tie. He had one gun in his waistband—mine, the .38 I'd left with Joanne—and another in his fist, a lightweight .25 Beretta. When he opened the door he stepped back one pace and pointed the toy in my direction.

"Come in, Mr. Crane. Shut the door behind you." If I was supposed to look startled I disappointed him. I just nodded and stepped across the threshold and made a wise-crack:

"What's a big boy like you doing playing with loaded guns?"

"I'm glad you've assumed it's loaded," he said. "It is." He had stepped back against the side wall so he could watch both me and Joanne. I gave her a quick glance. She sat in a low armchair, not mussed; she looked all right and she gave me a nod. She looked tense but not terrified.

I pushed the door shut behind me with my heel, and with my foot still braced against the door that way, I launched myself at him. He was a bit too far away for me to try the same trick I'd pulled on Mike Farrell, so I didn't go for the wrist. I counted on his amateur status; an amateur with a gun in his hand can be depended on not to shoot when he ought to; trigger-pulling is not one of the amateur's learned reflexes. When I made my dive, he reacted instinctively by throwing both arms up in front of him to protect his body, forgetting all about the gun.

He made it ridiculously easy. When I rammed into him with an open-handed stiff arm, he tried to bat me across the face with the gun. I stopped his wrist with my forearm, jabbed him under the chin and used my lifted left arm to spin him flat against the wall. Then all I had to do was reach out and pluck the Beretta from his half-numb hand. He went rigid when he saw the Beretta pointed at him. I lifted the .38 out of his waistband and stepped back across half the width of the room, covering him with both guns.

Joanne was actually chuckling. I glanced at her and said, "All right, who is he?"

"He didn't say."

109

I turned my eyes to him. He was massaging his wrist, making a point of not looking at me. When he got through with his wrist he rubbed himself under the chin where I'd hit him.

I said, "You heard the question. Who are you and what's this all about?"

He managed to meet my eyes. Glowering, he spoke without bothering to pry his lips apart. "My name is Robert Brown and I only wanted answers to a few questions."

I looked at Joanne. "How did he get in?"

"By my stupidity." She made a face at me. "I'm sorry, Simon, I'm not used to fending off men with guns. When he knocked, I let him in. I thought it was room service from the bar."

Robert Brown, if that was his name, took a breath and said, "This is all a mistake. I can save us all a good deal of trouble if you'll let me explain."

"Do that," I said. I clicked the safety on the Beretta and slipped it into my hip pocket, keeping the .38 pointed at him.

He directed a pudgy finger toward an early edition of the evening paper, lying open on the bed. One of the headlines, with photo, was: "AIELLO SUCCUMBS: ALLEGED RACKETEER FOUND SHOT."

Robert Brown said, "Mr. Crane, I don't know and don't care what your arrangements are with Aiello's friends, but I have to know what happened to the contents of Aiello's safe. It's very important to me—you could say vital."

"Everybody in town seems to be interested in that," I remarked. "Who told you the safe had been robbed? And why come to us to find out?"

"I won't fence with you, Mr. Crane." He said it coyly. He reminded me of nothing so much as an elephant trumpeting an unrequited love. "I spoke with Vincent Madonna an hour ago from my office, when I first heard of Aiello's death. I wanted to make sure the contents of the safe hadn't been disturbed. Madonna was quite frank with me; he told me the safe had been rifled and you were the person most likely to know where the contents were to be found. He told me where to find this lady, and wished me good luck, and asked me to forward to him any information I might obtain from you."

If I'd had time I might have stopped to puzzle over Madonna's reasons for telling all that to Robert Brown, but first there were more important things to cover. I said, "What's your connection with Madonna?"

"I wish to God there weren't any," Robert Brown said, sounding as if he meant it. "You must understand that we all make mistakes. There are some of us who are in positions where we can't afford to have our mistakes exposed. Unfortunately, evidence of one or two mistakes from my past found its way into Salvatore Aiello's possession. I have reason to believe that evidence was in his safe. I want to get it back. I won't breathe easy until I do."

I said, "You've got a wallet in your hip pocket. Take it out and toss it on the bed."

"What?"

I jiggled the gun at him. He wanted to put up an argument but he thought fast, gave it up, and did as he'd been told. He didn't look happy about it. I picked up the wallet and went through it, keeping one eye on him. The credit and membership cards identified him as Fred V. Brawley, M.D., member of various societies of surgeons, the A.N.A., Lions, Kiwanis, Chamber of Commerce, American Express, Diners Club, Yale University Alumni Association. The emergency ID card said he was forty-nine, allergic to penicillin, Blood Type B+, next-of-kin Mrs. Sylvia Brawley (wife) at 2744 Camino del Rodeo. There was a thick wad of cash, large-denomination bills, and two blank checks with his name and an office address at Cliff View Terrace. There were no photos of wife or children, but there was a handsome color snapshot of a cabin cruiser; it looked like about a forty-footer, with a flying bridge and marlin rigs on the open transom deck.

I put everything back in the wallet and tossed it back to the sportsman-surgeon. I said, to Joanne, "Doctor Fred Brawley. Mean anything to you?"

"I've heard of him," she said. "Very exclusive—high-priced and high society."

I said, "That right, Doc?"

He was mum, glaring not at me but at Joanne. I attracted his attention with a two-inch jiggle of the revolver and said, "Doc, I might suggest you're in trouble up to your lumbar region. I suggest you start over. Vincent Madonna didn't tell you where to find us. Who did?"

"Didn't he?" He was being coy again.

I only shook my head. It wasn't worth explaining to him. I said, "You told the truth about one part of it. Aiello had blackmail evidence against you in his safe, didn't he?"

"That's what I said."

"What kind of evidence?"

He managed a tight little smile. "I'd be a bit of a fool to tell you that, wouldn't I?"

I shrugged. "It doesn't matter much. Malpractice, maybe, or illegal abortions."

From the way he stiffened I knew I had scored a hit. I didn't press it; it didn't seem to matter. I said, "The point is, somebody pointed you at us. I have to know who it was, I'll get rough with you if I have to. How about it?"

He brooded at my .38 and finally said, "It's not only the evidence, you see. Aiello was the only one who had the background information that would have made the evidence useful against me. If anyone else turns it up, it won't be much use to them, because without knowing where to look for corroboration they won't be able to prove anything. I'll be honest with you, Crane. I had money in that safe. Two hundred and fifteen thousand dollars in cash, wrapped up in a bundle with my name on it, in Aiello's vault where no tax snoopers would find it. That money belongs to me and I mean to get it back. I don't care what happens to the rest of the money from the safe but I want my own property returned to me. I admit I made a mistake with you, letting you get close enough to disarm me, but I warn you that if I find out you've found that money and you don't return my share to me, I'll make it my business to kill you if necessary to get it."

It was pure bravado, coming from an unarmed man at gunpoint, and I had to admire it. But it also nicely masked his shift away from my question. I said, "That's fine, Doctor. If I find the money I'll think about it. In the meantime you haven't told me who sent you here."

"But I have. I can't help it if you didn't believe me."

"It won't do, Doc. If there's two hundred and fifteen thousand of yours in that loot, maybe Madonna would be willing to see you get it back, but he'd never have admitted to you that the blackmail evidence was missing. He wants that himself."

"I told you, it wouldn't be any good to him. He doesn't know the facts that Aiello knew, the facts he'd need to connect it up."

"If that's true, it gives you a motive to kill Aiello, doesn't it?"

His mouth drew back in disgust. "I won't dignify that with an answer."

"You just threatened to kill me," I pointed out.

"Mr. Crane, if I'd killed Aiello, I'd already have the contents of his safe in my possession, and I certainly wouldn't have any reason to come after you."

"Not unless you wanted me thrown off the track," I said.

He threw up his hands. "Suit yourself. We can stand here all day and argue like this, to no point. I've said what I came to say. I blundered clumsily, using a gun, I admit that, but there wouldn't be much profit in continuing this, would there? May I go?"

"As soon as you tell us who sent you here."

He considered me; by now he was disregarding the gun, assuming I wasn't going to use it on him unless he got violent. Finally he said, "I'll tell you what I'll do. I'll answer that question if you'll give me a straight answer to a question of mine."

I remembered something Madonna had said to me a few hours ago and I used it on him, only sorry that he couldn't appreciate the irony of it. I said, "Why should I bargain with you when I've got a corner on the market?"

For some reason that made him smile. Then he caught himself, straightened his face and said, "All right, I don't suppose it matters that much. The man who spotted Mrs. Farrell in the lobby this morning was indebted to me for various favors—I had treated his wife, brought her through a serious illness, and not charged the man because I knew there would be a time when I would want him to do me a favor. Those who are ignorant of medical procedures tend to be excessively grateful to a physician who, from his own point of view, was only doing a competent job of what he'd been trained to do. This man—"

"What's his name?"

"It doesn't matter, does it? If you want him, his name is Behrenman."

I looked at Joanne; she nodded slightly, confirming it.

Brawley continued: "Behrenman knew I had money in Aiello's safe, knew I had a vital interest in finding the contents of it, and felt duty-bound to me as the man who had saved his wife's life. He telephoned me at my office and told me that Madonna felt you were the most likely person to know what had happened to the contents of the safe. Behrenman didn't know why Madonna felt that way, but he did know that Madonna was sufficiently convinced of it to order elaborate surveillance on Mrs. Farrell to make sure the two of you didn't seize the money and make a run for it. I assume Madonna is hanging back in the hope that you'll lead him to the money, whereupon he'll pounce on you. That's none of my concern. All I want is my money. It's a rather small proportion of the total cash contents of the safe. Frankly I hoped I could force you at gunpoint to reveal the location of the money, or at least force you to go get my share and bring it back here to me while I held Mrs. Farrell hostage. As you see, it didn't work. I'm not very adept at that sort of thing, obviously. Another mistake to chalk up. But now I've told you what you wanted to know. You could return my frankness by at least telling me whether you do in fact have the money."

I shook my head at him. Either he was a fool or he just liked to hear himself talk. I said. "Go on, Doc, get out of here."

His face fell a bit. "What about my gun?"

"You won't need it," I said. "Chalk that up, too."

I pointed the .38 at him and pointed the other hand toward the door.

He gave up. Composing himself, he walked out stiffly. He closed the door behind him softly, ceremonially, like a mortician.

I went to the window and opened the Venetian blinds and watched him walk up the pavement and turn out of sight into the arched passageway. He must have left his car around front.

Joanne spoke at my back: "Do you think he was telling the truth?"

"Part of it, anyway."

"I could point out Ed Behrenman for you. I know him by sight. He's probably around here somewhere."

"No," I said, turning back and looking at her. "He'd deny it anyway—he couldn't afford to have it get back to Madonna from me. He might decide he had to kill you and me to keep us from telling Madonna."

"Telling Madonna what?"

"That Behrenman spilled the beans to the doctor. That wouldn't sit well with Madonna."

"Well, then," she said, "where does that leave us? What have you found out?"

"Not a hell of a lot. I had a long talk with Mike, but it didn't seem—"

I stopped because she had gone rigid at the sound of Mike's name. "Where is he? Is he all right?"

"He was fine the last I saw him. Stop shivering. Mike didn't do it, I'm convinced of that."

The sun was throwing long blades in through the Venetian slats. I looked at my watch—almost six o'clock. I waited for Joanne to go through a series of changes of facial expression and finally, when she seemed settled, I said, "You don't love the guy enough to remarry him but you're still fond of him and you've been scared to death I'd find out he was the culprit in this mess. Is that what you're trying to make me believe?"

"Trying to—I don't understand."

"Sure you do," I said. "But it isn't good enough. Joanne, you're letting public opinion push you around."

"I'm what?"

I said, "I told you just now that Mike didn't do it. You reacted. Vast relief, followed by confusion, followed by a mask. There's only one reason I can think of why you'd be all that relieved to find out Mike wasn't guilty. You're relieved because it means he doesn't have the contents of the safe. He hasn't seen the stuff—he hasn't seen the blackmail evidence Aiello had against you. It must be something pretty terrible to make you so anxious that Mike shouldn't see it."

Her only answer was a twisted smile. Behind it she looked cornered and violent. Her eyes shifted away from me and I said, "Why should you care what Mike thinks of you any more?"

"I can't help it," she said in a small voice. "I'm not all that self-sufficient that I don't give a damn what people know about me."

"Including me? Because if Mike had the stuff, I'd have found it, and I'd have known. Isn't that it, Joanne? Answer me."

She lowered her face slowly. Dark short hair swayed forward past her face and I couldn't see her expression; she had turned her profile to me. She said, very soft, "Yes . . . yes."

I went to her. Squatted on my heels beside her and slipped my arm in under the arm of the chair, sliding my band between her back and the back of the chair. I felt her spine beneath my fingers. I said, "You have got to trust me."

She shook her head, still not letting me look at her face. "Not with that."

"With all of it," I said. "What was in the safe?"

"I can't."

"You've got to. Because you're still holding something else out on me, and it's connected to this. Once you've told me the hard part, you'll have no more reason to hold back the rest."

"I just can't, Simon."

I stood up. I still had the .38 and now I put it down beside the newspaper Brawley had left behind. I said, "Madonna gave us forty-eight hours to find the stuff and return it to him. Forty-eight hours from noon today. That leaves forty-two. I don't have to give you chapter and verse of what happens to you and me, and Mike too I suppose, if we come up empty-handed."

She stirred. "They wouldn't—not all of us?"

"They would. I'm sure of it. They will. Not one of the three of us is important enough to cause much of a stir if we disappear. They'll make sure we're disposed of where our bodies will never be found. But before they get that far they'll do everything they can think of to make us talk. Matchsticks under the fingernails, chop off some toes one at a time—you've seen enough spy movies to know the techniques and you can believe they've seen the same movies. Whatever you know, they'll get it out of you, only by that time it will be too late to help us."

She took time to digest it. The first thing she said was, "What makes you so sure I know something that will help?"

"I'm not. But if I'm to have any chance at all I need every fact there is. Everything I can learn. Maybe I can put pieces together and come up with an answer. But not if you keep closing doors on me." Once more I went to her, took her hand in both of mine. It was ice cold.

She took a deep ragged breath, pulled her hand away and got up. She went to the farthest corner of the room and stood facing the bathroom door. When I shifted one foot she said, "Stay there."

I backed up and sat down on the bed. The revolver rolled down the depression my butt made. I picked it up and tossed it on the newspaper.

Joanne said, "I'll make this very short and leave out all the details—I'm sure you can fill them in from your imagination." Her voice was low, bile-sour.

I rubbed my chin. She took time to work up courage, then spilled it all out with breathless speed.

"A lot of cables run from Aiello's house to Madonna's. They're not all alarm systems. There's a closed-circuit television hook-up. You haven't seen Aiello's bedroom so I'll have to give you an idea of it—it's right out of *Playboy*, a big round bed in the middle and mirrors all over the room, even on the ceiling. The first time I saw it I couldn't help laughing out loud—I didn't really believe anybody actually went in for that girlie-magazine satyr stuff. But it's there. What I didn't know at the time—didn't find out until a long time later, when I tried to quit the organization—that bedroom is bugged from every conceivable angle by hidden television cameras. There's one behind every mirror."

I knew what was coming but I didn't speak. She had to say it, get it out. I waited, with a catch in my breath. She said, "Private dirty movies. Not for Aiello's entertainment, but for Vincent Madonna's."

She spat the name out as if it were venom.

She said, "I don't know what's wrong with Madonna but it's pretty obvious he doesn't get his kicks the way most people do. At first, when I found out about the television, I thought the idea was to have Aiello act as Madonna's flunky by testing girls in bed before passing them on to Madonna. But Madonna never went near me. It was just that one night, so damned long ago, and even though I'd been married a while I wasn't experienced enough to suit Aiello. He taught me things I'd never even heard of. I was drunk but I don't suppose that's any excuse at all. Mostly I was trying to prove what a brassy broad I was—trying to get revenge on poor dumb Milquetoast Mike. Hell, never mind—I did things, that's all. I did things."

Her voice trailed off but then she stiffened her spine and went rushing on:

"As long as it was private, just me and Aiello, I could live with it. But then Mike went to prison, and a couple of years later I divorced him. I was sick of the organization and I thought they wouldn't mind my leaving, since Mike and I were divorced and they couldn't reasonably use me as a hold over Mike any longer. But they didn't see it that way. Nobody ever quits the organization. I turned in my resignation, Aiello argued, I got stubborn and argued right back, and when they saw they weren't going to talk me into changing my mind, they trotted out the films and gave me a nice little private screening up at Madonna's house. I don't have to tell you what was on the film, do I? It was Technicolor and it had sound. It was a very professional job and it didn't leave anything out."

I said, "And Aiello kept it in his safe."

"Yes."

"They must have threatened to do something with it if you didn't cooperate. What was the threat?"

"Well, my mother and father for openers. They live in California now. Madonna knows how to find them. Then there was Mike, of course. And you."

She had maintained her rigid, averted pose throughout. Telling it didn't seem to have taken the load off her. She stood taut as ever, as if waiting for me to explode. "They made it clear," she said, "that if I ever decided to get married, no matter who it was, he'd have a chance to see the movie if I didn't do everything they told me to."

When I made no reply, she said, "There's just one more thing, because I think you've got to know the good part too, if that's what you can call it. It's about Aiello and me. Aiello didn't really like me much—in bed, I mean. We got along all right in the office, but I was too young for him, too inexperienced. He wanted hot stuff—girls who really knew what to do. I imagine Madonna had some influence there, since—since he liked to watch it, on TV, and Aiello liked to be watched."

I thought of Judy Dodson and the way Mike had described her—a hot-pillow girl.

Joanne said, "The next day, the day after it happened with Aiello, I walked out of the house feeling as if I needed to spend twenty-four hours scrubbing myself with Lava soap. I was trying to get the car started and Aiello came out and leaned his big hairy arm on the window and said some nasty things about the night before, so I pretended to be getting a cigarette out and I punched the dashboard lighter. When it was good and red hot I pulled it out of the dash and jabbed it against his arm. He still has—had—the scar. But when I did that he just laughed at me and stepped back and waved me off. Said I was third-rate in bed anyway and I could forget any ideas I might have about giving him a repeat performance. He meant it, too. It was stupid, ignorant luck, I know that, but he never came near me after that. I think I—amused him. He must have thought I was a funny, audacious little girl, still clumsy and wet behind the ears, branding his arm with a cigarette lighter. I could imagine him later, roaring with laughter, telling all the boys how he'd hung big tough men out to dry for less provocation than that. I'm only guessing at that part, of course."

She had been talking too fast, trying to salvage some small absolution. Finally she stopped talking and slowly, fearfully, turned to look at me.

I was giving her a silly grin. Her face changed. She said, in a different and somewhat bitter voice, "Don't pretend it doesn't matter to you, Simon. I don't want sympathy. I only wish you hadn't forced me to tell you, because no matter how you rationalize it, it's sordid and it has to spoil something. It has to." She added, more quietly, "Don't forget, you haven't seen that film yet."

"I don't intend to look at it, even if I get a chance," I said. "I'd only get jealous."

"Don't make jokes."

"It has never failed to amaze me," I announced, "the crazy things some people are sensitive to. Push the right button with almost anybody and you'll get instant panic. Joanne, let me make it as loud and clear as I possibly can: I don't give a good goddamn how you and Aiello amused each other back in the dark ages."

"I don't believe it," she snapped.

"Believe what you want," I answered, just as flatly. But when I kept staring at her she lifted her head; our eyes locked, and then, slowly, her mouth became soft and lost its bitter downturn, her eyes widened and then became drowsily heavy, and she whispered: "Oh, Simon."

Chapter Seven

I held her in my arms until she stopped honking and trembling. When it seemed safe enough, I lowered her into the armchair. I said, "Okay, you sit still a minute and collect yourself."

I picked up the phone and gave the operator a long distance number at the state capital. After the usual confusions between the switchboard at my end and the switchboard at the other, I finally made connection with Jerry Sprague, a former cop-colleague of mine who now held down the city desk on the *Sun-Telegraph*. He was happy to hear from me. After dispensing with amenities I said, "I'm trying to pin something down, Jerry. Can you give me a fast tracer on the movements of Stanley Raiford and Frank Colclough over the past thirty-six hours? I understand they're up in your bailiwick."

I heard his chuckle. "Minute-by-minute, you mean? How come you always want the hard ones?"

"Do I?"

"I don't know if we've had legmen on them straight through. You may be asking for the impossible."

"With parsley," I agreed. "But it's important. Mainly what I want to know is if either one of them had an opportunity to leave the city last night sometime around midnight, by plane, and return before dawn."

There was an underlayer of excitement in his voice when

he shot back: "You're sitting on something, Simon, I can smell it."

"When it's available for publication I'll let you have it first. If it gets there. It's probably nothing—I'm just trying to rule things out."

"The time period you're asking for—that would be the time Salvatore Aiello was murdered. For Christ's sake, you don't think—"

"I don't think anything, Jerry, and your guesses are your own. I didn't mention Aiello's name, you did. How about it?"

"I'll see what I can dig up. It may take time—most of the legmen are home by now, we're wrapping up the early edition now."

"Okay. I'm not sure where I'll be so I'd better call you back. When can I catch you in the office?"

"I'll be here till midnight. After that—here, I'll give you my home number."

I took down the number on a motel notepad, tore it off and pocketed it. He asked a few more questions and I put him off without specifically denying anything; as long as I left the bait dangling and let him jump to conclusions he'd be excited enough to dig for the answers I needed. We traded a few wisecracks and I hung up and smiled at Joanne.

I had been watching her face during the conversation with Jerry. She had reacted when I'd mentioned the names. I said to her, "What about it?"

"About what?"

"Colclough and Raiford. When you heard the names, you jumped."

"Did I?"

I shook my head. "Do I have to pry everything out of

you with a can opener? Look, you and Mike and I are all in the same boat with no bait and no hooks. Forty-one hours and ten minutes to go. How much of it do I have to waste arguing with you?"

She was apologetic. "Keeping secrets gets to be such a habit I've learned automatically to pretend I don't know anything. I'm sorry, Simon. You want to know about those two greasy politicians. Certainly. I've seen both of them, at different times, at Aiello's house. Naturally Aiello impressed on me that I was to forget I'd ever seen them there. You know what the penalty was to be if I ever mentioned it."

I nodded. "Good. Okay. Now let's go back to the safe for a minute, the things in it. Do you want to change your story? You told me this morning you'd never seen the inside of that safe, but I don't believe that."

"You're right, of course. But what makes you so sure I didn't tell the truth about that?"

"One or two things I've picked up about Aiello's character. He loved to show things off."

She made a face; obviously she was thinking about the TV-bugged bedroom. I hadn't been thinking about that; I'd been thinking about what Mike had said about the way Aiello had shown him the contents of the safe and bragged about it. If Aiello would be that expansive with Mike, it wasn't reasonable to suppose he hadn't displayed the wealth for Joanne.

She said, "I've seen the safe, when he had it open, quite a few times. Most recently two days ago. DeAngelo was there putting some money in, for Madonna, I suppose. Aiello never missed a chance to point to the little black steel box with the roll of film in it. He didn't have to say anything because I knew what was in the box and he knew I

125

knew. He just pointed and grinned."

"This may disappoint you," I stated, "but I'm not particularly interested in that. What I want to know is what else
you saw in the safe."

"Money, mostly, and half a dozen metal boxes." Her answers were coming easier, more smoothly, all the time.
There was no hesitation. She went on: "The boxes were different shapes and sizes but they were all the same kind.
Black-painted steel with locks. Like safe-deposit boxes.
Each one had a little cardboard label in a brass slot, like the
labels on office file drawers."

"And there was a name on each label," I said.

She nodded. "I suppose you want to know whose names
they were. I wish I could remember, Simon. You've got to
understand, every time he opened that safe and dragged me
up to look inside, there was only one thing that drew my
eye. It was that little square box with my name on it. He always kept it right out front, on a shelf at eye level, so I
couldn't possibly miss it. The rest of the boxes were farther
back inside, on different shelves, and you had to walk inside
to see what was written on them, all but one or two, and
one of them just said 'S. Aiello.' I suppose it was his personal property, and the other one had Frank Colclough's
name on it, but you already know about him."

"How about bundles of money with people's names on
them?"

She nodded. "There were four or five of those. I don't
remember seeing that doctor's name anywhere, what was it,
Brawley? I've never seen him before, I'm sure. Of course
I've heard of him. He's very high class in the trade, the kind
of surgeon all the rich, fashionable people go to. He's on
the boards of both hospitals and he's active in charities. I
suppose if you don't read the society page you might not

have heard of him, but believe me, he's well known by all the Somebodies."

"But you never had reason to suspect any connection between him and the mob before."

"That's right," she said.

"Can you remember any of the names that were on the bundles of cash?"

"I'm afraid I can't. There's a reason, of course. You just said Aiello liked to show things off. But obviously there were certain things he wouldn't want to give away, and those would include the names of people who had money in his safe, wouldn't they? Usually the bundles were turned so that the names didn't show. Once or twice he got careless and flipped one over by mistake, but I don't recall—no, wait. Yes I do. The other day, when DeAngelo brought the briefcase full of cash, Aiello had to make room for it, and he moved several of the bundles. He stacked them up on a front shelf down at the bottom, and three of them had the names showing. Now let me think. One was Colclough, I remember that, and another one—yes, I'm sure it was Raiford."

"What about the third one?"

She shook her head, concentrating. I said, "Brawley?"

"No, I'm sure it wasn't." She looked up at me and shook her head again. "I just can't remember. Maybe if we leave it alone it will come back to me."

"Okay. Let's try something else. When you went to the house this morning the safe was empty. Did you mean that literally? Everything gone?"

She nodded. "Of course the shelves were still there and I didn't get down on my hands and knees to make sure they hadn't left something on the floor at the back, but it looked to me as if everything was gone. The works."

"All the money and all the black lockboxes."

"Yes."

"All right, now think a minute. If all that stuff were stacked up in one heap, instead of spread out on shelves, how much space would it take up?"

She gave me a puzzled look. "What do you mean?"

"What I mean is, could you fit it all in the trunk of a car, or would you need something bigger?"

"Oh—I see. Well, of course I don't really know. I'd imagine if you had a big car with a big trunk compartment, and you didn't mind stuffing wads of cash in all the funny little nooks and corners, you might get all of it in. But it would have to be big."

"Like, say, a Cadillac?"

"I suppose so. I don't think I've ever looked inside the trunk of a Cadillac."

"Who do you know that drives a pink Cadillac?"

"I—I'm not sure I know anybody. I don't really pay much attention to the make of cars. I can't tell one make from another."

Neither could I, any more. Fifteen or twenty years ago you could, but nowadays they were all pressed out by what looked like the same cheap stamp mills. I said, "Any large pink car, then. Pink cars aren't all that common."

She took a while to think about it and there was no doubt she was giving it full effort, but she came up empty. I said, "It's okay," and went back to the phone. This time I gave the switchboard Vincent Madonna's number.

I had to run the gauntlet of Freddie, the Neanderthal, and DeAngelo, whose hoarse whisper sounded a bit out of breath, before I got put through to the big cheese. Big, I thought, green and moldy. Madonna snapped at me without friendliness and I said, "I need a fact. It may help both of us get what we're looking for if you can answer a question."

"Where are you?"

I grinned at the phone. "Don't play games. You've got Ed Behrenman and I don't know how many other goons glued to this place. You know damn well where I am."

I had to hand it to him. He actually chuckled into the phone. Then he said, "What fact?"

"Who do you know that drives a pink Cadillac?"

"What?"

I just waited, seeing no point in repeating it, and after a moment his *basso profundo* resumed: "Offhand, I don't know anybody who'd be seen dead in a pink Cadillac. Are you serious?"

I recalled the classic Continental in his drive and knew I'd hit on a sore spot. If Madonna had any taste, aside from his weird preoccupations with voyeurism, it seemed concentrated in his worship of fine automobiles. I could see how a car painted pink might offend him. It also indicated he would probably have noticed it if any of his acquaintances had driven into his driveway in such an abomination.

I thanked him and got off the line after he recited the expected litany of veiled threats. Naturally he didn't commit himself to anything actionable over the telephone but the meaning was clear to both him and me. I couldn't help feeling more shaken than ever when I hung up, and Joanne couldn't help but notice it.

She was giving me a cool stare. She said, "So you did go to see him. What kind of deal have you made with him?"

"You don't trust anybody, do you?"

"Simon, I want to."

Her faith was so tattered I couldn't keep attacking her. Instead, I gave her a brief resumé of the day's unhappy events. I condensed it but left out nothing important. At the end I said, "There's no question I've been floundering. We're still in that boat without hooks or bait. The only clue that makes any sense is that pink Cadillac Mike saw leaving Aiello's when he went there the second time last night. If he was telling the truth, and if it was a pink Cadillac. He was a bit vague about it and it was the middle of the night. Head-lights might make a car look pink even if it was orange or red or yellow. Of course, the chances are even if we do find a pink Cadillac we'll discover it was stolen three hours be-fore the robbery. But it's just about the only lead we have, and we've only got"—I looked at my watch—"a little over forty hours to settle this."

I got up, picked up the .38 from the newspaper on the bed, and stuffed the gun into Joanne's handbag. It made a tight squeeze and I thought of substituting the little .25 Beretta I'd taken from Brawley, but decided against that for a variety of reasons, one of which was that if a woman unfa-miliar with guns has to shoot one, she's better off with something that makes a lot of noise; it may scare off an at-tacker if it doesn't hit him. Another was that a .38 police bullet will make a man stop and think even if it just pinks him, while a pipsqueak .25 is only a bee sting if it doesn't hit a vital spot.

So I gave her the .38 and told her to use it if she had to, trusting she'd learned from the mistake with Brawley. When I handed her the handbag she said, "Where are we going?"

"Dinner, first. Even if we find the loot we can't carry it on an empty stomach."

She shuddered a little. "It's all so—callous, Simon. We keep talking about the money and never say a word about the man who was murdered."

I said, as harshly as I could, "I don't gave a damn about

130

the poor unfortunate victim and I see no reason why you should. If ever a man deserved to be killed—"

"All right," she said, snappish. "Let's not argue about it."

"I just want it clear. We're not a couple of hawkshaws investigating a murder mystery. The only reason it might help us to know who killed Aiello is that it might lead us to the loot. I've got no interest in bringing anybody to justice—if there is such a thing—all I care about is your life and mine. Understood?"

"Yes." She nodded. "Yes, of course. I get stupid sometimes."

No wonder, I thought dismally. Buffeted back and forth by one shock after another. Most of the girls I knew would have ended up in a rubber room long ago, going through what Joanne had had to suffer the past few years. Yet, through it all, she remained vivacious, even wholesome to the casual eye—certainly not undone to the point of hysteria.

I put an arm around her shoulders and held her tight, walking her to the door and outside. The sun was going down behind a layer of diaphanous cirrus clouds. I made a remark about the spectacular sunset and she was not too immersed in fright to agree, even stop a moment to stare and drink it in. With sudden savage conviction I said to myself, We will make it through this.

We ate in the motel dining room. We didn't have much to say. I was trying to work out the next moves, and Joanne drew into herself and huddled over a whisky sour until the food came. The only time she roused herself to speak was when there was motion at the bar, beyond the fake flower planter, and she nudged me with her foot and told me not to look but she knew the girl at the end of the bar—she'd seen the girl at Aiello's several times in company with Tony Senna. I nodded and went on chewing celery. When the time seemed right I glanced over my shoulder. She was just another girl who probably spent half her time working the bars and the men in them, a brittle, black-haired borderline alcoholic. She was making a point of not watching us, staring instead at the Geriatric Five on the bandstand. But the tip-off came when she rejected a pickup. The guy shrugged and went away.

I had spotted one outside when we'd walked to the lobby from the room—a paunchy, purple-nosed man standing with his hip against the fender of his car, trying not to look interested in us.

When we were out of his earshot Joanne had identified him for me—Ed Behrenman. So we were well-covered—Behrenman in front, with the car; the girl in the bar; watching us; and doubtless a third man somewhere in back where he could watch the room and my Jeep and Joanne's car.

I wanted to get us out from under Madonna's surveillance, perhaps for no reason other than that it made me nervous. But this wasn't the place to do it. If we'd had a reliable friend with a car we might have pulled it off, and I thought of two or three but ruled them out. On the road was better, I decided. So while Joanne did her lips, I went out into the lobby and paid the room phone charges at the desk, telling the clerk we planned to leave very early in the morning and wanted to take care of this now. By the time I paid the dinner bill at the dining-room cashier's desk, Joanne was up and walking. We went outside without paying any attention to the bar girl, who followed us at a discreet distance until she made sure we were out the front door and within Behrenman's view.

We went through the ice-machine alley and as we approached the room I said, "We're not going inside, but make it look as if we're headed for the room until we get parallel with the Jeep."

"Where are we going?"

"We'll drive around and ditch our friends, then go pick up Mike. I want to hide both of you out."

She didn't get inquisitive. We walked past the winch on the front bumper of the Jeep, walking as if we intended to turn into the room, but then I grasped her elbow lightly and gave her a half-turn, making it look as if I'd changed my mind at the last minute. I climbed into the driver's seat and by the time I had fitted the key into the ignition, Joanne had walked around and got in. I backed out and headed diagonally across the concrete parking area, not wasting time but not in an obvious hurry. We drove around the back of the place to the far end and went out to the road there.

It would take the watcher in back a few moments to hot-foot through the alley to the front and alert Behrenman, who had the car. I didn't want to make it obvious we were trying to shake them, so I didn't pour it on when I pulled out on the road and headed south, toward the freeway interchange. It took us right past the front of the motel and of course by the time we started up the ramp Behrenman was rolling out onto the road. Now I knew where I'd seen him before. It was the same green sedan that had buzzed past when I'd driven out of the motel before noon. He'd probably spotted me coming out of the place, recognized either me or my Jeep, and made a U-turn beyond the cloverleaf to come back and investigate. That must have been when he'd picked up Joanne, phoned Madonna and then phoned Dr. Brawley.

The freeway had a moderate after-dinner traffic load. Teeny boppers and men from the nearby Air Force base cruised up and down the pavement in hopped-up cars, looking for competition for drag-race money. It was a good Southwest night, stars glistening, moon on the rise, the sky vast and velvet; at such times, under better circumstances, a vehicle as open all-around as a Jeep was worth twenty closed Detroit sedans.

But the Jeep wasn't built for acceleration or speed. I couldn't ditch Behrenman by running away from him; he had a big car with probably five times as much horsepower under the hood as he would conceivably need for any purpose short of breaking the land-speed record. Still, a freeway—particularly one going through the heart of a city with interchanges every quarter-mile—was virtually the ideal place to ditch a tail. Behrenman knew that; he was sticking much closer than is usually done—partly because he didn't care if I spotted him, partly because he was afraid of losing us. Madonna had probably made it clear what would happen to him if he blundered.

I swung out in the far left lane—there were three lanes in each direction—and stayed there, doing sixty-five, judging the gaps in the traffic roaring along the two lanes to my right. I had to pass four interchanges before the cars were spaced right. A glance in the mirror placed Behrenman for me, and I was glad to see he was in my lane, separated from me by one car. With a little more experience and brains, he'd have known enough to stay in the middle lane, from which it would have been easier to maneuver.

It was simple. I waited till we were perilously close to the exit, then dodged into the center lane through a narrow gap in the long line of cars, cut sharply in front of a big semirig—earning a blat of his air horn—and squealed wobbling into the off-ramp. I had to hit the brakes hard to bring it down from sixty-five to thirty-five, and even at that we almost lifted two wheels off the ground on the sharp ramp turn. But the traffic had blocked Behrenman from getting to the right fast enough, and he would have to go on to the next exit. We had lost him.

I drove under the freeway and got back on, going in the opposite direction from my previous heading. We went east three quarters of a mile and got off to head north. I kept an eye on the mirror but we had no company. I turned into Las Palmas at nine forty-five and found the boarded-up hideout without too much trouble—a feat accomplished only because I'd spent most of my thirty years in this town and knew the back streets by heart.

We were going slowly enough so that Joanne could speak without fighting the wind. She said, "That was very neat."

"Thank you, ma'am. For my next number I whistle and the Jeep gets up on its hind legs and dances in time to the music."

"Are you as collected as you're trying to make me think you are, Simon?"

"No," I said shortly, and turned into the gap in the high oleander hedge.

The place was dark and silent, which meant nothing. When I turned the engine and lights off, I sat motionless long enough for him to get a good look at us from whatever crack he was using in the boarded-up windows. Then I got down and walked to the door, avoiding the broken glass easily by moonlight. The door was open, sagging. I waited outside and said, "Mike? It's Simon. Joanne's with me. Okay to come in?"

No answer; no sound at all. I went inside. It was black in

there, I stayed near the door and lifted my voice—possibly he was asleep. "Mike!"

Finally I went back to the Jeep and got the flashlight from its clamp under the seat, told Joanne to wait, and went inside with the light. He wasn't in the front room. I made my way through the rest of the place, picking a path carefully over piles of fallen ceiling plaster. After fifteen minutes I was satisfied he wasn't there. It left me in a sour mood; I didn't want to waste half the night tracking him down. I went back into the main room and flashed the light around once more, ready to leave; the flashlight beam picked up something out of place on the seat of the old couch and I went to have a look.

It was a piece of paper torn off the corner of a newspaper. On the white margin was written in pencil, in a crabbed hand, C—I'm going to your place. Meet you there. Mike.

I took the note outside, got into the Jeep and showed it to Joanne. She said, "I suppose 'C' is you?"

"I can't think of anybody else it's likely to be. But it raises a question or two. Why my place? And where could he have got transportation from here to there? He left his car up in the foothills."

She said, "Something may have frightened him. That's his handwriting, I guess, but it's much shakier than I remember it." She stirred, hugging herself; nights cool down fast in the desert. "Do you suppose he's remembered something important?"

"We'll find out," I replied, and pushed the starter. Might as well head home, anyway, I thought; I needed a quiet place to think and if Madonna thought we were on the run after ditching Behrenman, my house was the last place he'd look for us.

I kept a careful eye out for surveillance on the way but spotted none. We took back streets and roads across town— the Jeep was too conspicuous. It took forty minutes to get to my dirt road, and when we passed Nancy Lansford's lonely outpost I turned off the headlights and drove the rest of the way by moon and stars. It was no great feat, with the silver desert glowing with pale reflection.

From a mile away I could see there were no lights on at my place, and I applauded Mike for having that much sense. In some ways it doesn't pay to have a home which is also a goddamn beacon. The view of the city from the house is marvelous; the view of the house from the city, of course, is equally distinct.

There was no car in the yard. "He must have hitched a ride. Who with, I wonder?"

We dismounted from the Jeep and I called out, "Mike?"

There was no reply. Joanne looked at me. I said in a murmur, "Stay put," and went forward, pulling the Beretta out of my hip pocket, not liking the distant sensation that had begun to crawl through me—a feeling like ice across the back of my neck. I headed for the nearest corner of the house, got into the shadows where moonlight didn't reach and sidled along the wall toward the door.

The screen was shut but I heard the buzz of flies heavy in a swarm, and as I got closer I saw them, hanging angrily in a knot above a thick mound on the doorstep. I took in my breath sharply and bent down to look.

The body lay drawn up, fetal. The side of his head, above the ear and just behind the temple, was a sickening, jellied crater, faintly glistening in the starlight. Death had sucked all expression off his boyish face. The sour odor was subtle but impossible to disregard, any more than the lurching of sick spasms in my belly could be ignored. One sock, bunched, had fallen down around his ankle; the trouser leg was crushed up to the knee and the hairy leg was a spiderweb of half-scabbed blood. His left hand, visible, was twisted awkwardly, with the thumb, and index finger bent back beyond the natural possibilities.

I rolled back his eyelid but there was no need. There wasn't any question of his death. He had been tortured, systematically bludgeoned and lacerated. Automatically my stricken mind catalogued the evidence and calculated the method: brass knuckles, a knife and something heavy enough to cave in his head. The blood on the rest of him was ample indication that the other injuries had been sustained before the final massive blow which had, mercifully by then, killed him.

The first I was aware of Joanne's nearness was when I heard her begin to choke. I straightened, wheeled and got an arm around her, pushing her back away from it.

She forced enough control of her voice to say, "It's Mike, isn't it?"

"Yes."

"He's dead."

"Yes."

"Oh, my God, Simon." I heard a faint jangling and after a moment recognized it—the ring of the telephone in the house. It rang a second time, and stopped. My head snapped up; I stepped out into the yard and threw my glance downhill, and spotted it—the hill-crest overglow of headlights, coming up, and mingled in the glow the rhythmic flash of red and blue. Police car, with the rooftop dome light flashing.

Joanne had one arm outstretched against the wall of the house, bracing herself, looking faint. I put sympathy aside and snapped at her: "We've got five minutes, maybe less.

You're going to have to act a part. Come on, snap out of it—we've got a lot to do and no time."

She stirred and blinked. "Yes. All right. What do you want me to do?"

I told her, in a rush of words; and we did it.

Chapter Eight

The city patrol car, air-conditioned and overstuffed, slewed into the yard. The cop drove with more ferocity than skill; he sent a spout of dust forward when he stopped. I waited till then before I turned on lights and stepped out, holding the screen open for Joanne.

The cop sat in the car, switched on the spotlight and swung its lancing blade of light across the hilltop until it zeroed in on the two of us, blinding us. I shaded my eyes with one hand. After a moment I heard the car door open. The spotlight switched off and the man got out: Sergeant Joe Cutter. I had scars to remember him by.

Cutter was a wide brute, shaped like a fire plug. Hairy and heavy—maybe 225 swarthy pounds on a five-foot-ten frame, fierce and thickly muscular. His jaw was blunt, flesh thick around the lips and nose, eyes set back deep in crude massive bones. Cutter, musky and ugly as a rhino, radiated a constant force of danger like heat.

Speaking, he revealed a chrome-hued tooth. "All right, Sy. Where is it?"

"Where's what?"

"Mike Farrell."

"Does this look like a hotel? I don't keep a register." I could feel Joanne tense beside me. I didn't look at her.

Joe Cutter said, "Okay, then we do it the hard way." He

reached into the car and brought out a long five-cell flash-light.

"Hold it," I said. "Before you do any searching you can show me a piece of paper signed by somebody—and you can explain what you're doing up here outside city jurisdiction. Since when are you working for the sheriff?"

Joanne said spryly, "No tickee, no lookee." Her eyes danced—too brightly. I shook my head slightly.

Joe Cutter shook his head with an air of exasperated and disgusted patience. "Come off it, Sy. We can be friendly about this or I can get tough, whichever way you want it. You know better—this time of night I can't get a warrant, but you make a stink and take it to court and I'll have a warrant to show the judge with tonight's date on it, and I'll have some county cops to testify they gave me authority to work outside the city because the Aiello case is a joint effort, right? So why make a nuisance out of yourself? You butt out and shut your flap or I knock both of you right on your enchiladas, okay?"

As he spoke, Cutter pushed the button of his $80 holster; the molded clamshell popped open and he lovingly lifted his .357 Magnum, not pointing it at anything in particular.

I gave him a flat look and said, "Put that thing away. We've got a witness this time."

Cutter shook his head again. "Where's the dead guy?"

"What dead guy? Somebody gave you a bad tip."

"Sure."

"Tell me who tipped you and maybe we can get it straightened out."

"Try another one, Sy. You killed Farrell and you haven't had time to get rid of the body."

I had put lights on in the house. The draw on the batteries brought the diesel generator to life. It began to thud and pound. I lifted my voice to carry above the racket: "Somebody lied to you."

"Nobody lies to me," he said, walking forward. "Not even you, Sy." Straight-faced, he gestured with the Magnum. "Let's go inside and look, okay?"

I gave in with an elaborate show of disgust; held the door for Joanne and went in ahead of him. Cutter went through the house with efficient speed, keeping the gun more or less pointed at us and herding us with him as he searched. Cutter wasn't a ransacker; he had a compulsion toward military neatness; he left nothing disturbed, but didn't miss a single place where a corpse might fit. He looked inside the refrigerator, checked the cabinets, opened every closet door and pawed through, got down to look under the couch and the bed, looked behind the Army-blanket drapes, poked his nose in every corner, even climbed on a chair to shine his flashlight into the swamp-cooler ducts.

When he was satisfied he exploded in a few choice phrases and took us outside. We went around the house, Cutter shining the flashlight in every direction. At the back of the house he lifted the lid of the generator enclosure and aimed the flashlight beam inside. The diesel exuded noise and heat and pollutant odors. He banged the lid down and went on around the house, making the full circuit, examining the edges of the stone foundation for signs of openings. He glanced into the Jeep, then shooed us up toward the rock-polishing shack. Joanne waited until he was looking the other way before she gave me a weak grin of relief. We went into the shack and Cutter stood still a moment, sizing it up. He found the light switch and turned it on.

The shack was cluttered with gear—workbench along

one wall, most of the door occupied by tumblers driven by electric motors. The largest of the tumbler barrels was about the size of a ten-gallon keg. They rotated slowly on their tracks; the noise was soporific, a quiet swish and thud, gemstones revolving through viscous abrasive solutions of pumice and silicates. It took months to bring a tumbled stone to high polish; each stone had to be moved from coarser to finer solutions through the series of five tumblers.

Cutter said, "Where do you shut this stuff off?"

I pointed to the master switch. "Why? You expect we cut up your imaginary dead body and put the pieces inside?"

"I wouldn't be surprised," he said, deadpan. He opened the switch and lifted the lid on the large barrel. The polishing solution was the color of cement. He put down the flashlight, rolled up his sleeve, and plunged his hand inside. After he felt around, he withdrew his hand, shook it and looked around for something to clean himself with.

Joanne picked up a rag and handed it to him. "Thanks," he said absently, wiped his forearm and hand meticulously, and tossed the rag aside. He followed pattern by sealing the barrel shut and turning the machinery on.

It was always hard to detect expressions on his immobile face but I had the feeling he was boiling with rage. It seemed a good time for it so I said, "What makes you think Mike Farrell's dead? What makes you so sure it wasn't Farrell himself who gave you this bum steer to keep you occupied while he gets out of the state? He probably killed Aiello and now he's just making waves so he can get away in the confusion."

He gave me his hooded glance and gestured with the Magnum. "Outside."

He took us all around the hilltop, spending a half hour at

it, walking a regular search pattern with flashlight and eyes to the ground. He didn't find anything more than Ed Baker had found twelve hours earlier. Joanne slipped her hand into mine while we trailed along with him. Her fingers were slick with cold perspiration.

When we circled back to the front yard Cutter's scarlet face was composed into such a parody of indifference that I was sure he was outraged. He lifted the lid of the galvanized trash can and poked around inside with the flashlight, replaced the lid and turned to face us, playing with the gun. He was standing with one foot crushing a rose stem.

He said, "I've got half a mind to run both of you in. Material witnesses."

"To what? You've got half a mind, period."

I baited him because he expected it, and because he knew as well as I did that he had no grounds to arrest us. *Habeas corpus.* He had already admitted to himself that he'd lost this round.

He said, "I'd like to pin the Aiello hit on you, by Jesus."

Joanne said, "Simon didn't kill Aiello."

"I didn't say he did. But I can pin it on him if I take a notion to. Maybe I won't take a notion to, Sy, if you do what you're told now—don't mess in the Aiello thing any more, okay? We'll find Farrell, or whoever did it. We don't need amateur help. Understand?"

I said, "You had a bum steer. You've had your fun. Now you can go."

He stepped across the roses and stood close before us, shaking his head like a patient father chastising an errant child. "You got to learn manners, Sy," he said, and plunged the barrel of the Magnum into my stomach just under the ribcage.

I hadn't been expecting it. It knocked me back against

Joanne. She lost her balance and fell.

I choked down a sudden belly-lurching heave; pain flooded me. I should have been ready for it: Cutter was a creature of grudges.

I gave him a dismal stare and braced, knowing he wasn't through. The .357 Magnum gave him total control of us, but knowing it, he did not smile—his sadism didn't take the form of visible amusement. He grunted, blinked, feinted with the gun and kicked me in the shin. His boots had metal combat toes. Agony exploded in my shin; off-balance, I went down.

Joanne was on her knees, hissing words, and Cutter whipped the gun around toward her. "Freeze."

The heavy boot came swinging at me; I rolled away but he took one step and kicked again. It caught me on the shoulder blade. He knew just where the tender spots were; he worked with scientific, methodical brutality. He crouched, elbows on knees, waiting for me to complete my roll; when I did, he cracked the steel Magnum lightly against my kneecap just a tap, but enough to blind me with pain. I felt coiling spasms.

Cutter's voice was a soft low insinuation: "You're digging yourself a grave, see? Next maybe I break a few bones you need the most. Sy, you know you're going to talk. Don't make me crack you."

Joanne said, spitting it, "All you need is thumbscrews and a rack to complete the picture."

He ignored her; he said to me, "If you can't talk when I get through, you'll write it with your toes. How about it, Sy?"

I was half blind. I managed to shake my bead. Joanne, keeping herself under thin control, spoke through her teeth: "How does it make you feel to torture an innocent man?"

"About as guilty as the President feels killing them by the thousands overseas," he replied without heat, without even glancing at her. "Now that's all the idle conversation we're going to have. Sy?"

"I don't know—anything now that I didn't know the first time you asked."

He bounced the Magnum suggestively in his fist, stood up and suddenly plunged the weighted boot-toe into my ribs.

I stifled a cry of anguish. He kicked again and I made a grab for his leg, got it, hung on, twisted his foot until he fell. I got my knees under me but then the Magnum came whipping across, flat along the side of my head. I fell over, lights flashing inside my skull; I heard Joanne yell something. I rolled away from him—anything to get beyond the reach of his steel—rolled across a rosebush and felt thorns cut through my shirt, lacerating my chest. A red wash filmed my vision. I heard the crunch of earth, somebody moving quickly. There was an abrupt white-hot blade of pain where my neck joined my shoulder—he had whacked me across the collarbone with the barrel of the gun.

I never thought it possible to feel such pain. I scrambled away, blind; my mind jumped the track and I felt the unreasoning helplessness of real blindness, the panic and terror. My nerves twanged, a desperate mindless compulsion to retaliate—to smash and slash, kick and maim. For the first time I fully understood the compulsion to kill, the unthinking fury of total rage.

I shook my head violently, trying to clear my vision. My shoulder banged against the rock wall of the house; I clawed my way upright, turned, plunged my hand into a hip pocket and tugged out the .25 Beretta, the automatic I had taken from Dr. Brawley.

As the red wash drained from my eyes I saw Cutter, on one knee, frowning in a crazy, dazed way. He looked stunned. Beyond the doorstep Joanne was stooping, her face white; she was clawing a fist-sized rock out of the ground and I saw a depression beside it where there had been another rock. She must have thrown a rock at Cutter and hit him in the head.

Cutter was shaking his head; I saw the spittle running from his mouth. He wiped it off with the back of his wrist and turned the Magnum toward Joanne. He had forgotten all about me.

I pushed the Beretta out in front of me and bellowed at him:

"Hold it!"

He froze; his small eyes shifted toward me. For a long broken moment nothing stirred. Then Cutter took a deep breath. He lowered the Magnum and got up, stuffing the long flashlight under his elbow and rubbing his right temple with his free hand. He had the Magnum at arm's length, down at his side; with slow stubborn movements he pressed it into the clamshell holster and snapped the holster shut. He shifted the flashlight from one hand to the other and said expressionlessly, "Okay, Sy, put that thing away."

I didn't move the gun a half-inch. I gave Joanne a quick glance: sweat dripped from her face and there was a white, knotted bulge at her jaw hinges.

Cutter gave me his long deadpan stare, as if fixing my face forever in his dark mind. He turned without saying a word, opened the car door and got in. The engine came on, then the headlights; the car wheeled around, throwing dust, and crunched away downhill. Darkness swallowed it.

Joanne made sounds in her throat. I put the Beretta in my pocket and croaked, "Jesus, he knows how to hit."

"The bastard. I wish I'd killed him."

"Yeah." I staggered to the front step and sat down, all my movements slow; I felt like a hundred-year-old man. I closed my eyes and stifled a moan. Red waves of pain pulsed through my bones. I felt Joanne's warm hand on my shoulder.

After a little while I summoned strength and got to my feet. I felt rickety and weak. Still throbbing with angry, hot pain. I climbed into the house and went around shutting off all the lights. I felt my way back to the front door and found Joanne on the step, fooling with her handbag. She pulled my .38 out and held it pointed at the place where Cutter had stood. I sat down by her and put my hand over hers, depressing the gun. "Okay," I said. "Okay."

"He'll come back."

"No. He's too conceited. He thinks if he searched the place and didn't find what he expected to find, then it isn't here. He wouldn't have given up if he hadn't been convinced. Showing a little muscle before he left—that's just his way."

"He's an animal."

"Yeah." With cops like him, who needs gangsters? I guess if you're far enough away from the Cutters, if you haven't actually come under their guns, you can find all kinds of Freudian explanations for them. It's a cop's job to handle garbage. He has to deal with vicious, ignorant, hysterical, self-important gutter people. He sees so much casual violence he becomes indifferent to cruelty. You could look at it that way. You could, but I couldn't. To hell with the psycho-sociological explanations. I didn't want the Joe Cutters in the same world with me. They didn't have any right to life.

Then, I thought, why hadn't I used the Beretta on him?

There had been a time when I understood killing. I'd have understood it, without questioning, if I'd shot Cutter, or if he'd shot me. But something along the years had taught me words—mercy, justice, responsibility, pride, dignity. I had learned the words and I didn't understand any more. The words had turned me into a human being. Simon Crane vs. the inevitable.

I became aware of the soft rhythm of Joanne's breathing beside me. I had been thinking—compulsively, to mask pain, to hold myself together. Angry, I stood up fast. Weakness flowed along my fibers. I walked around, testing my legs. I felt needles; there was a little tremor behind my knees. Tender here, stab of pain there. I walked a small circle, waving my arms around. When I came back to Joanne she pushed her lower lip forward to blow hair off her forehead and then turned her face away from me; I didn't understand why until she said, with a lurch in her voice, "I wish somebody would invent a mascara that wouldn't run."

She had been through so goddamn much in a few hours. I lowered myself beside her and turned her head with one finger, at her chin. Her face hovered before me. The wind kept a mesquite branch scratching on the side of the house. I felt the faint touch of something we had once had—the soft warm, nesty feeling of love.

The lights had been off long enough; the diesel generator had stopped. I squeezed her and said, "Maybe you'll want to stay here, I've got to take care of—Mike."

She shook her head. "I couldn't be alone, Simon."

"It's got to be done."

"I know. I'll help. Oh, God, poor Mike."

We buried Mike far back in the desert mountains, near a place where some hopeful hardrocker had tried to strike it rich. We had tugged the tarp-wrapped body out from under the diesel generator platform in back of the house. Cutter hadn't been able to look down there while the engine was running; he would have risked an ear against the engine's whirling, bladed fan. We had loaded the body into the Jeep and come lurching across country, using four-wheel drive.

It was three in the morning and the ground was full of stones under its thin layer of dusty topsoil. I ached in all my joints; every stab of the shovel into the resisting earth plunged pain through me.

I tucked the tarp around him as tightly as possible and piled high-mounded rocks over him, to keep the animals away. It didn't matter if someone found the grave; the body could not be traced to me, now that it was away from my home. The tarp was Army surplus, ten years old; in work gloves I left no fingerprints, even if there had been surfaces smooth enough to retain them.

When it was done we both stood by the mound, not speaking. An owl drifted above the saguaro cactus and the wind rubbed itself against us, cooling the sweat on my unclad torso. I was caked with dirt; my hair was matted when I ran fingers through it. Back here in the hills it felt as if civilization was a thousand years away.

In the moonlight Joanne was wan and pinched, near her limit of endurance. I told her to get in the Jeep and drive it down as far as the old rutted mining road a quarter of a mile below. I came along after her on foot, sweeping away tire tracks with a mesquite branch, taking agonizing punishment from the simple exercise of stooping and walking backward to sweep. When I climbed into the Jeep I put my shirt on and let Joanne drive us home. Her hands were locked white-knuckled on the wheel but she drove with steady competence. She astounded me; she seemed to have no breaking point.

We reached the old rock fort before dawn. Getting out of the Jeep and letting her reel past me into the house, I said, "You're fantastic."

There was a trace of her old laugh, hearty and mellow—just a trace; she shook her head at me, the laugh dwindling to a wan smile. I said softly, "You're pretty deep in my guts, you know."

She rubbed her face with both hands, closed her eyes very tight and let them spring open. She said, "I know you don't like coffee but you need some." She went into the kitchen, turning on lights.

I sat down by the phone. I had to think but my brain was stunned. Finally I fished from my pocket the number I had jotted down and dialed long distance. The line rang five or six times before Jerry Sprague grunted fuzzily into the mouthpiece and I identified myself.

"Jesus Christ. You know what the hell time it is, Simon?"

"I know. I'm damn sorry about it, but I'm telling you the literal truth when I say it's a matter of life or death."

"Crap. Whose?"

"Mine," I said. "About Raiford and Colclough—what have you got?"

"A headache," he said. "I waited at the office till damn near two o'clock, expecting your call."

"What about Raiford and Colclough?"

"Neither one of them has left the city in the past forty-eight hours. They've been here straight through. I know it positive, because—oh, hell, you want the details?"

"No. As long as you're sure neither one of them could have come down here for a few hours."

151

"And bumped off Sal Aiello. Simon, what's the score down there?"

"Nothing to nothing," I said, and added with addled wit, "two hits, no runs, a million errors. Go back to sleep Jerry. Profound apologies. If I live long enough I'll buy you a steak dinner at Porfirio's."

"I'll hold you to it. Listen, Simon, is there anything I can do? I mean, this has got to be something serious, and if I can help—"

"If I think of something I won't hesitate. Jerry—thanks."

When I hung up I sat, drained, my hand draped forgotten over the telephone. Joanne came in with coffee. I took one swallow and put the cup down. I said, "I've got to wake up. Maybe a shower." I went into the bathroom and stripped and turned on the water, full cold; stepped in, holding breath against the icy shock, and stayed just long enough to soap away the larger cakes of sand-grit. When I went dripping into the bedroom Joanne was standing by the door, unclothed, indifferent to her own nakedness and mine. She said, "You're too beaten to think straight, Simon. Go to bed. Don't try to think about it—don't think about anything. Forget. Sleep." She walked into the bathroom and shut the door. I heard the shower begin to splash.

I thought with dismal rage of Mike Farrell, maimed and murdered. Why? Had he found out something and confronted the murderer with what he knew? Had Aiello's killer murdered him? But why the maiming, the evidence of torture? Somebody had tried to force him to talk. To talk about what? Earlier in the day I had left Mike, convinced I knew everything he knew. What piece of information was there in Mike's story that could point to the killer who had robbed Aiello's vault?

Images of pink Cadillacs, guns, open vaults spun kaleidoscopically through my brain. I lay back on the bed and tried to concentrate. My muscles throbbed with pain. Trying to focus my mind, I closed my eyes—and sleep struck me like a club.

Chapter Nine

I woke up drowsily when she came burrowing down under the sheet with me like a warm, furry, inquisitive pet, creeping into my arms, fitting against me with close-together warmth. I felt the soft tickle of her hair on my skin. Burning slivers of daylight lanced into the room through cracks at the edges of the blanket-drape. I looked at her over a stretching interval. Her flushed, unsmiling face was inches from mine. Inside, I felt a visceral quiver, the slow coil and press of wanting her. The macabre ghost of Mike threw a shadow across my thoughts, but the terrifying threat that hung over us, the urgency of hard danger, created in me—and in her—an urgency of blood needs. Joanne sighed and wriggled and gave me a serene unhurried kiss; she stirred against me, her mouth softened and parted; we were drugged with panic. Her short breaths beat a fiery rhythm; her throat pulsed. We moved together and I felt the pound of her blood and mine. The cruel drive of urgency: she gave herself to me with a newer, deeper, more brutal abandon than ever before.

Afterward she said, "Love is a tough animal," in a puzzled, drunken murmur. "This was crazy—my God, we just performed a funeral! I think now I understand why people have wakes. We—needed this. Am I babbling?"

"Yes. Go on and babble."

"God, Simon, I'd forgotten all about your—about that

son of a bitch last night with his combat boots and his huge revolver. You must hurt like hell."

"I wish I was one of those movie cowboys who take eight tons of punishment and come right back without a hair out of place and wreck the whole saloon. What time is it?"

"You asked me that yesterday morning, remember? It must be about eight. I slept on the couch because you'd passed out and I didn't want to disturb you. But I woke up with the sun in my eyes and it was—lonely." I remembered the tumultuous months we had had together, in what now felt as if it must have been a prior incarnation, a different world—a world without grim, frightful terror.

We dressed and went outside under the burning sky. Heat pressed down. I drove her down to Nancy Lansford's. Nancy came around from the back of the house, big and shapeless and happy to see both of us. I told Joanne to stay out of sight—I would return by midnight at the very latest; I left her in Nancy's care and drove alone toward the city.

Almost half my forty-eight-hour grace period was gone, but I had set my own deadline well in advance of Vincent Madonna's. If by midnight I did not feel substantially closer to finding the loot than I was now, I would give up the search; Joanne and I would run for it. I hadn't decided where, or how; I knew we had to disappear. I still had in my pocket the name of the plastic surgeon Mike had mentioned, but surgery required more money than I had. As for Mike's $5,000 roll of cash, only the murderer knew what had happened to it; I hadn't found it on Mike's body.

I couldn't assume that Mike and Aiello had been killed by the same person. It was possible—if Mike knew too much, he could have been killed to shut him up. But the waters were muddled by the unmistakable signs of torture. The obvious questions, then, were: (1) what had Mike's murderer expected to learn by torturing him, and (2) had the murderer learned it?

I stopped at a filling station near the freeway, its price war pennants flapping. The attendant ambled forward with much less enthusiasm and haste than he would have displayed had I been driving an $8,000 Kluge with a slurpy twenty-six-gallon tank. While he filled the Jeep I put a dime in the newspaper vendor and pulled out a copy of the morning paper. I scanned the Aiello story—three front-page columns, cont. on p. 5—but there wasn't much I didn't already have. The police had found a station wagon abandoned a mile from Aiello's house. It had been wiped but they had found two fragmentary fingerprints identified as Michael Farrell's. Farrell was being sought for questioning. There followed a garbled version of Farrell's history and hearsay assumptions that Farrell had a gripe against Aiello. No mention anywhere that Aiello had a safe, or that it had been robbed. Either the cops still hadn't learned that part or they were saving it. There were a few details I hadn't known, like the bullet that had killed Aiello: a 9 mm bullet fired by a "German automatic pistol," unspecified make. That would probably be either a Luger or a Walther. So far, in my encounters with various personae, I had not seen any German automatics.

There was something obscene about the way the gas station attendant shoved the hose nozzle into the gas tank tube to sell me the last possible drop. I paid him, looked up an address in a phone booth by the curb, and drove under the freeway and across the north side of town toward the fashionable foothills.

Cliff View Terrace was a middle-sized shopping center built on the leveled top of a steep hill. The buildings, all one story, were faced with the pink-streaked gray brick that is used when you want to be ostentatious about your construction costs. There was a good deal of landscaped greenery; shops and offices fronted on eccentrically laid out walkways under awnings and shade trees. I parked the Jeep in a strip of shade and spent five minutes on foot finding what I sought. I finally located it near the back of the shopping center in a small quadrangular building introduced by a tall signpost from which, on chains, hung the names and occupations of occupants: Sylvester Johnson, D.D.S.; Julius Stein, M.D.; Fred Brawley, M.D., F.A.C.S.; and six more.

Brawley had a corner office at the back of the square. A narrow asphalt lane went past the backside, near the door marked PRIVATE; I saw I could have parked right there, on the lip of the hill.

I walked into the front office. The waiting room was just a waiting room. Indirect lighting, modern furniture built for design rather than comfort, magazines mildewing with age, carpet and walls done in pale hospital green. The receptionist-secretary was a starched fat blonde girl with an antiseptic polite smile, seated in a small cubicle behind a little glass window like a bank teller's. There were three patients waiting—a teenage girl and a matron, both reading magazines, and an old woman with cyanotic skin who sat with her legs crossed and stared at the tremor in her left hand.

I put an elbow on the sill of the receptionist's window, stuck my head in and said, "Doctor in?"

"Do you have an appointment, sir?"

"No, I'm not a patient. But if you'll—"

"Doctor Brawley sees pharmaceutical salesmen only on Thursday afternoons. If you'd care to leave whatever literature you have and come back Thursday afternoon, I'm sure—"

"I'm not selling," I said. "Look, just tell him Mr.

Crane's here about the missing property he wanted investigated. Will you do that?"

"Mr. . . . uh . . . ?"

"Crane. Simon Crane."

She masked her confusion by reaching for the phone, pushing a buzzer and turning away from me in her swivel chair so I couldn't hear her speak.

When she put the phone down she gave me a startled look and said, "He'll be right out Mr. Crane."

"Thank you." Obviously she was dying to know what missing property it was. I didn't oblige; I went to a chair and sat.

It took six minutes. Then Brawley appeared in a doorway and beckoned. The old woman beside me started to get to her feet and Brawley said, "I'll be with you in just a moment, Mrs. Chandler."

I followed him down a corridor. Doorways on both sides led into examination rooms, an X-ray room with a fortune in equipment, two labs, several bathrooms, a small operating room. At the back in the corner of the building, he had his office and consultation room. It was large and luxurious, like the office of a senior corporate executive. Picture windows in two walls gave a wide view of the city, a few hundred feet below. Brawley's desk was placed in front of one of the windows, just enough to one side so that a patient looking at him wouldn't be blinded by the glare behind.

He didn't sit, or offer me a seat. As soon as he closed the door behind me he said, "Well?"

"I'm still looking for your money," I said, which was true enough as far as it went. "Maybe you can help me find it."

"Me?" He laughed; he was trying to act affable but he was too ill at ease to bring it off; he hadn't quite settled down yet from the minor manhandling I'd given him yesterday. Trying to look casual, he leaned a crooked elbow across the top of a brown metal filing cabinet. Just behind him, set in the wall, was a three-foot office wall safe, the combination-dial showing. On an impulse I said, "Is that safe locked?"

"Not now. I only lock it when I'm out of the office."

"Mind if I look?"

His eyebrows went up. "Certainly I mind." Then he waved a hand through the air. "But go ahead if you must." He pulled the round door open. There wasn't much inside—a green lockbox and two stacks of papers and a row of small bottles which, it could be assumed, contained prescription narcotics.

I nodded. "Just a stab in the dark. Obviously I can't be sure you didn't steal the money yourself."

"I'd hardly be looking for it if I already had it."

"Smokescreen," I replied.

He smiled. "Have it your way. What progress have you made?"

"I don't know yet. But you were tied up with Aiello one way or another—don't bother to argue the point, Doctor—and you must be acquainted with some of the other prominent people who had dealings with Aiello."

"Assume whatever you want. It may not get you very far."

"Let's put it this way. You must have visited Aiello's house quite a number of times."

"I did, yes. To put things in his safe and get things out. They weren't social calls. If he had other people in the house he didn't introduce me to them—he kept them out of my sight, or vice versa. What are you trying to do, compile a list of his associates? I'm a rather poor subject for that sort of interview, I can assure you."

"Just tell me this. On your various visits up there, did you ever notice a pink Cadillac parked near his house?"

Brawley's eyes gave away brief alarm. He frowned to cover it. "What's that got to do with my money?"

"What kind of car do you drive?"

"Why, a Jaguar. Didn't you see it parked outside? An XKE sports model."

"Yeah. You're quite the image of a sport, Doctor. Who owns the pink Cadillac, then?"

"I'm sure I don't know."

"Try again. You telegraphed the first time I mentioned it. It rang your bell."

He clamped his mouth shut. I pulled the Beretta out of my hip pocket and got tough. "I'm not playing a game. It would be a shame if you got shot with your own gun, Doc, but it's important to me to find that car. You're the only one I've met who knows anything about it. Now let's have it."

He licked his lips; his eyes were fixed on the gun. I took a pace toward him and lifted the Beretta, making an effort to look menacing, and after he backpedaled and put up both hands, palms out toward me, he said, "All right—all right. I do know a man who owns a pink Cadillac, but I'm sure he couldn't be the man you want. He couldn't have stolen my money."

"Why not?"

"He's too rich to need it."

"Nobody's too rich to need three million dollars."

"Three million? Good Lord, is it that much?"

"Who is he?"

Brawley frowned at me. "Look, I'm sure it's not the man you want. This man is very rich, very prominent. He's an old friend of mine, and I must say a lucrative patient—he's a notorious hypochondriac."

"The name, Doc."

"Baragray."

"John-Ben Baragray?"

He nodded, tight-lipped.

I said, "Well I'll be damned."

John-Ben Baragray was a sort of ambulatory national monument. I had never seen him, let alone met him, but I was well versed in the Baragray folklore. He was a mossy-horn Texan who'd made his first fortune in east Texas oil then come west. One of those sleepy old back-porch kingmakers who owned half the land and most of the politicians in his rural bailiwick, he lived on a sixty thousand-acre ranch in the next county, fifty miles from the city. His fortune allegedly measured in the hundreds of millions. Among other things he was one of the state's most powerful bankers. His wealth was mostly tucked away in a variety of tax-dodge foundations that owned not only most of his own county but half the capital city as well.

When I stopped to think about it, it seemed only natural there could be a connection between a man like Baragray and the Madonna-DeAngelo-Aiello mob. Both were exponents of political bossism; both exemplified the feudal way of life.

It took me an hour and a half in the Jeep to reach the gate of Baragray's fence. It was a working gate, thrown across a cattle guard, built into a four-strand barbwire fence that stretched in both directions along a straight line to the horizons. This eastern county of the state was plateau land, six-thousand-foot high country carpeted in tall yellow grass. Darker spots on the distant hills were Hereford and Brahma cattle grazing. Three small airplanes buzzed around in the sky—modern cowboys, air-dropping rock salt, herding cattle, reconnoitering the herds.

Beef-raising, for those in the know and those rich enough to do it on a scale of massive efficiency, was one of the most highly profitable ventures available to a man with large capital—certainly by far the most lucrative of all agricultural pursuits. John-Ben Baragray, on this ranch and seven others scattered throughout the West, was one of the country's biggest cattlemen.

I drove several miles on Baragray's property, on a road he must have paved at his own expense, before I reached his headquarters. It was more of a village than a ranch. There were an airfield, a filling station, a company store with post office, and a town-sized scattering of small but sturdy frame houses for married employees, as well as a bunkhouse and a far-flung litter of workshops, barns and miscellaneous outbuildings. A forest of windmills sprouted throughout the camp. Most of the vehicles in sight were pickups, Jeeps, trucks and power wagons. There were a few souped-up automobiles.

It was, all together, a nice little baronial empire, all belonging to one man. The master's mansion was in keeping and in scale. It was a three-story splendor of sprawling wings, screened-in verandahs and balconies.

The ground floor of one wing was a garage, its five doors open against the heat. All five stalls contained cars. A Rolls or Bentley, an Alfa Romeo, a Jeep station wagon and two Cadillacs.

Neither Cadillac was pink.

A butler, in livery, answered my knock and looked me up and down without expression. It was the first time in my life I had ever met a liveried butler. I gave him my name. He asked what it was with reference to. I said it was personal and private and I had been sent by Dr. Brawley. He said I could wait in the parlor, showed me in and went.

The walls were studded with Renoirs. It was the sort of house which could easily have been ugly and baroque, but whoever had decorated it had owned taste enough to stop well short of that. Impressive as it was, the house—at least as far as I could tell from this part of it—had been designed with one paramount purpose: comfort. The furniture was massive, upholstered, but not overstuffed; most of it was covered with leather. The high ceiling was supported by dark beams at least eighteen inches thick. The carpet was the most enormous Chimayo Indian rug I had ever seen.

The room was cool, fanned without drafts by unobtrusive central air conditioning. The far wall, to which I walked now, was floor-to-ceiling bookshelves.

By their books shall ye know them. John-Ben Baragray had a catholic collection on his bookshelves. Philosophy, science, literary scholarship, and one section very heavy on military history. There were three shelves of novels, but none of them could have been classified as light reading. All the books looked as if they had been read. None seemed to be rare or expensive editions; they were books that had been accumulated by a reader, not a collector.

There was a deep leather reading chair, well worn, and a chair-side table that supported two cork coasters and a collection of pill bottles. I bent down to look. There were nitroglycerine pills, stimulants, depressants and amyl nitrate capsules. I frowned. Brawley had called him a hypochondriac—but you didn't prescribe nitro and amyl-nitrate for psychosomatic disorders. Those were remedies for severe heart disease. A violent murder, transportation and burial of the body—all these committed by a man with a weak heart? It didn't—

"Mr. Crane? Simon Crane? Do I know you, sir?"

The voice was a deep round boom. I straightened up and turned.

He was an enormous old man. He towered over me. He wore shirt and trousers of what looked like death-wish black. His hair was a full gray mane; he had a sweeping mustache. His face was crosshatched with weathered creases, and his hand, which he offered, was powerful and horny.

"I'm John-Ben Baragray. You mentioned Fred Brawley's name."

"How are you?" I said by way of greeting.

He answered the question literally: he made a good-natured groan, which resonated off the rafters, and said confidentially, "Truth told, I'm a sick man. A very sick man. You were looking at the pharmacy over there—I've got a bum ticker of course. If I was a building the doctors would condemn me. Do you know how close I am right now to having a coronary? But to hell with it. Modern medicine—hogwash. Of all the false gods we worship, the most false is the idea that man progresses. An African witch doctor has as high a percentage of cures as the highest-priced physician in the world today."

He lowered his head to examine me from beneath his heavy unruly eyebrows. "You're not falling apart with sympathy at all. Hell, that's the penalty for being an oversized man—you don't get appreciation of your misery when you're ill. Well, if you let me I'll spend the whole day talking about my numerous ailments, and I suspect that's not what you came here for. You've had a long drive in an open Jeep under a goddamn hot sun and therefore I deduce it must be something too important for the telephone. Can I get you a drink?"

He was already walking, with short paces for a long-legged man, to a bar beyond the front window. I said, "Just beer, if you've got it."

"A man shouldn't drink anything but beer on a day this hot," he agreed. He removed two bottles of beer—some foreign brand I'd never heard of—from a small concealed refrigerator. It wouldn't have surprised me if he'd opened the bottles with his teeth, but he used an ordinary five-cent church key, handed me a bottle without bothering about a glass, and lifted his bottle in toast. "I drink to you, sir. Your life expectancy is longer than mine."

That was doubtful. I tasted the beer and it was excellent. John-Ben Baragray pointed to a chair. We sat, facing each other; I said, "I've got a crapshooter's instincts and sometimes I play by them. I came here with something in mind but I've changed my mind."

"You're not a doctor, of course, even if Fred Brawley did send you."

"He didn't send me. He suggested your name when I put a question to him."

"What question?"

I considered his wise, tough, worldly face. I said, "You've probably heard, Salvatore Aiello was murdered."

"Yes." He watched and listened expressionlessly, slightly skeptical but not aroused. I felt disconcerted.

I said, "I'm not a cop, but I've got an important stake in finding out who killed Aiello. The only lead I've got is a pink Cadillac that was seen leaving his house at about the time of the murder. Brawley told me you had a pink Cadillac."

"I did," he said, without emphasis. "Anything else?"

"What's your connection with Aiello?"

The bushy brows lifted; nothing else moved. After a moment he said, "None whatever. Of course I know who he is—was. I won't deny I've had a few dealings with an associate of his, but I've never had anything to do with Aiello."

"Vincent Madonna?"

"If you like naming names," he said. "Yes."

"Politics?"

"Naturally," he said. In the back of his tone there was the hint of a Texas drawl, but it wasn't pronounced. He had a voice like a bassoon. He said, "Madonna and I are on different sides of the fence. It's no secret. He wants to bring the gamblers into our state, legally, and I want to keep them out. I've met Madonna a few times, tried to negotiate the question, but he doesn't believe in negotiating. That's all right—I can be pretty stubborn myself. I don't like those bastards but I respect them. Do you want to know anything about my pink Cadillac?"

"Sure."

"I sold it a month ago." He gave me a look that might have passed for a fleeting smile; he said, "I can prove it if necessary."

"Who'd you sell it to?"

"The Cadillac agency. I swapped it for a new car." His chuckle was a thunderous rumble. "Naturally the word went around that I traded it in because the ash trays had filled up. That's the curse of wealth in this country. The fact was, the car was several years old and I don't treat cars gently. It needed replacement. Well, never mind. The rich are always hated, you know, and I've learned there's no way to prevent it. You can donate a lot of money to good causes but you're accused of dodging taxes. You can drive around in a cheap used car and wear old clothes and act like one of the boys and they say you're cheap or phony or trying to suck up to somebody or crazy or insecure. If you've got good manners you're a snob and if you've got bad manners you're nouveau riche and that makes you a slob. If you live according to your income you're conspicuous and vulgar, and if you don't you're a tightwad. There's only one answer to it and that's to quit giving a good goddamn what anybody thinks and just do the hell what you feel like doing, because that's the only thing money can do for you anyway—buy you freedom."

He stopped suddenly and gave me a sharp glance. "Hell, you didn't come here to listen to a sick old man bleat about the poverty of riches. Is there anything I can do for you besides tell you about pink Cadillacs? Another beer? A bite of lunch?"

"No. No, thanks." I got up, feeling like an intruder. "I'm sorry I bothered you. I had a feeling before you walked in the room that I'd been given a bum steer."

"It happens," he said, "all the time. I'm sorry I couldn't help more. You're sure you won't stay and put on the feedbag with me?"

"No, I've got to—"

"Nobody around here eats with me any more," he said, overriding me with the parade-ground strength of his big voice. "The hired help think it ain't proper and I've got no family left. My wife died two years ago and my only son was an Air Force colonel, shot down in Vietnam. How about a bite of lunch? You look like a man who can make good conversation."

The poor, sick, lonely old fossil. I shook my head and declared, "I'll take a rain check. If we're both still alive next week I'll take you up on it."

"By God, I'll hold you to that." He smiled for the first time.

Heat clung to the ground like melted tar. It was past one o'clock; I felt the crowding press of time as I drove out the front gate and turned left on the highway, pushing the Jeep up to speed. One or two thoughts had begun to jell in my mind and I knew where I wanted to look next.

Ten miles west of Baragray's gate the plateau ended abruptly at the Mogul Rim. The desert lay beyond, below the three-thousand-foot scarp. The highway made several sharp turns and went down the face of the rim with long slopes and hairpin switchbacks, hugging the cliffs. I'd started down the steep narrow pitch, with the sheer drop at my left, and a green car ahead of me pulled out onto the road, going in my direction. I braked and mouthed an oath. The car ahead built up a little speed but after that I knew I was stuck. He wasn't much of a mountain driver. I had to keep it down to twenty-five to accommodate him, and I couldn't see any place to pass. I chafed. This was no time to get stuck behind a schoolteacher. I could see vaguely past the sun glare on his back window the faint shape of his head and shoulders hunched nervously over the wheel.

The road bent around a promontory and kept going down; we crawled around two tight hairpins and then I spotted a straight stretch approaching, where I might be able to get by. Impatient, I moved up close behind him, downshifted, hit the horn button and pulled into the left lane, gunning it.

It was downhill; the Jeep shot forward. But as I pulled parallel, the green car accelerated.

I turned my head to yell at him—and saw his wide, florid face.

It was Ed Behrenman—the tail I'd shaken off last night.

The crimson face broke into a taut grin. I saw a gun in his right hand, coming out across the sill, a big Army .45 automatic. He tugged the wheel over, bringing his car across the white stripe, crowding me onto the edge.

Chapter Ten

A few times in my life I have done things for which I would like to have taken credit, as if I had reasoned them out beforehand, prepared for them and accomplished them with cool deliberation, unruffled and supreme. The truth was, in each case I acted with unthinking reflex, and it happened to work. Call it luck; call it fate. Call it a natural endowment of good reflexes.

Behrenman swung his car against me. We were both streaking toward a sharp right-hand bend, with the 2,500-foot drop at my left. I hit the brakes hard and it was those unthinking reflexes that made me crab the wheel—not away from him, but toward him.

He was expecting it but he was a shade slow reacting. My bumper banged along the side of his car with a garbage can racket. He slammed his brakes and slewed across the road at an angle, trying to shove me off the cliff with the superior weight of his big car. He might have done it, if the Jeep had had a longer wheelbase. I heard the crack and roar of his pistol. A glazed star appeared in the windshield before me. I was crabbing the wheels over hard, fighting the weight of his car, and as he slid forward the protruding edge of the Jeep bumper swung into the scalloped fender opening over his left rear wheel. There was the sudden sharp stink of burning rubber as the bumper shredded his back tire; then the hooked edge of the bumper caught the inside of his fender. I held the brakes down hard. The green car skidded, swiveling on the pivot. He spun left. His front wheels went over the edge—I saw terror on his suddenly white face. The .45 boomed and roared. In that broken instant of time my reflexes sent messages to feet and arms: I gunned the Jeep forward, got free of his fender, spun around with my rear wheels skidding to the right.

The gun was still thundering. A ricochet screamed off the Jeep's hood. Freed of bumper-hook restraint, the green car pitched forward over the rim and turned a slow somersault.

The Jeep shuddered and stopped, skewed across the road at an acute angle. My front wheels were inches from the edge. I jammed the shift into reverse, backed onto the pavement and set the hand-brake. I got out on wildly trembling legs and made my way to the edge. I could still hear the bang and crash of the tumbling car.

It was still falling. The cliff was not quite perpendicular; the car went down end-over-end, each somersault slow and ponderous. It was hardly recognizable as an automobile—squashed, foreshortened, both ends pleated like an accordion's bellows.

Four hundred feet below, it pitched out over a rock outcrop, hung suspended in the air, and crashed down like a pancake on a reverse-turn of the highway. From where I stood it didn't seem to bounce at all. It hit the pavement flat, on all four wheels, with a sound I never forgot—deafening, but more crunch than crash. Like the amplified crump of a distant field mortar.

Pieces of sharded glass winked in the sunlight down the length of the car's vertical path. One door lay intact, hardly dented, forty feet below me. One wheel, with part of an axle, teetered on the lip of a rock a few yards below that.

I retreated from the edge and braced both hands on a flat fender of the Jeep, taking deep breaths. After a while I opened my eyes and climbed numbly into the seat, got the Jeep moving and crawled downhill at a feeble pace. My arms shook violently. My mouth was sticky with dry fright.

The unrecognizable remains of the green car were splashed across the width of the road, more or less in one piece fused together by impact. The thing was upright but the final blow had driven the remaining wheels and underparts up into the body; it was squashed almost flat, not more than three feet high at any point.

It was a useless gesture, but I tried to pry into the wreckage to find him. All I could find was a hand, severed, the fingers locked around a mangled pistol. I went to the side of the road and vomited.

The wreck blocked the road. I would have to move it. I unwound a length of cable from the winch-drum on the front bumper of the Jeep, found a corner of the wreckage on which to set the hook, went back to the Jeep, set the brakes and worked winch levers.

It was no good. The wreck had smashed completely into the pavement. The only way to move it would be to get above it with a wrecker and lift it out.

I caught myself uttering a blank monotone of curses. I clamped my mouth shut, rewound the winch cable, and turned around to drive back up to the top. There was another highway that would take me around, past Baragray's ranch and down another cliff road thirty miles to the north. It would cost me three hours.

I phoned the Highway Patrol from a lonely filling station to report the wreck, giving them a fake name, and went on. Driving through the mountains, threading menacing dark stands of pine, I put my mind on Ed Behrenman, who had not tailed me up to Baragray's from the city but who had known where to ambush me, and by the time I started down the steep canyon highway I knew where to look for Aiello's killer and where to start looking for the $3 million.

Only it wasn't my day for speed. Halfway down the canyon a tire went flat.

I turned the lurching Jeep into a graveled cliffside overlook and got out, cursing loudly now, to change the tire. It was easy to see what had caused the flat—somewhere in the tangle with Behrenman's car the tire had been raked by steel, the sidewall cut almost through.

Changing the tire was a half hour's work. I went around the Jeep to inspect the other tires but found nothing to alarm me; and went on my way, uneasiness turning to a sour belly-taste of fear as the sun moved steadily toward the mountains across the desert. There were a lot of places to search. I knew who had the money, but not where.

It was well after five when I left the freeway and crossed town on the Strip. I had seen the address some time ago and hadn't forgotten it. Blue, lime, red and pink neon winked and flashed along the Strip. Girls and uniformed men in cars went recklessly fast, squealing into broad parking lots in front of the places where they could spend or otherwise separate themselves from their money. I went by the Moulin Rouge without slacking, thinking momentarily of Mike Farrell—I thought I had that figured out, too, but it would take checking and I didn't have time for that.

Near six o'clock, after fighting the outbound traffic rush and two miles of unsynchronized traffic lights, I turned up a quiet street and drove slowly, seeking house numbers. Going past one house I saw a television screen, blue through the window, flickering as an airplane went overhead, an old woman sitting there, bending toward the set, trying to hear. The house I wanted was next door. I stopped the Jeep and put my hand in my hip pocket, on the Beretta.

There was wrought-iron furniture on the front lawn. I went up a curved pavement to the door and tried the knob without knocking. It was locked. I pushed the doorbell and heard chimes inside. After a minute without response I backed up and walked around the side of the house into the gravel driveway. There was a two-car garage. I looked into it through a side window. There was one car inside, a Jaguar coupe with a slinky look of speed. I went back to the side of the house and looked in. The view through the kitchen showed me part of the living room beyond, and I saw a woman walking toward the front door, not steadily, belting a bathrobe around herself and brushing back uncombed hair.

I went back around to the front and was there when she finally opened the door; evidently she had stopped to put away her hairbrush before answering the chimes. Her mouth was sucked in with a tight look of disapproval. She barred the door with her body, a feline redhead with an amoral half-drunk look. What had been a pretty face ten years ago had hardened.

She swept me up and down with a practiced look, and stepped back. "Come in." She hadn't asked me who I was or what I wanted—just, "Come in."

I came in and pushed the door shut, looking around past her. The place was decorated in Miami Modern, expensive but hideous. Had I been in any condition to do so, I might have reflected at some length on the fact that the sole original meaning of the word "luxury," in Elizabethan times, was "lust." The house, with its careless, tasteless opulence, and the woman before me would have told me all I ever needed to know about the master of the place, even if I had never met him.

I said, "I'm looking for your husband. I assume he's your husband."

"Won't I do?" She ran her tongue along her lips. "I'm Sylvia." Heavy-breasted, she twisted her ungirdled hips, wanting sensation. She sat on a Naugahyde couch and plucked a cigarette from a case on the coffee table. She eyed me as if I were a side of beef and said, "Mix me a drink and we'll talk about my husband. Mix yourself one while you're at it."

"Where is he?"

Her shoulders stirred. Her breasts handled the bathrobe seductively. "You're a lovely man."

"Where is he?"

"Who knows? There was a phone call. An emergency case, he said. He's got my car, his is broken down. He'll probably be gone most of the night, as usual. I don't think I even want to be bothered to know what her name is. You don't know, do you? Her name?"

"No," I said, biting it off. As I looked around the room it occurred to me he might have the loot hidden right here in the house. A good place to start looking—but she, Sylvia, could make it difficult. I said, "I'll mix drinks, but let me use your bathroom first."

"Sure." She smiled and pointed vaguely.

In the bathroom medicine cabinet, as I'd suspected, there was an assortment of medicines. I found the one I sought, dumped six capsules into my palm, flushed the toilet and went back to the living room with the capsules in my closed hand. "Where's the bar?"

"I've got an open bottle in the kitchen. Scotch—I hope it

suits you because my husband keeps the bar locked when he's not home." She tittered. "Make mine straight, one ice cube."

As I crossed to the kitchen I saw she had sat back on the couch and adjusted the bathrobe. She had nothing underneath but skin. The lapels were parted, displaying a wealth of pale, soft breast. A lot of men I knew chose their wives with less care than their barbers. In the kitchen I made drinks and emptied the contents of the capsules into hers. I stirred it up and took the drinks into the living room, gave hers to her and was about to retreat to a chair when she patted the couch beside her. "Sit here by me. What's your name?"

"Simon."

"That's nice. It's—different, you know? Sexy." She picked up her drink, watching me over the rim of the glass, and slugged down a good big swallow. "The way you came in, I thought you might be the wronged husband of some broad he's shacking up with. But you said you didn't know her name."

"That's right, I don't."

"So you're not the wronged husband. Who are you?"

"Does it matter?" I said. "You're sure you don't know where I might find him?"

She shook her head, giving me a while-the-cat's-away leer. Her upper body stirred, twisting toward me as she set the drink down; her nipples made hardened dents against the robe. When I didn't react in keeping with the invitation she pouted with her mouth and looked down at her drink. "I'll bet he's keeping one of those cheap Mafia broads— some gangster's gun moll. He's thick as thieves with the mobsters, did you know that?"

"Yeah. I know that."

"Why, I'll bet you're one of them."

"One of what?"

"A hoodlum. Is that what you are?" She seemed more excited and pleased than alarmed. She laughed. "That would just serve him right, wouldn't it?" Then, quickly, she shifted her seat and tugged at the cloth belt. Her garment came apart; the heavy breasts burst free. She touched her damp palm to my cheek and whispered, "I'm a woman, Simon. I need what every woman needs."

"Right now," I stated truthfully, "I feel like having sex about as much as I feel like having a cucumber sandwich."

"In that case," she said, undismayed, "I'll just have to seduce you." She gripped my shirt collar and pulled me close.

I extricated myself and stood up. She growled a hoarse obscenity and reached for her drink, and upended it defiantly. Her expression didn't change. She said, "I drink a lot. Do you mind? It helps keep your guts in." Her tongue was starting to thicken.

I said, "Tell me about him and the Mafia. You said he's thick as thieves with them."

"Did I?" Her head was slightly tilted. She put the burning cigarette in the corner of her mouth and it sent a thin slow jet of smoke past her half-shuttered eye. Squinting up at me, she said, "Who the hell are you, anyway?"

"An interested party."

"You're one of them. I knew it. A hoodlum. You want to find him so you can kill him."

"Why should I want to kill him?"

"You know perfectly well." She was glazed, mumbling in thickening syllables. "He told me he had some kind of—he called it a beef, against the Mafia. He said he had a lot of evidence against them and if he can't straighten things out with them he'll release some of it to the newspapers. He says it's enough to blow the Mafia sky-high, and a lot of politicians with it."

The stuff I had put in her drink, chloral hydrate from sleeping capsules, wasn't supposed to act as a truth serum, but it seemed to be having that effect. Either that or the alcohol had entirely wiped out her inhibitions against disclosing dangerous secrets. Or maybe she was just getting revenge on him.

It didn't matter any more; she crumpled slowly and lay inert. I straightened her out on the couch, tested her pulse, closed the bathrobe around her, and began to subject the house to a painstaking search.

The sun threw a last burst of light along the horizon. I emerged from the house empty-handed except for a key case I'd lifted from Sylvia's purse. I used it to let myself into the garage, and spent ten minutes climbing rafters and seeking cubbyholes. Nothing. I went back to the house and put the keys back in her bag. Where else? His office, I supposed. Or the car he was driving—her car, she'd said. There was no question in my mind what kind of car it was. I'd never seen it but it had to be a Cadillac and it had to be pink

I left her on the couch, snoring, and let the lock click shut behind me when I went outside. In plum-colored dusk I drove up toward the foothills. I stopped once, to telephone Nancy's house and talk to Joanne. I told her, in a voice so weary it alarmed her, that I was on a warm trail and would see her soon. "Don't set fire to your hope chest just yet," I said lamely, and hung up, and got back in the Jeep to climb the foothill street.

On the way up I paid no attention to the bright neon display on the flats below. It was fully dark by the time I drove across the deserted parking area, past the brightly lit windows of the expensive shops that were closed for the night but lighted against burglars. I didn't park in front this time; I found the service road and drove around back, out along the narrow asphalt path that hugged the rim of the hill the way the mountain road hugged the cliff where Ed Behrenman had made his plunge. Quite a bit of light flowed up here from the illuminated city below.

The back door of a pharmacy had a neon sign that spattered and fizzed.

The pink Cadillac four-door sedan was parked at the end of the service road. I rolled the Jeep to a quiet stop behind it. The adrenalin pumping through my body made my hands shake.

I had to walk past the Cadillac to get to the back door of the place, but I was interrupted by the sight of the man slumped in the driver's seat of the big car. I stopped, lifted the Beretta, and gingerly reached inside to shake him. It was Dr. Fred Brawley, but what the hell was he doing asleep in the Cadillac?

He wasn't asleep. He was dead. When I touched him he pitched over on his right shoulder and didn't move. I opened the door and examined him by the light of the dash and map lights. He had been shot in the back of the head by a bullet of sufficiently small caliber and low velocity to lodge in the skull; it had made no exit wound in front.

I felt sinking disgust and a coiling tension in my groin, the acid sense of failure. Somebody had beat me to him. Somebody else had found him out, killed him and taken the loot. I was right back where I'd started.

The corpse was still warm; he hadn't been dead more

than a few minutes. Maybe there was still a chance. I withdrew from the car, glancing into the back seat—a suitcase and an overcoat. I opened the suitcase: just clothes. Brawley had been traveling light.

The quadrangular medical office building had been locked up for the night, I supposed, but when I glanced up at the corner picture-window ten feet above my head I saw the wink of a small light traveling across the glass in reflection. Someone was inside Brawley's office with a pencil flashlight. Blood pumping, I walked around the Cadillac to the back door of the building.

The metal door had been jimmied open; it stood slightly ajar. I pushed softly inside, taking the Beretta off safety and holding it at ready. As I climbed the stairs toward the upper floor—that was the ground floor if you entered from the front; the pitch of the hill made the difference—my nostrils detected the lingering firecracker scent of cordite sulfur.

The stairwell was dark. I went up on tiptoes. At the head of the stairs the door stood wide open, giving out into the long corridor. At the end of the hall I could see the faint reflections of the moving flashlight around the corner in the office. I went forward along the soundless carpet, gripping the Beretta, taut with the knowledge that if the man was still searching for it then he hadn't found it.

I eased up to the open office door and slowly put my head around the jamb, and saw him.

He had his back to me. He was trying to get the safe open. He had tools; the pencil light was in his teeth and he was using both hands on the tools. The little electric drill was whining with the particular whine of a diamond bit. I had a drill like that; I use it on rocks.

There was a click as the drill plunged through, and as he withdrew the bit and set the drill down on the chair beside him, I heard him grunt—a breathy, falsetto sort of grunt caused by the old injury to his larynx.

I said, "Stand still, Pete. Freeze."

DeAngelo wheeled. In the flickering strange light of the tumbling flashlight I had a glimpse of his grin, a spasm of clenched teeth and drawn lips. His hand, as quick as a diamondback's strike, was spinning a silencer-weighted pistol toward me.

He wasn't allowing any argument. I pulled the trigger, too much in haste, and saw vividly the jump and puff of his shirtsleeve as the flesh received the bullet. It stung him but he was still moving, diving toward the desk. The automatic in his fist made a little puff of sound and I heard the solid whack of the bullet driving into the wall above my head. I wheeled back, flattening against the outside of the door-jamb; slid down to the floor and went into the room on my belly, gun out in front. But he took me by surprise: he launched a chair through the picture window, and in the crashing confusion went out through the jagged opening.

He had a ten-foot drop to the ground. I got my feet under me and crossed the room fast. The leg of a chair, un-seen in the dark, tripped me; I sprawled, cursed, got up and peered down through the shattered window.

I had a glimpse of him, running with a limp past the neon drugstore sign, his face a twisted ugly mask of fury. He stopped and fired at me, just once; I ducked, put my head out again and watched him disappear at a shambling run. The only explanation I could think of was that he must have been running out of ammunition.

He would probably summon help from the nearest phone. I didn't have much time. I went to the wall safe.

Luck, this time in my favor. He had broken the lock with his drill just before I had surprised him. The door swung open. I picked up his pencil light from the floor and played it around the inside of the safe.

There was only one thing inside that hadn't been there when I'd looked inside this morning. The addition was a gun—a Walther 9 mm automatic.

I took it out, checked its loads, and put it in my pocket.

I tested the safe for false walls or bottom, but it seemed sturdy, and there was no money in it. I looked around quickly, going through drawers and the brown filing cabinet. The loot wasn't in the office. I spent only five minutes going through the rest of the examining rooms and closets; what I sought was bulky and I didn't waste time on small enclosures. There was no money, and as far as I could tell there was no evidence lying around that could, in Sylvia Brawley's words, blow the Mafia sky-high.

It had to be somewhere. Brawley had had it; DeAngelo hadn't found it.

I went back outside, very scared now, but remembering what Joanne had told me—the loot might have fitted into the trunk of a car. I got Brawley's keys from the ignition and went back and opened the trunk, all the while keeping my senses alert for sign of DeAngelo's return or the arrival of reinforcements.

It was all there, stuffed into the trunk of the pink Cadillac, crammed tight into every inch of space.

From the linen closet of Brawley's office I took a stack of folded bedsheets, the kind that nurses used to cover the examination tables. They weren't too large but they had to do. I opened the sheets one at a time and made laundry bundles of the money from the Cadillac trunk, tying the sheets up by their corners. I put them all in the bed of the Jeep and put the metal lockboxes, seven of them, on top to weight the sheets down; I slammed the Cadillac trunk, tossed the keys on the seat beside the dead man, and went around the Cadillac wiping fingerprints. I did a fast job and headed for the Jeep with a gun in my hand—I had spent far too much time here.

Then a sound rocked my head back: the wail of a siren's idiot laughter, somewhere close by.

I backed the Jeep down the service road to a wide spot, turned around, and headed up toward the shopping center plaza, which was the only way out.

I came out from between two buildings in second gear, pushing the gas, but the police car slithered across my path and squealed to a halt. The door slammed open and the driver leaped out—Joe Cutter, lifting his .357 Magnum.

DeAngelo must have called him in. I ducked my head, spun the wheel and braked the Jeep. Cutter's gun boomed. My windshield took another bullet hole, the second for the day; by then I was out, diving flat, hitting the asphalt painfully on one shoulder and rolling. I rolled past the Jeep in time to see him shift his aim toward me; he had the Jeep's headlights in his eyes and he was squinting with a ferocious scowl crouching down on one knee to aim. I used Brawley's Walther pistol. My steady, firm pressure on the trigger made it go off. It caught me almost by surprise, as it should. Magically, as if by stop-motion photography, a dark disc appeared on the side of Cutter's heavy face. Blood burst from his cheeks; his head snapped to one side under the bullet's impact.

He pitched to the pavement, full in the cone of the headlights.

I sprinted across the fifty feet that separated us. The hole in his cheekbone was rimmed by droplets of crimson froth. His expressionless eyes blinked twice and stayed open, focused on my knees.

There didn't seem to be anyone about. I turned a circle on my heels to make sure. As I completed the turn, my eyes fell on Cutter's heavy .357 revolver. Of all the people I'd known, Cutter had been most likely to die by the sword. Sometimes I had thought he was just batting around seeking a place to die. He had found it.

I picked him up and put him in the squad car, put the Magnum in his hand and drove the squad car through the alley; I parked it behind the Cadillac and left Cutter dead behind the wheel. Then I walked over to the pink Cadillac and pressed the Walther pistol into Brawley's dead hand. Paraffin tests would prove Brawley hadn't shot him, but a superficial investigation would suggest he had. And I had no doubt the Walther was the same gun that had killed Aiello. It had been in Brawley's safe and I presumed it was registered to Brawley. Let the cops figure it out. There was nothing to tie me in, except DeAngelo, and he wasn't likely to finger me for the cops.

I had things in mind for DeAngelo. I walked back out to the Jeep and drove away; in the bed behind me, wind rattled the bedsheet bundles of money.

Chapter Eleven

I eased Joanne's beige convertible to the curb by a roadside phone booth and switched off the ignition. The morning sun whacked the boulevard, traffic swishing by. Joanne said, "Are you sure we have to do it this way?"

"Yes. Scared?"

"Yes."

I patted her hand, got out, and went into the phone booth. It was Freddie's dull voice that answered my ring and I asked him to call Madonna to the phone. Madonna came on the wire growling. "Where are you?"

"Is that the only question you know how to ask?"

"Listen, Crane, I—"

"Let me do the talking. You want to know where that missing property is, don't you?"

"You son of a bitch."

"Sure. Look, the reason I'm calling first, I don't want to get mown down by artillery on your doorstep. I'm coming up to your house and I'm bringing Mrs. Farrell with me."

"Come ahead," he said. "I'll be waiting."

"Not like that," I snapped. "I know where that property is, but you'll never find it if you don't give me a chance to talk to you."

"You'll have plenty chance to talk to me, Crane. I promise you that."

"Not under a gun," I said. "You may recall there were

185

certain items in that shipment of property which could make things a little uncomfortable for you if they got released to the wrong parties. Some of those items are in the care of a person who'll release those items at midnight tonight unless I intercept that person and give instructions not to release it. And don't think I can be pressured into giving you that person's name, because even if the muscle boys went to work on me they wouldn't be able to get to this person in time to keep the stuff from being released. You understand?"

The cold bass voice said, "Crane, you're talking into a dead phone. Get the hell up here. I'll listen to what you've got to say but let's quit making threats. I don't like threats."

"Sure—just so we understand each other. One more thing. Don't believe everything Pete DeAngelo tells you."

"I don't believe everything anybody tells me. You've still got till noon to close our deal. It's ten o'clock now. When will I see you?"

"We'll be there in twenty minutes," I said, and hung up.

I slipped into the driver's seat. Joanne said, "All set?"

"All set."

"Put your arms around me, darling."

I did. Nose to nose, we drowned in each other's eyes. I grinned at her. I felt jumpy but alert; I had taken a speed tablet, one of Nancy Lansford's diet pills. We had been up all night, busy.

We kissed at length, right out in what Mike would have called bare-ass daylight, and when Joanne straightened out and arranged herself on the seat she said, "I'll probably never stop thanking you for what you did with that film."

I turned the key and pulled out into the traffic, heading for the foothills. I had burned the movie film at my house at midnight and flushed the ashes down the toilet. It had made a terrible stink, the burning film. I hadn't looked at it before destroying it.

It was the only part of the loot I hadn't examined, in detail; that was what had taken all night. That, and arranging for the safekeeping and possible release of the material—my weapon against Madonna and DeAngelo.

We turned onto the Strip. Joanne said, "I'm still scared to death. I will be until it's over."

"It'll work," I said. I grinned at her. "If you can't join 'em, lick 'em."

"I know, but something could go wrong."

I didn't answer. We were underdogs against the organization, of course. But the weapon of an underdog's survival is cunning. With a little luck we might come out all right. But she was right, there were risks. I was sure DeAngelo had spent the night trying to find a wall to nail us to. It would be a bad mistake to underestimate him.

By the time we crunched to a stop behind the beautiful old Continental in Madonna's driveway, Freddie the Neanderthal had the door open and was standing there, leaning forward like Buster Keaton, wearing a rumpled sports jacket over his gun and glowering at us. I saw DeAngelo's Mercedes and the blue Ford that Senna and Baker had visited us in. That was all right; the more muscle in the house, the better—if my scheme worked.

I got out carrying the briefcase, walked around and opened Joanne's door. She turned sideways on the seat and came out legs first, moving prettily, a girl of supple grace. With my back to Freddie, I tried to reassure her with a smile. She reached for my hand and clutched it hard. We went up to the door and Freddie said in a monotone, "I got to frisk you."

"Frisk me if you want. But the briefcase stays locked and

you'll keep your paws off the lady."

"Now you know I can't—"

I cut him off harshly: "You've got enough torpedoes inside the house to cut us to pieces before we make the first half of a false move. Hold your gun on us if you want."

He looked us up and down. Pointing to the briefcase he said, "What's in there?"

"Papers. For the Don's eyes only."

The husky rasp of Pete DeAngelo's ruined voice shot forward from the room behind Freddie: "Okay, Freddie, never mind. Let them in and keep both eyes on them."

Freddie stepped aside. We walked into the house. I felt the cold clutch of Joanne's tensing hand in mind.

There were deep vertical lines between DeAngelo's eyebrows. He wore a short-sleeved shirt and his arm was thickened by a bandage where I'd shot him last night. Cold, ruthless, hard and direct, DeAngelo gritted his neat white teeth in a satanic grin. He pointed to the antique Seth Thomas clock above the marble mantel and said, "The race is just about over, Crane, and you're about to finish out of the money."

So he had decided to bluff it through. That was all right by me.

Two men walked in from one of the house wings and posted themselves, without comment, on either side of the door through which they had just come. Ed Baker and Tony Senna. They both wore guns in unconcealed shoulder holsters. Senna looked into the doorway and nodded his head, and only then did Vincent Madonna make his entrance.

Madonna looked tired. His wrinkled suit jacket was undone and, as before, he wore no tie; his open collar revealed a tangled mat of dark hair. Big-rumped, he moved to the fireplace, ten feet in front of us, and set himself in a hipshot pose with one arm on the mantel. There was no preamble; he only said, "Okay, you've got the floor."

I squeezed Joanne's hand and set the briefcase down on a chair-side table by my right hip. I said, "You want to know who made the hit on Salvatore Aiello. You want to know who robbed his safe, and where the loot is now. Okay, that's what I'm going to give you. But I'm going to give it to you in detail, because you'll want to be able to check my story and find out if it's true, and you can only do that if I give you all the details. It's going to take a little time and it'll go faster if there are no interruptions. If you've got questions save them till I'm finished. Check?"

"Go ahead," he said, expressionless.

"Some of this is guesswork but if I'm wrong you can correct me. The important facts I have. It's the background that's guesswork because I haven't had time to check it out. All right, here we go. Background. Aiello had an important appointment for some time after one in the morning, the night he was killed. You can check that with Judy Dodson. She doesn't know who the appointment was with or what it was for. I'm not sure myself what it was for, but I know who it was with. Doctor Fred Brawley. Brawley went to Aiello's house late at night because a man in his position couldn't afford to be seen going there in broad daylight. The appointment was all set up and Brawley arrived, probably carrying some important information that Aiello wanted—blackmail, evidence against the lieutenant governor, who up to now has been opposing your attempts to get gambling legalized. I assume that's what Brawley had because that evidence is part of the loot from the safe, but if it had been there earlier than that night you'd have used it, and the lieutenant governor would have switched his stand before now. Okay. That explains why Aiello was anxious to see

Brawley, and why he let him into the house at that hour. What Aiello didn't know was that Brawley had a beef against him. I don't know why but I can guess. Aiello was probably screwing Brawley's wife. Am I right about that?"

"Keep talking," Madonna said.

"If it wasn't that it was something else, but Brawley definitely had a beef. He went to Aiello's and got Aiello to open the safe under the pretext of putting the blackmail evidence in and maybe getting some money out. As soon as Aiello opened the safe, Brawley shot him. I suspect that when Brawley first worked out the plan, all he wanted was to get back the abortion-malpractice dirt Aiello had in the safe. But then he got greedy. Three million dollars is an attractive lure to anybody, let alone a man saddled with a wife like Sylvia Brawley. Brawley probably figured with all that money he could disappear, go to Europe with a new identity and live like a king. So when he went to Aiello's house he didn't take his own car, which is a sportscar without much space in it. He took his wife's car because it was a tremendous big Cadillac with plenty of room in the trunk. He put Aiello's body on the floor of the back seat and filled the trunk with the loot from the safe. Then he buried Aiello out on the road project so that if the body did get found, it would look like a mob hit."

Madonna's head was lifted; he was listening to the run of my voice. I glanced at Pete DeAngelo, whose eyes were narrowed to slits. Nobody asked any questions so I went on: "Brawley thought he was in the clear. Nobody had known about his appointment with Aiello except the dead man, and as far as he knew, nobody had seen him go in or come out. One person did see him, though. Mike Farrell. He didn't recognize Brawley but he remembered the pink Cadillac."

I heard DeAngelo grunt but I didn't wait. I said, "Brawley wanted to make sure nobody was on his trail. He planned to wait around town until the heat died down, then disappear. He was planning to disappear last night—but we'll get to that. In the meantime, the morning after the murder, Brawley made some arrangements with a man named Ed Behrenman, a minor soldier in Aiello's regime. Brawley gave me a cock and bull story about how Behrenman owed him a favor. The truth was Brawley probably had blackmail evidence against Behrenman and forced him to cooperate. At any rate, it was Behrenman who spotted me and Joanne at the Executive Lodge the other morning. While I was here talking to you, you got a phone call. It was from Behrenman, right?"

"You're telling the story," Madonna said, but then his lips peeled back and he said, "Yeah, it was Behrenman. Go ahead."

"After I left you called Behrenman back and told him to stake out the motel."

"Sure."

I nodded. "It all fits together like a watch. Behrenman phoned Brawley and told Brawley he had instructions to stake out Joanne and me. That gave Brawley an idea what was up, and he went over to the motel. He wanted to talk to us because he had to know how much we knew, how close we were to finding him out. He must have felt fairly satisfied when he left, because he didn't panic. He figured he'd thrown us off his trail for good with his elaborate yarn about the money he had in the safe that he wanted to get back. It almost worked—he was a good actor. Almost as good as Pete DeAngelo."

I shifted my attention to DeAngelo. He had his slitted eyes on me like blades, motionless but ready to cut.

191

I said, "I can't prove this but I think DeAngelo must have talked to Judy Dodson after I did. She thought I was working for DeAngelo but when DeAngelo told her I wasn't, she told him everything I'd said to her. Right, Pete?"

"Go ahead. Dig your grave."

I went back to Madonna. "DeAngelo knew Mike Farrell was mixed up in this somehow. He found Farrell sometime in the afternoon, probably about the time I was talking to Brawley at the motel. Don't ask me how DeAngelo found Farrell. He probably just used his head and went looking in all the places he expected Mike to hide, and found him. DeAngelo put the screws to Mike. I don't know if he had help but I suspect he did. Mike was roughed up pretty hard and it probably took at least two men to give him that kind of going over. You, Tony? Ed Baker? It doesn't matter. DeAngelo squeezed Mike Farrell dry. He found out everything Mike knew, which wasn't a hell of a lot, but he did learn that Mike had made a deal with Joanne and me, that the three of us were working together to find the loot. That must have convinced DeAngelo that none of the three of us actually had the loot. From that point on we were expendable—all three of us. He didn't figure we had any better chance of finding the loot than anybody else, so why leave us around to mess things up?

"By this time Farrell was so badly tortured they couldn't do anything else but kill him. DeAngelo had to get rid of the body, and he wanted Joanne and me out of the way, so he did the obvious thing: he planted Mike's body at my house, then phoned the cops and talked to Joe Cutter because he knew Cutter had a personal grudge against me. Cutter came up to my place but he didn't find the body."

My eyes roamed from face to face. I returned to Madonna and said, "Now this is important. Everything I've told you can be checked—by you, not me. You've got the leverage and the manpower for it. Now here's a question for you. I've just told you what Pete DeAngelo was up to. How much of it has he told you?"

Madonna's glance whipped across to DeAngelo. DeAngelo opened his mouth and began to say something; Madonna said, "Sit down and give your mouth a rest, Pete."

DeAngelo closed his mouth slowly, gave me a dark scowl and held it on me while he moved to the nearest chair and sat. Freddie the Neanderthal moved up to stand behind his right shoulder, only a few feet to my left. I turned to keep them in view, and resumed:

"If DeAngelo didn't keep you posted on events, it was because he wanted to find the loot and keep it for himself. He's too ambitious to be satisfied with being anybody's number two man. He remembers how you took over this mob and he figures to do the same to you. With the money from Aiello's safe, and the incriminating documents that went with it, DeAngelo would be in a hell of a strong position to move right in and take over the organization. Wouldn't you, Pete?"

DeAngelo's left hand reached the table beside him and gripped its edge. He didn't speak.

To Madonna, I said, "Nobody likes to think himself a poor judge of human nature, and you probably don't want to buy this, especially since Pete's an old friend and I'm just a troublesome outsider. But think about this. The other night when I phoned you to ask you about the pink Cadillac, DeAngelo answered the phone. He sounded out of breath. I'm willing to bet he had just come in after planting Mike Farrell's body.

"DeAngelo had learned one vital fact, either from Mike Farrell or from my telephone call here. The pink Cadillac. He knew, or he made it his business to find out, who owned that car. It's my guess he had to do some detective work to find out, because otherwise he'd have gone after Brawley sooner than he did.

"In the meantime, yesterday morning, I went to Brawley's to ask him who owned a pink Cadillac. Brawley's own car was a Jaguar, and that threw me off. He sent me off on a wild goose chase to the boondocks. I was coming back from that when Ed Behrenman tried to run me off the highway over a cliff. Behrenman ended up dead at the bottom of the cliff. There was only one way Behrenman could have known where to find me. Brawley was the only man alive who knew where I'd gone, and I already knew there was a connection between Brawley and Behrenman. So then I knew who'd killed Aiello and taken the loot. I searched Brawley's house but it wasn't there, so I went straight to his office. DeAngelo knows what I found when I got there, because DeAngelo got there ahead of me. DeAngelo probably waited out back of the office until the last of Brawley's patients and employees left for the night. Then, when Brawley came out the back door, DeAngelo shot him. He had a silencer on his gun and he knew nobody was likely to hear the shot. He was so sure he'd find the loot in Brawley's office he didn't even bother to keep Brawley alive long enough to make sure. The pink Cadillac was parked right there and that was all DeAngelo wanted to know. He put Brawley's body in the car, jimmied the door and went inside. He was working on Brawley's safe when I got there. That's how he got that hole in his arm, in case he's told you something to the contrary. We had a little shoot-out and DeAngelo went out the window. He didn't stay long enough to find out what was in Brawley's safe, but I can answer it if he's still interested. There wasn't anything interesting in the wall safe except a gun. It was a Walther nine millimeter and I suspect it was the gun that killed Aiello."

"That's fine," Madonna murmured. "Only where's the money?"

"It was right where it'd been all the time. In the trunk of the pink Cadillac. Brawley had a suitcase and a coat in the back seat. He was ready to take off for good when DeAngelo found him. Too bad DeAngelo didn't keep him alive long enough to ask him a question. Incidentally, by now I'm sure you know they found not only Brawley's corpse but Joe Cutter's. I think DeAngelo must have shot Cutter, too."

DeAngelo shot erect in the chair. "That's a goddamn lie," he rasped. It was the first reaction I'd had out of him.

Madonna told him to shut up and said to me, "Where's the money now?"

I heard the raspy growl in DeAngelo's throat before I saw him start to move with the corner of my eye. He had a gun under the loose tail of his sport shirt and he was hauling it out. Big Freddie, slow to react, was taking a surprised backward step when I shot my arm out, extracted the gun from Freddie's shoulder holster, and snapped it downward just as DeAngelo's gun leveled on Madonna's belly.

The report of the gun was startling in that enclosed space. Bone fragments and blood sprayed from DeAngelo's head. His bodily functions instantly lost their control; his sphincter relaxed and there was immediately the stink of human urine and manure.

Chickens will suspend their pecking order whenever one of their number gets sick. They all turn on the weak chicken and peck it to death. Ed Baker and Tony Senna had their guns in their fists before the echo died, but they were pointed at DeAngelo, not at me. DeAngelo's actions, and the expression of his face, had been all the admission of guilt any of them would ever need to see. Before the body even began to slump in the chair, Senna and Baker had put bullets into it.

Tony Senna and Freddie herded us outside to the pool; the stink inside was offensive. Baker was doing something about the body. Madonna came outside behind us and we all stood ranged around the poolside furniture. Nobody wanted to sit down. Joanne trembled violently and clung to my arm. She said to Madonna, "Nobody double-crosses you, do they?"

"Not more than once," he said with a grimace. "You have to understand the rules of the game, honey. The winner is the last one left alive." He said it with a straight face.

I set the briefcase on a round metal umbrella table and opened the hasp with a key. Senna tugged out his gun and trained it on me but I only glanced at him, and upended the open briefcase to dump its contents on the table. Folded documents, photos and two packages of recording tape tumbled across the table in a littered heap.

I said, "That's a sample, mainly to prove to you that I really do have the stuff. You can do whatever you want with this. Most of it's worthless now. The blackmail evidence against Doctor Brawley is somewhere in here, and quite a bit of stuff that would have nailed Aiello for tax fraud if he were still alive. Now, of course, it's useless. The film you had on Joanne has been destroyed. The evidence on Frank Colclough and Stanley Raiford has already been mailed to the FBI, so I doubt those two will get very far with their primary election campaign before they're indicted."

Madonna gave me a hooded glare. "That'll buy you a ticket to the graveyard. You know that."

"No. The rest of the documents from Aiello's safe are still under my control. They'll be turned over to the appropriate federal agencies if my contact doesn't hear from me regularly. I've got you over a barrel. You know as well as I do what's in that collection. If it's released, some prominent noses are going to bleed, yours included. It'll crack the whole state open like an oyster—it'll blow your whole stinking mess of an organization ten miles in the air."

"Then why don't you release it?"

"Because it's my life insurance. Mine and Mrs. Farrell's."

"You're a pretty smart son of a bitch, aren't you? What about the cash?"

"It comes to three million, one hundred and eighty-five thousand dollars, in unmarked, untraceable bills."

"That's not what I asked and you know it."

"It's in a safe place," I said. "You don't need it. And I can't think of anybody it ought to be turned over to. If it went to the law it'd just end up lining some crooked politician's pocket. So I'll tell you what's going to happen to the money. Mrs. Farrell and I plan to honeymoon in Las Vegas a few weeks from now. I plan to win one hell of a lot of money when I'm there. Say a quarter of a million dollars, this trip, and I'll repeat it every year or so until I've won three million, one hundred and eighty-five thousand dollars across the roulette tables. I'll declare it as income and pay taxes on it. I leave it to you to make the arrangements and see to it that Las Vegas comes across. Any slip-ups and a few pieces of warm information will start to dribble into the

FBI's hands until you straighten out."

I grinned a tight grin at him. "Any questions?"

He said in a low growl, "What the hell do you need all that money for?"

"I want to buy my kid brother an operation so he can play the trumpet again."

I took Joanne's arm and walked her around the pool to the back gate. Madonna said something behind us, and Tony Senna was there with the key by the time we reached the gate. He opened it and let us through. I heard the gate click shut behind us, and the snap of the lock. We walked around the end of the house, across the lawn, and got into the car. Joanne gave me a long slow smile. I started the car and pulled out of the driveway. I looked in the rear-view mirror, but nobody was following us.

The Marksman

By Way of Introduction . . .

This story was written in the mid-1980s as an original screenplay. The producer to whom it was delivered sent back a note indicating his disappointment with the script. He wrote, "The story is too old-fashioned. It has a beginning, a middle and an end." I'm not making that up. In that estimable gentleman's honor, I have divided this narrative version of the story into three acts, labeled—well, you've already figured that one out.

The organization that was to have filmed this one tumbled into Ozymandian ruins, like most independent movie companies, and *Marksman* went to a shelf in my house where, like most unfilmed scripts, it remained unread by anyone except a producer and the author's agent and the author's wife.

In its original form the script is 105 pages in length. It would have made for a movie about 95 minutes long; but a screenplay contains a great deal of white space. It is in fact no longer than a novelette, or extended short story. A screenplay is nothing more than a sheet of instructions for filmmakers and actors to keep at hand while they assemble their movie out of such components as they may have gathered. Often it's true that the tricks attributed by cineaste critics to "marvelous directorial touches" are in fact specified clearly in a writer's screenplay before a director ever gets near the picture; but generally speaking, a screenplay does not (or at least should not) tell directors how to direct, actors how to act, cinematographers how to photograph, or audiences how to feel. The screenplay simply tells us what happens. It's up to the actors, the director, the photographers and the sound team, the editors and the audience to interpret these happenings. The writer creates the story, but everyone has to bring something to it—the writer alone does not make a movie unless he also happens to be producer, director, cast and crew.

Screenwriting Rule One: A script is a blueprint for illusion, and its every sentence must meet one of two criteria—it must be dialogue, or it must begin figuratively with the words "we see" or the words "we hear".

If the camera can't see it or the microphone can't hear it, then it cannot be filmed, and therefore it doesn't belong in the screenplay.

In preparing this story for publication in narrative form, I've eliminated the abbreviations and jargon that may make screenplays annoying or confusing. (How many readers can be expected to know that because of an obscure Hungarian director's pronunciation in the 1930s, "MOS" means "Mit-Out Sound," which is filmese for "without sound" or "silent"?) I've added bits and pieces in order to clarify events—a few lines or words here and there, in the effort to make it readable. But I have not tried to disguise its origins; it remains quite staccato. In movies people rarely talk in long paragraphs—everything's a one-liner. It's best to leave those essences alone.

I think most screenplays that are padded into novels turn out to be anemic novels at best; a movie script is a simplified form of storytelling because it is external—it cannot go inside a character and feel what that character feels, nor can it deal very effectively with ideas of any complexity.

This was not yet a shooting script; it was a second or perhaps third draft, and because of minor revisions it contained a few loose threads, unnecessary characters and incomplete thoughts. Those probably would have been caught by the writer on the next go-round, or by a director or producer, or at least by a script supervisor on the set. In the present situation, however, if the reader should chance upon an incongruity or mistake, please blame it not on the writer—never on the writer!—but on the Optical-Character-Recognition scanner that rendered the script into computer-editable form.

The Marksman is an action-suspense story, in which changes in the main character are triggered by violent events. It contains very short scenes and jump-cuts; I haven't tried to smooth them over. It does not confine itself to the viewpoint of any single character in a scene, as narrative fiction ought to do. It makes leaps in logic, understanding that actors can bridge those by creating appropriate shifts in the ways their characters change their minds about one another and therefore change the ways they behave with one another. It asks the reader to become camera and microphone—to imagine and visualize the people and events that are depicted in blueprint form—and it provides plenty of leeway for the stunt wranglers and FX enthusiasts who have become the tail that wags the dog of commercial cinematic storytelling. All this may make more work for the reader; I hope it does not harm the story.

—Brian Garfield
Los Angeles: October 2002

A Beginning . . .

On a sagging cot in a flyspecked room in an inner-city flop-house, a man tosses and turns. In his sleep he's hearing a racket of combat—explosions, automatic weapons, screams. Against his eyelids images flash like the intermittent flare of artillery on a battlefield at night.

He pushes the half-awake nightmare away. The effort is enough to exhaust him. After a few moments his breathing steadies and he rises in a sweat, disoriented for a moment before he recognizes his drab surroundings.

He hasn't shaved in a while. His brown hair is stringy. There's a wicked long scar across his temple; the old wound makes his head ache—makes him wince when he bends over to get into his rumpled old clothes.

C. W. Radford—that's his name. He's got the remains of a good constitution but he looks barely one step up from a homeless tramp. The jeans and work-shirt are threadbare. His shoes are utterly worn out. He laces them up with bo-vine listlessness. The headache makes him dizzy.

In the rickety bedside drawer is a small case that was de-signed to be a diabetic's insulin kit—its ersatz leather worn away at the corners now, cardboard showing through the edges. He flips open its lid on loose hinges to expose the syringe within, and the small rubber-topped bottle with its prescription label: "every four hours as needed for pain."

Radford draws liquid into the syringe and injects himself with its needle.

Radford trudges across a filthy street in a bitterly silent part of the city—beat-up cars and derelicts human and inanimate. The corner is dominated by an all-night joint, Charlie's Cafe—in its original incarnation a drive-in burger joint; subsequently expanded to a quarter-block sprawl of counters and Naugahyde booths, all of it much the worse for wear now—neon beer ads in the windows.

A dealer, wearing a wild shock of red hair and clothed in what used to be combat fatigues, transacts business with a skinny teenage girl. Radford glances at the two of them, shifts his glance away and continues walking toward Charlie's Cafe.

With the deftness of a sleight-of-hand artist the dealer pockets the girl's money, looks warily around and slips her a tiny package. When she hurries away, the dealer sizes up Radford with a bellicose challenge but Radford shuffles past, appearing to ignore him.

Reflections glitter off the license plate on a parked van— 7734 OL—and above the plate two men sitting in the van watch Radford. They both wear shirts, no jackets; collars unbuttoned, ties at half mast. The guy in the passenger seat is polished, neat, fortyish and smoking a cigarillo. Next to him the driver bats ineffectually at the smoke. This driver is big, tough, a body-builder. The van is a custom camping job—drapes etc.

It would appear that Radford gives them no more attention than he gave the redheaded dealer.

The two guys in the van watch while Radford approaches the side door of the cafe. The guy with the cigarillo has a file-folder open in his hand; in it is a print-out dossier—he squints against the curling smoke to see a military mug-shot photo of a younger, neater Radford clipped to the file.

Radford climbs up onto the curb as if it's only another step half way along a wearisome journey up a mountain-high pyramid. As he turns painfully toward the door of the cafe, a young dude comes rushing out of the alley, flailing an expensive attaché case in one hand and a heavy Glock automatic pistol in the other.

The dude is immaculate in a flashy tailored suit—the uniform of a drug wholesaler or a pimp, or both—but he's hardly more than a child: a teenage kid trying to look like a big shot.

Radford stops. The dude is right in front of him, arm's length. He's laughing hysterically but behind the laughter the dude is able to make an instantaneous judgment: he dismisses Radford and wheels, grinning, laughing, and aims his automatic back at the alley. He's wild: spaced out.

A pursuing policeman runs into sight—sees the dude; reacts, skids, ducks, and the dude's shot goes wild overhead.

A lot of noise now, people dodging to cover and shouting inarticulate warnings—the two guys in the van dive beneath their dashboard out of sight and the dealer flattens himself back against a wall as if trying to press himself back through it into invisibility, and Radford stands bolt still.

The dude laughs on, full of wild bravado. He is trying to steady himself to take aim on the policeman when the sound of screeching tires brings his head whipping around in time to see a squad car squealing to a slithery stop behind him.

The dude's gun swivels to meet the new challenge as two cops pop open the doors of their unit and brace their weapons across the tops of door and car, aiming at the dude.

One cop says, "Drop the gun."

The other gestures. "On your knees, asshole. And then on your face. *Now*."

Radford stands unmoving, without expression, while across the street the redheaded dealer slides around a corner like an eel and disappears. Radford appears to pay more attention to that than to the confrontation between dude and cops.

"*Drop* it, asshole!"

Now there's the policeman at the corner—the one who was chasing the dude on foot—and there's the pair of cops at the car, and there's the dude, and they've all got their handguns up but the dude can't quite decide which of them to aim at and he swings his pistol back and forth, first one cop and then another, and presently he stops with his finger whitening on the trigger and the muzzle of the Glock leveled toward Radford's scarred forehead.

Radford faces the gun with utter indifference.

The cops hesitate, probably fearful that any move could get the bystander shot dead.

The dude keeps laughing. His head whips around in a frantic effort to keep all the cops in view. His arm wavers; he starts to drop into a crouch and his automatic goes off—

The bullet unzips a crease in the pavement within an inch of Radford's foot.

Radford doesn't flinch. He doesn't move at all.

Within a single broken instant of time all three cops fire simultaneously, and the dude is physically blasted off his feet by the combined firepower. The bullets drive him down hard . . .

In the wake of it, the echoes of the gunshots fade into a stunning silence.

In the parked van the two guys sit up and appraise the

situation with scientific interest.

From their various directions the three cops cautiously approach the dude. He lies broken across the curb. Guns out, two of the cops walk past Radford with only a glance; they're intent on the dude, whose brains are all over the sidewalk. One of the cops mutters dispassionately, "Angel dust. Laughing his head off."

His partner says, "Where's it say a spaced-out maniac can't have a sense of humor?"

Radford trudges to the side door of the cafe as if there'd been no interruption. He knocks.

One of the cops is saying, "Get Forensics."

Charlie the cook, who owns the cafe, opens the door from inside and stands in his apron, peering out cautiously. Charlie has a prosthesis in place of one hand. He recognizes Radford—they go back a long way together—admits him.

The two guys in the van consult rapidly and the driver turns the key and crams it roughly into gear. The van lurches. The passenger's voice is pained: "Hey—Easy with my van."

One of the cops is calling in on his car radio. The partner is swiveling full-circle on his heels, gun half raised, waiting for another shoe to drop. The foot-patrol cop strides across to the dude and kicks open the attaché case that the dude dropped. He looks dryly at the dead dude. "You have the right to remain silent."

Charlie the cook holds the door open. Several sleazeball waiters trail tentatively out to study the carnage.

Radford moves past them and goes inside. He pulls down an apron off a peg, ties it on without hurry and proceeds to stand all alone washing dishes.

Later in the day Radford, still in his apron, swabs the

floor. Two or three scuzzy waiters move past him, carrying trays in and out. Cooks and other kitchen staff are at work—the place is busy.

Radford keeps to himself, talks to no one, looks at no one. A beer-bellied bruiser named Don—pack-leader of the waiters—sneers at Radford. Other kitchen staff are watching. Knowing he has an audience, Don picks up an open can of tomato juice, then steps on Radford's mop, stopping it. Radford just looks at him. Don deliberately pours tomato juice on the floor. No reaction; Radford merely begins to mop it up.

"D'you used to mop up for the I-raqis like that?"

Don reaches for the side of Radford's waistband, pulls it out past the apron and pours tomato juice inside the front of Radford's pants. Radford pulls away but does not fight.

Don shouts at him—"What's with you—fuckin' coward?"—trying to get a rise out of Radford.

It's loud in the room but Radford barely hears what Don says; what he hears, interspersed with clatter of dishes and silverware, is the growing sound of explosions and automatic weapons and the dreadful screams of the injured and dying.

Radford picks up a tray of dirty dishes. Don sticks out his foot. Radford can't see it—the tray blocks his downward view. He trips over Don's foot. In his head the sound of battle fades as dishes tumble with a loud clatter.

Don waits, taunting, hoping Radford will fight. Don's one of your martial-arts types and he just knows he can beat up anybody—especially somebody who won't fight back.

Radford is picking up the scattered dishes. He doesn't even look up at Don.

Charlie the boss strides across the aisle and grips Don roughly by the arm. "Hey, bozo. Bust my dishes, you pay for 'em . . . I told you leave him alone."

Don gives him a look, decides not to make anything of it right now, and walks away.

Charlie helps Radford to his feet. "You got to remember to fight back."

Radford thinks about it, visibly. He has to marshal the things swimming around in his head before he can formulate an answer. Finally he says, "Don't want to hurt anybody."

"C.W., you gotta look out for yourself."

"Doesn't matter." Radford resumes picking up dishes.

Charlie pulls him up straight and makes motions as if dusting him off. "Go get yourself cleaned up."

At the sink of the tiny employees' washroom Radford stands in his shorts scrubbing tomato-stain out of his trousers. Then he locks the door. His head aches terribly. He takes that same insulin kit out of a pocket and injects himself with painkiller. He's hearing again that sound of sporadic combat fire.

He sees a Middle-Eastern town, arid, devastated by war, and a gaunt undernourished teenage girl moving silently through the night, alert, weapon ready, her face lit by sudden distant flashes; we hear continuing sound of combat fire. The girl takes a step forward—steps on a mine—abruptly Radford's memory explodes in a white flash as the girl disintegrates . . .

He sees himself, then, watching from up in the gaping skull-like third-story window opening of a bombed-out shell of an apartment house. He holds a 'scoped sniper rifle. He's very young (22), in camouflage uniform, face blackened, revealing no feelings except fear. Scared . . . sweating in the bitter cold, frightened, he aims his rifle at something in the distance. He can hear its approach, the Iraqi helicopter, and he squints into the scope, aiming up into the sky—steadies his aim and fires. The recoil rocks his shoulder gently; he's used to that. When he lowers the rifle, his expression has gone blank—he seems no longer afraid. The sound of the helicopter rotors changes, becomes rattly and uneven, and Radford watches while the machine begins to sway from side to side as if on a pendulum before it shatters against the slope of a jagged rock hillside. The explosion lights up Radford's face like daylight and he shrinks back into the shadows of the bombed-out building.

. . . In the cafe bathroom he puts the syringe and bottle away in the case, and pockets the case, and straps on his grease-stained uniform. In his aching head the sound of combat fades. He tries to open the door. It won't open. Won't budge. He shoves hard at it. Nothing now, except after a moment he begins to hear men chuckling beyond the door. He kicks the door. The voices outside begin to laugh aloud.

The harder Radford tries to open the door, the louder they laugh.

He feels as if the room is closing in on him . . .

Outside the door, in the cafe hallway, are grouped several waiters, including Don. They're the ones who're laughing. A chair is propped under the door handle, wedging it shut.

Don opens a fuse box on the wall. His finger flips a circuit-breaker from "on" to "off."

Inside the bathroom Radford is plunged into darkness and panic overtakes him. He thrashes at the jammed door.

Out in the hallway the waiters' laughter stops abruptly when the door is kicked out in splinters.

Radford comes exploding out through the smashed wreckage.

They gape at him.

In a sweating panic Radford stands panting.

Don backs away in sudden fear.

—And Radford walks away.

The waiters try to laugh again, but it's uneasy and it trails off . . .

After nightfall the cafe's trade changes. More of an up-scale crowd now—thrill seekers looking for something they won't find behind a velvet rope in the more trendy sections.

In a corner booth sit the two guys who earlier were in their van watching Radford on the street. Their names are Conrad and Gootch. Conrad's the dapper dandy who likes to smoke cigarillos but he can't smoke inside here so he's drumming his fingers on the Formica tabletop, an unlit cigarillo between his fingers. He's watching Radford swab the floor, mopping under tables. Conrad, the body-builder, is facing the other direction, intent on something or someone. Conrad asks, "What you lookin' at?"

"Curly, Larry and Moe over there."

Conrad swivels, hikes his arm up over the back of the booth and twists his jaw to look back over his shoulder. He sees three tough-looking punks drinking beer at the counter. "Uh-huh." He looks at his watch. "You know that's what I hate about theater. You bust your ass to get there on time and the fuckin' curtain never goes up when it's supposed to. Fifteen, twenty minutes later they get all the stragglers seated and some dickhead gets on the mike and says please turn off your fuckin' cellulars and pagers. Where the hell's our leading lady tonight?"

Back in a doorway, half hidden in shadow, Don the

waiter swigs beer and watches everything.

Now a slim woman enters—attractive, blonde, thirties, well put together and nicely dressed; too sophisticated for this place. She looks around nervously.

Radford glances at the woman, looks away, continues to mop the floor.

Conrad says under his breath, "Curtain going up."

And now—quickly . . .

Conrad and Gootch look toward the counter where the three punks sit.

The three punks—Curly, Larry and Moe—drain their beers and get up. Their path toward the exit just happens to take them near the blonde.

Don from his shadowed corner watches everyone.

Curly, the leader of the three, does a take as he play-acts recognizing the blonde.

She doesn't look at Curly; she's seen them out of the corner of her eye and she's alarmed. Abruptly Curly shouts: "Your brother owes me two large."

The blonde at first doesn't look at him. Then, startled to realize it was addressed to her, she tries to conceal her fear. "Were you talking to me?"

Curly bellows, "He owes me money!"

Curly jerks the blonde forward roughly, his face an inch from hers.

"Let go!" She looks around frantically for help but there's only Radford, mopping the floor.

Curly grips the blonde's throat. She tries to fend him off but Larry grabs her wrists and stands behind her, immobilizing her arms, and Moe moves in close, menacing. The blonde whispers, "Somebody please . . ."

Curly says, "Let's take it one more time from the top. Start with where's your brother at?"

The blonde in terror finally blurts, "I don't have a brother!"

Radford watches but makes no move.

Curly slaps the woman's face hard and tightens his hold on her throat. Larry pulls her arms up behind her back. She cries out. Moe kidney-punches her from the side and Curly slams his fist hard into her midriff, doubling her over. "Let's try one more time."

The blonde can barely gasp. "What're you talking about? . . . Please . . ."

Moe gets set to hit her again and then suddenly rocks back—something has hit him hard in the back—and as he falls away from the blonde his fall reveals Radford. He's jabbed Moe with the end of the mop-handle.

Radford says, "Hey man, please."

The punks react. All three turn on Radford. By the swiftness of their reaction, and the way they suddenly ignore the blonde, it doesn't take a rocket scientist to see this whole set-up has been rehearsed. The one they're really after is Radford.

As the three attack him he stabs the mop handle toward Larry's eye and it makes Larry flinch away and in the flow of the same motion Radford swings the pole against Curly's cheek, hard enough to knock the man off his feet, but now Moe has recovered from the kidney punch and he swarms toward Radford and all of a sudden the three of them are on him like bears on a honey pot and the pain in his head is beyond unendurable but still, somehow, moving faster than anyone ought to be able to, Radford protectively pushes the blonde into a booth before he swings to face them and speaks before any of them can nail him:

"Hey, guys, I don't want to hurt you."

That provokes Curly's harsh laugh. They come at

Radford and he backs away, looking for a way out, really a coward . . . And all three punks pile on him, beat on him, lock him in a hold that a crowbar couldn't pry loose . . .

Conrad and Gootch are watching with keen interest. They see when Radford knows he can't get out of it and begins to give in with unhappy resignation.

Conrad speaks under his breath to Gootch: "Now we see if he's a player."

The three punks have Radford pinned. His mind is screeching, running off the track now—All of a sudden he's in a chilly fog as he comes heaving up out of a basement under some derelict building like a monster creature. He's young, in combat fatigues, hauling his sniper rifle—he tries to slip away in the night but abruptly there's the gleaming point of a bayonet against the back of his neck and he reacts . . . turns his head slowly to see a child holding a rifle at the other end of the bayonet. A boy, not more than twelve or thirteen, looking half stoned, wearing wretched street clothes but a soldier's *kepi* on his head.

A blank mask descends over young Radford's expression. With resignation he lifts his hands in surrender.

Curly is whipping toward the blonde's booth while Larry and Moe keep Radford locked in their grip but now, seeing where Curly's headed, Radford explodes. He hammers backwards with one heel against somebody's shin and, with that opening breached, skillfully kicks his way out of their hold and now he goes after the three punks with the silent cold precision of a demolition ball. There's no question of "fighting fair;" Radford swings a leg toward Curly at the booth, kicks Curly in the groin and flashes around to face the other two. He uses anything as a weapon—steel paper-napkin holder, table, bottle of ketchup, chair, his own hands and feet—this isn't a neat clean choreographed thing. It's a brutal fight; Radford fights dirty.

The blonde watches this, wide-eyed. Conrad and Gootch watch with clinical interest. Don the waiter stares, inscrutable. Charlie the owner comes from the kitchen scowling, drawn by the racket; picks up a kitchen knife and comes around the counter lofting his prosthetic hand, but by then the fight is over. Charlie is pleased with him—pleased for him. "O-kay."

Radford has knocked the living shit out of all three tough guys.

Charlie says, "Finish 'em, C.W. Bust up their knee-caps."

But the three are down, and Radford backs away.

Curly and Larry painfully pull themselves together and try to rouse the semi-conscious Moe.

Radford hardly even seems to be breathing hard. The scar on his face glistens with sweat.

Don the waiter fades back, disappearing silently.

The blonde seems to be looking for a way to sneak out without being noticed.

Curly and Larry help Moe outside.

Radford watches Conrad and Gootch as they cross to the door and exit.

Outside on the street, the redheaded dealer appears from shadows while Conrad flicks his cigarillo into the gutter; he and Gootch get into their van. This time Conrad takes the wheel (it's his van). He says to his companion, "That'll do it. They do a background, they'll find out he just about beat three guys to death."

Inside, Radford looks out through the cafe's big picture window at the three punks who're staggering away down the sidewalk. His attention is drawn to the van when its engine revs up. What he sees, reflected in window glass, is a puddle behind the van. In the puddle he can see an upside-down backward reflection of the van's license plate—a reflection within a reflection. The plate number is 7734 OL, and seen upside down and backwards it reads quite plainly "To hell." Even Radford may remember that . . .

The van drives away, rippling the puddle, destroying the image.

The blonde comes toward Radford's shoulder. "Hey, I really—I'd like to . . ."

Ignoring her, he carries his mop back toward the kitchen.

Mystified, the blonde looks at Charlie. "He always so sociable? . . . What's his name?"

"Radford. C. W. Radford." Charlie shrugs, smiles and goes away toward the back, where he finds Radford washing out the mop as if nothing had happened. Charlie takes out roll of cash, peels off some, tucks them in Radford's shirt pocket. "All right. Take the night off, will ya?"

Radford's only acknowledgement is to hang up his apron and head for the back door out.

Charlie says, "See? You can still take care of yourself. Think about it, C.W."

Radford doesn't look back; he opens the door and goes out.

Outside as Radford trudges away from Charlie's, the redheaded dealer intercepts him. "Hey, my man. You was pretty cool back there. This mornin' and now those guys. You want to buy?"

Radford shakes his head "no" and walks on.

A car approaches him from behind. Its headlights throw

his long shadow ahead of him. It seems ominous because of the slow pace with which it catches up to him but he only glances at it—particularly at its rent-a-car plate holder. The car paces him. Then its window opens and we see it's the blonde who's driving.

"You never gave me a chance to thank you."

"Wasn't looking for gratitude." Radford's voice sounds rusty, as if from disuse. Then he looks directly at her. "Lady, it's three in the morning and this is no neighborhood to go driving around with your windows open."

"I know. I'd feel ever so much safer if you were in the car."

He looks back over his shoulder. He can't be sure—is that slow-moving shadow back there the same van as before?

He keeps walking until the woman guns her car forward and pulls into the curb to block him. She gets out and confronts him.

He says, "Uh-huh?"

"You restored my faith—I was starting to think chivalry was dead, or at least traded in on a second-hand Toyota . . . That's a pun, son. Not even a chuckle?"

She opens the passenger door. After a beat, with no break in expression, Radford gets in the car.

When she shuts the door on him Radford glances at the door's wing mirror. The van's still back there. Pinpoint glow of a lit cigarillo.

The blonde gets into the car beside Radford, behind the wheel, but before she puts it in gear she leans close and gives him a deeply questioning look. She runs her hand along his coarse beard stubble. "C. W. Radford. That what you call yourself?"

"Mostly I don't call me at all."

"Me, I'm Anne. Anne with an 'e.' " Then after a momentary silence she says, "You're supposed to ask if I've got a last name."

It doesn't inspire a response in him.

She says politely, "It's Hartman. Anne Hartman."

"All right."

In the streaming hot water of Anne Hartman's shower, Radford stands with a borrowed Gillette ladies' disposable, shaving by feel. He's not alone, naked in the steam. Anne is scrubbing his back. She's laughing.

And then in her bed he's clean and shaved and mostly ignores the woman while very gently she explores his many injuries. "All these scars—kind of sexy."

Through slitted lids his eyes explore the room. It's a stodgy furnished flat on the ground floor of an apartment court, impersonal as a hotel room. She says, "Where'd you get 'em?"

"What? The scars? Place called Kurdistan."

Anne gets out of bed and crosses into the bathroom. Radford doesn't stir; he lies on his back with hands over his eyes—that headache again.

Anne's voice chatters at him from the bathroom. "Yeah, so I work for a political action committee. You know. Fundraisers, campaign literature, get out the grassroots knuckleheads."

On the pillow he rolls his head back and forth in pain. Then he hears the woman approach—her voice growing louder: "C.W.? Hey—you okay?"

Anne sits down on the edge of the bed and gently strokes his forehead. "You don't have a hell of a lot of small talk, do you? What're you thinking about?"

"Nothing."

"You can't think about nothing."

"Yeah," he says. "You can. You can teach yourself to do that."

"Why would you want to?"

He's thinking about that detention camp on the northern border of Iraq—primitive; stark. Watchtowers. Tangles of barbed wire. Prisoners dying slowly in filthy rags, Kurds mostly, a few volunteers from Kuwait and Armenia, and two gaunt Americans, one of whom is himself, Radford, just a kid then really, covered with suppurating bruises and cuts, and the other of whom is Charlie the cook—also that much younger, and even more beat-up—with a bloody stump, hardly staunched with rags, where his hand used to be.

She brings him back from that camp. She bends down gently to kiss his scarred forehead.

He says, "Lady, don't waste sympathy on me. I broke."

She doesn't quite understand.

"I talked. You know? Went on the telly . . . Iraqi TV."

And in the black-and-white TV monitor in his mind he can see his whipped young self speaking straight into the camera with lifeless calm. He says to Anne, "I told the world how wonderful life was in Saddam's paradise. I recited all the lies they told me to tell."

She's stroking him. "I see." Then she says, "No one can blame you for wanting to stay alive."

"Nobody stayed alive."

She takes his face in both hands and kisses him. After a bit, he begins sluggishly to respond . . .

In the daylight he stands at the window in his stained trousers, sips coffee and looks out at parked cars and little kids splashing in an inflated wading pool. As the phone rings, Anne enters in a robe, toweling her hair. She makes a face when she looks at the condition of his trousers. "Let's get you some new clothes." And she's picking up the ringing phone. "Hello? Oh—hi. Ha, right. Well none of your nosy business . . . What? Now? I, uh, I forgot. All right, okay, sure. I'll be there in, like, an hour?"

She hangs up and says to Radford, "I promised some friends I'd go target shooting. Want to come along?"

He only looks at her, without any change in his expression.

The sign in the old building corridor announces the path to "Alvin York Memorial Gun Club—Open Mon–Sat 6:30 a.m. to 10 p.m. Closed Sundays." The sign is on a door, and Anne opens it. She's very sexy, painted into skintight jeans. Radford, in new trousers and shirt, follows her in.

The foyer needs paint. Its scratched metal reception desk is unoccupied. The decor consists of gun ads, hunting prints and NRA posters. A long window separates Radford and Anne from a shooting range where they can see the backs of three men wearing ear-protector headsets and shooting rifles at targets; the snap of each shot is barely audible in here.

Anne leads the way through the inner door onto the indoor range. A big guy looks up—Harry Sinclair, 50, bearded, muscular and rough—from where he's handloading ammunition at a work table. The thick beard hides most of his face. When he smiles, he has a badly discolored front tooth, second left from center.

Anne says *sotto voce,* to Radford, "Come on—lighten up."

Harry says, "Hi."

Anne says, "Hi yourself. Harry, this is C.W."

"Ha're you?" And, to Anne: "You havin' any trouble breathing?"

"No. Why?"

"That outfit of yours so tight I'm havin' trouble breathing . . . Got a weapon you want to sight in?"

Radford shakes his head. "No. I'm just a spectator."

Anne teases him: "Oh come on." And to Harry: "C.W. told me he used to compete in target matches."

Harry looks at him with sudden recognition. "C.W.— Wait a minute. You're, what's the name, no, don't tell me, I'll get it—"

On the range one of the shooters looks this way. All three wear goggles; perhaps Radford recognizes Conrad, from the van. Conrad pretends no interest in Radford or Anne; so do his two companions. One is Gootch; the other is Wojack, 25, dapper and Ivy League in a high-priced suit.

Harry is going right on with his recognition exercise: "You were just a kid, you won the Wimbledon Cup on the thousand-yard range at Camp Perry . . . I got it. Radford. C. W. Radford. Am I right, hey? Am I right or am I right!"

Harry claps Radford amiably on the bicep. Radford's reaction is stony but Harry doesn't seem to notice.

Harry puts on a pair of thin gloves before he selects a 308 target rifle from the rack. "Damn gloves—solvent on my hands, don't want to soil the goods." He turns, smiling, and proffers the rifle to Radford. "Here, try this 308. I'd admire to see you shoot."

Radford shakes his head, refusing the rifle. "You go ahead."

Harry is taken aback, then puts on a smile and ushers them forward toward the firing line. Anne and Radford watch Harry load the 308 rifle; he still wears the gloves.

The three shooters are intent on their own target-aiming. Their faces are concealed by goggles and ear protectors; Radford never gets a clear look at any of them.

Harry says, "This here's the rifle, for my money. Shoot across rooftops or shoot across the street. Great support for a GPMG team. Your perfect weapon for urban area combat."

Anne says, "Harry's the world's greatest combat expert. That's because he's never been to war. But boy, just let 'em invade Tenth Street and Main . . ."

Harry gives her a look. He and Anne put on ear protectors. Then abruptly, with a grin, Harry tosses the rifle to Radford.

Reflex: Radford catches it. He scowls at Harry, then studies the rifle briefly, then turns and aims casually and fires one shot downrange.

Harry puts his eye to a swivel-mounted telescope to spot targets.

"Jeez. A perfect bull's eye. Wow. Awe-some!"

By this time Conrad, Gootch and Wojack are watching Radford with intense interest, but Radford doesn't seem to notice this. With distaste he shoves the rifle back into Harry's gloved hands. "No thanks."

Harry says to Anne, "Fantastic. Dead center, perfect bull's eye, like there wasn't nothin' to it."

And now, behind Radford's back, Harry and Anne exchange glances.

Anne's car draws up outside the big sign of Charlie's Cafe.

"Thanks. For the lift and—everything." Radford is about to get out. Anne holds him in place while she takes something out of her handbag.

It's a key. She slips it into his shirt pocket and gives him one of those bright smiles that can light up your whole day. Radford just looks at her—a grave beat. Then he gets out and she watches him walk to the cafe. She doesn't drive away until he's disappeared completely inside, but he never once looked back at her.

Night again, and the street's deserted until Charlie's side door opens. Radford, untying his apron, pokes his face out into the night air and takes a deep breath in an attempt to clear away his headache. Charlie appears behind him and takes the apron. "G'night, C.W. Take care."

"Yeah." It's a noncommittal grunt. Radford walks around the corner, then past two hookers, then past the redheaded dealer, who gives him a glance. Radford is tired and everything hurts. When he puts his hands in his pockets, he discovers something in one pocket and takes it out and looks at it.

Anne's key. He thinks about it.

But he goes back to his flophouse and finds it unchanged, the cot as always unmade. Radford rummages through the few paltry possessions in his duffel bag, finds a worn envelope, takes a creased photograph out of it and sits looking at the photo. He was very young then, handsome in his tailored class-a uniform, posing proudly with his arm around his best girl.

Dorothy McCune. In the photo she's quite young and very beautiful in a cocktail dress. On her other side stands her father, a very distinguished guy. They're at a posh political rally; big banner reads "Tom McCune for Senate." They're all happy.

Radford broods at the picture, then puts it back where he got it.

★ ★ ★ ★ ★

Outside Anne's apartment court near the wading pool Radford stands in the night for a long silent stretch of time before he finally goes up to Anne's door and pushes the bell. He waits, and when there's no response he turns to leave. That's when the door opens.

She's in a nightgown, sleepy.

He's apologetic, hesitant. "Hi. Sorry."

"Well don't just stand there." She draws him inside.

In the afternoon Charlie's Cafe kitchen staff go in and out on their errands. Don the waiter stacks dishes—and watches the aproned Radford scrub a griddle.

Charlie enters—with Harry. Charlie says to Radford, "Fella wants to talk to you."

"Harry Sinclair. Gun club—remember me? Look, there's a turkey shoot-out on the hill range tomorrow—small potatoes, but I'll put up the side bets and you take a third of my winnings. Nobody around here knows you. We can make some bucks. What do you say?"

Radford studies him. "I guess not."

Charlie razzes him. "Shit, go ahead, C.W. Shoot some bull's eyes—have some fun."

"Charlie, I haven't shot targets in years. What if I get the shakes and come up Maggie's drawers?"

Harry says, "Then I'll eat my losses. But it won't happen."

Charlie says, "Man's got confidence in you, C.W."

Harry looks satisfied. "Tomorrow morning. Pick you up at eight. Hey. What d'you say?"

"Do it, C.W. I'll give you the day off—hell you don't even have to ask, you know that."

Radford thinks it over.

* * * * *

On a general-aviation runway, the executive jet taxis to a stop. Its door opens. The motorized stair extends down and locks in place. A couple of cops stand at the foot of the steps, watching the horizon.

Led by motorcycle cops and flanked by squad cars, a limousine draws up—little flags above its headlights. Diplomatic flags. Several suits come down the stairs from the plane. We can tell by his carriage that one of them is the VIP and by his clothes that he's foreign. Threading the phalanx of security people, he walks toward the limousine.

All this is being watched from the parked van by Conrad, smoking, and Wojack, who focuses binoculars on the activity at the plane. Conrad looks over his shoulder into the gloom of the van and he sees Slade still back there, a fat cop nearly busting the seams of his uniform, on the bench side seat looking uncomfortable with his wrists dangling over his knees.

Conrad says to Slade, "It's on. You be in the building early."

"Don't sweat it, Conrad."

"You'll ice the perp in self defense. Just make sure he's all-the-way dead, right? If he's alive to talk—"

The fat cop waves it off. ("Sure, sure.")

Harry Sinclair drives his SUV off the main road onto a rutted dirt track. Beside him Radford sits strapped in, not talking, not seeming to notice the scenery. Harry parks by a lean-to shack and gets out. He's wearing gloves. He takes that familiar 308 rifle out of the back seat and walks around the car and hands the rifle up as Radford gets out. Then, talking, Harry walks away, past the shack. "Come on—it's just up the hill."

Hidden from Radford's view behind the shack, Don the waiter and Conrad's partner Gootch pull stocking masks over their heads to hide their faces.

Harry's still talking: "We're an hour early. I figured you'd want to get the feel of the place, maybe squeeze off some practice rounds."

Radford, following without much interest, comes around the corner after Harry—and suddenly, without warning, is jumped: expertly attacked from behind by the masked Don and Gootch. One pinions his arms while the other's hands grip Radford's throat front and back with expert pressure, clamping off the flow of the carotid arteries. That's when Harry grabs him around the knees to keep him from kicking.

Radford, taken by surprise, tries to struggle but it's no good: the rifle drops away and the carotid hold renders him unconscious. He slips to the ground . . .

Harry sits back and, in relief, peels the phony beard and stage make-up off. Now we see him clean-shaven.

Don produces a syringe, which he fills from a phial while Gootch rolls up the unconscious Radford's sleeve . . .

A Middle . . .

The office building is a high-rise with a multi-story parking garage connecting to one side of it. Inside a fourth-story office, vacant of all furniture, Conrad and Wojack stand at the window looking down at the street below. Both wear surgical gloves. Wojack looks like a bright Ivy League college senior dressed for a job interview. He has a suction cup against a lower corner of the window; he's working around it with a glass-cutter. Finally he pops the glass disc loose and sets it aside on the windowsill, leaving a neat, open hole in the window. We notice he leaves the glass cutter and the suction cup on the sill. He picks up that familiar 308 rifle and screws a 'scope sight onto it. Conrad doesn't smoke here—he's too professional for that. He wears a headset-and-mouthpiece cell phone. He listens to his headset and talks back to it: "Affirmative." He turns to Wojack: "It's on. It's a 'go.' "

Conrad looks at his watch. Wojack aims his rifle down through the hole in the glass at the street below. Conrad steps forward beside him to look down out the window. Wojack says, very dryly, "Do I get fifty points for a little old blind lady in the crosswalk?"

Down there through crosshairs he's peering at the steps of the government building across the street. On the fringes of the 'scope's image he can see a gathering of cops, officials and reporters with their TV cameras and microphones,

229

all waiting for the limo to arrive . . .

Now Conrad and turns to look past Wojack into the darker recesses of the unfurnished office. He sees Gootch and Harry bracketing the unconscious Radford. Harry is pasting his phony beard back in place.

Conrad says to Harry, "Time to give him the upper. Wake the son of a bitch up." Then, to Gootch, "Lock the elevator and go start the van."

Obeying, Gootch exits.

Conrad watches Harry take a disposable syringe from its package and begins to fill it from a phial.

At the window Wojack, sighting down through the hole, tightens his aim.

In the 'scope sight he can see the windshield of the limousine—the one with the foreign flags—as it pulls up, escorted by cops on motorcycles. Reporters crowd against a cordon of cops; a wedge of security people surrounds the man emerging from the limo—that same vaguely foreign VIP from the plane. Wojack's practiced grip zeroes in the crosshairs on the center of his torso and there is the sudden sound of the shot: the image jerks upward in recoil and then settles down again as the VIP falls dead on the steps.

By the time the VIP has fallen dead to the steps, Wojack has already wheeled back away from the window and is jacking a fresh cartridge into the chamber of the rifle.

Conrad and Harry drag Radford across the room, stooping to remain below sill-line, dragging the groggy man directly beneath the window.

In the street there's a crowd around the body; people are pointing up this way. Cops rush across the street toward the building.

Quickly and efficiently, Wojack and Conrad prop Radford against the wall and place the smoking rifle in his hands. Harry takes a quick look out the window.

Conrad murmurs, "Let's go . . ."

The three run to the door.

Radford stirs—a twitch . . .

In the fourth floor corridor, an elevator stands open. Gootch waits there, holding the door. Conrad, Wojack and Harry run into it. Conrad turns a key. The doors close . . .

Down on the ground level several cops swarm across the lobby and up the emergency stairs. Two or three stand guard in the lobby, watching the elevators. The indicator of one elevator shows that it's descending from the 4th floor . . . 3rd . . . 2nd . . .

In the vacant office Radford struggles to wake up.

Cops thunder up the echoing stairs, guns up.

In the lobby, cops watch while the indicator of that descending elevator passes the ground floor. A cop punches the button in angry frustration. The indicator stops at "B." The cops look at each other; suddenly two of them bolt for the stairs and go running down the stairs out of sight . . .

In the vacant office Radford lurches to his feet, dazed.

In the garage Conrad's van roars past a doorway, heading out the exit. Its license plates, smeared with mud, are unreadable. A split second after it disappears up the ramp, the two cops come running out of the stairwell in the office building next door. They see nothing.

In the vacant office the fat cop Slade busts the door in and drops to a two-handed crouched shooting position. He sees:

—no Radford.

Nothing.

Slade has just enough time to be amazed before Radford jumps him from behind the door, slamming the buttstock of the 308 rifle against the back of Slade's head. Slade goes

231

down. Radford drops the rifle, scoops up Slade's revolver and nightstick, and bolts out of the office . . .

Out in the corridor, he lurches groggily and stumbles out of sight around a nearby corner just before two cops come racing out of the stairwell. As they run forward, elevator doors open, decanting several more cops into the corridor. All of 'em squeeze into the vacant office, because it's the one whose door stands open—the cops go in fast, guns up, and the first ones trip over the stunned Slade, who lies clutching his injured head.

Even more cops enter; they part to make way for a veteran sergeant, Dickinson. He takes in the scene with a quick look around. Then he makes a face; it expresses volumes.

Below, in the lobby, there's a willy-nilly darting of cops. A uniformed bald cop, having lost his hat somewhere, burrows into a crowd of officials and reporters and cops. Among them is Dickinson. There's a babbling racket of simultaneous conversations. The bald cop approaches Dickinson. "Who's catching?"

"All the way to the top. Commander Clay."

"Oh shit." The bald guy immediately straightens his uniform and examines his brass and shoe polish.

Up in the unfurnished office the scene is very busy. A technician threads his way through the throng, struggling to reach Commander Denise Clay, forties, a black woman in immaculate uniform. She is homicide chief of detectives. She's talking to an officer: ". . . Probably still in the building. I want double security on every exit—doors, windows, roof, basement, every rathole. Go."

Now she turns to face a handsome business-suit gent—Colonel Vickers. He's near 50—very youthfully so. A uniformed cop is talking on a walkie-talkie.

The officer behind Commander Clay talks into a cellular

phone: ". . . Got the outside exits covered. She wants to start a sweep in the basement, work your way up—"

Vickers grabs the officer. "What's going down?"

"Who the hell are you?"

Clay and Dickinson approach on collision course just as Vickers swings violently around in anger. They nearly butt heads. Vickers is roaring now: "What the fucking hell's going on? You let him get loose?"

Dickinson snaps, "Who're you?"

And Clay says to the officer with the cell phone, "Officer, show this gentleman out."

Vickers shows his ID. "No ma'am. Not me. Colonel Vickers . . ."

Clay gives it a glance. She does a take and examines the ID. "White House?"

The officer with the phone is on it again. "I said he's loose in the building! Bottle him in . . ."

Down there, outside the building, squad cars and motorcycles squeal into sight, bringing massive reinforcements . . . Cops push a growing corps of press and TV back across the street, farther from the building . . .

In a law firm's low-partitioned bullpen typists at computer terminals watch as cops, with guns up, search methodically. Corners, closets, under desks.

The lobby now is utterly still. Armed police stand guard at the entrances in silent tableau . . . The elevators . . . Paramedics carry Slade out on a stretcher . . .

And in the multi-story garage a sudden deafening noise precedes the appearance of white-helmeted cops on motorcycles who come roaring up the ramps.

And up in the unfurnished office Clay is barking at the uniformed officer with the cell phone: "Shut down every elevator . . ."

The officer begins to relay the instructions into his phone . . .

In the elevator shaft Radford clings to a narrow perch high up inside the shaft. He's got a firm grip with one hand; in the other he holds Slade's service revolver. Several elevators are at various levels; two or three are moving. Then suddenly, jarring the cables, all the elevators stop. Radford reacts to the sound of men's footsteps in a nearby corridor. He can hear voices but can't make out the words.

On the double doors nearest him is stenciled the legend "7th floor." Abruptly the point of a crowbar appears, sliding through between the doors. It begins to pry the doors apart . . .

Radford reacts. Reaches out, nearly loses his balance, gets a grip on one of the thick cables, swings out into space . . .

The revolver falls from his grasp, tumbles down into darkness; after a significant and scary length of time he hears the sound when it hits bottom.

The crowbar has slipped, allowing the doors to close again, but now it's prying them open again . . .

Radford clings to the swaying cable . . .

No choice. He allows himself to begin sliding down the cable. He goes faster and faster, dwindling downward . . .

The crowbar has pried the doors open enough for a cop to stick his face through; several hands hold the doors apart for him. He looks up, around, down.

All the cables are swaying.

And after a moment the cop speaks. "Nothing. Let's go."

In the dark at the bottom of the elevator shaft, Radford picks himself up slowly. His hands are bleeding. He lurches to one side, finds his balance uncertainly, begins groggily to feel his way around the concrete walls, searching for a way out . . .

In the unfurnished office frantic activity continues: Clay, Vickers, Technician. Vickers now holds a CB radio; he's trying to listen to it while he badgers Clay: "What've you got on the assassin?"

The technician talks to Clay, overlapping: "Remington 40-XC National Match. Caliber 308."

Vickers scowls. "That's a target rifle."

The technician says, "Yeah. We're trying to raise the serial number. Acid."

Vickers says into his radio, "You can assure the director we've got the lid screwed tight." He cups the mouthpiece and glares daggers at Clay. "The United Nations Secretary General wants to know what the fuck's going on here."

Clay hasn't got time for him. She's tagging Dickinson: "How many men on the roof? Where's that chopper?"

In a basement corridor a cop prowls with a nightstick past a large metal ventilation grille in the wall—a return-duct for the air-conditioning system, through which Radford, hands bleeding, filthy and grease-stained, peers out while he tries to dry the blood from his palms on his shirt. He sees the cop open a door on the opposite side of the hall and looks in: glimpse of a utility-furnace room. The cop shuts the door and comes toward Radford's grille and turns; he posts himself on guard, his back to the wall, half blocking the grille.

Radford looks up . . . the inside of the duct is constricting, claustrophobic.

He's sweating.

The cop beyond the grille doesn't budge.

Dickinson and the bald cop walk into the unfurnished office with a uniformed Army medical corps major—Dr. Huong Trong. Dickinson walks the doctor up to Clay. "Commander—this is Major Trong . . . Doctor Trong."

Clay is glad to see Trong. "Okay!" She takes the doctor by the arm and steers him toward the cut-glass hole in the window. "C. W. Radford. One of yours, I think."

"Used to be," Dr. Trong concedes. "Belongs to the V.A. now . . . You believe he's the assassin?

"Smoking gun—literally, Doc—his fingerprints all over it—and the injured cop gave us a positive make on his Army photograph. Doesn't leave much reasonable doubt."

Dr. Trong says, "Did anybody actually see him do it? Because if they didn't, you might want to keep an open mind."

Vickers scowls at Dr. Trong. "What're you, Major? Japanese?"

"Korean."

"Yeah."

The cop stands with his back to the grille. Two SWAT officers jog quickly past, toting riot shotguns; they nod to the cop; he nods back. They jog out of sight . . . Abruptly the grille comes slamming out from the wall, knocking the cop off his feet, and behind it Radford explodes from the duct, elbow-chops the cop and drags the insensate man (including nightstick) through a doorway into the utility-furnace room . . . When the door closes behind them the corridor is empty and silent . . .

Dickinson is bitching to Clay. "Reinforcements getting

jammed up in the afternoon rush hour."

Clay says, "I called a shift for traffic control . . ."

Vickers is menacing now. "Commander Clay—if you let the scumbag get away—"

Clay tells him, "If you're upset about something, maybe you should call the police."

"Ho, *very* funny. Do you have any idea the international repercussions—?"

"You people can play global politics," Clay snaps. "I don't care if the stiff was left or right, east or west . . . Colonel Vickers, I know what the situation is, here. You are not helping."

A uniformed cop with two nightsticks climbs the stairs from landing to landing. At each floor an armed cop is posted. The cop with the two sticks waves a careless hello to a cop on duty, and turns to climb the next flight.

It's Radford, in cop's uniform.

On a higher landing there's a fire emergency station with a coiled high-pressure hose. Beyond it is another uniform standing guard. When Radford climbs into sight the cop starts to smile and greet him, then scowls—recognition. Something not quite right in the way Radford wears the uniform.

"Hey—!"

The cop draws his gun . . . And on other landings the other cops hear his cry . . . And—

Radford kicks the revolver from the cop's hand, takes the nightstick away from the cop, then—all this with lightning speed—busts the fire-hose loose, opens the valve and just as cops start shooting, he uses the high-pressure blast from the hose to drive 'em back above and below.

Bullets ricochet . . . He hears a cop cry as he tumbles

downstairs . . . The cascading flood obscures his view . . .

On an upper floor of the garage near the top of its spiral ramp, half a dozen police motorcycles are parked on their kickstands. A helmeted motorcycle cop stands guard over the bikes, and watches everything at once. He can hear a lot of activity—distant voices; sirens in the city; running feet . . .

Now a uniform approaches from some distance away. He carries two nightsticks. The helmeted motorcycle cop sees him coming, but is not alarmed until Radford walks up and abruptly slams him upside the helmet with the two heavy nightsticks. The blow knocks the cop to his knees. In a flash, Radford is bestride a motorcycle.

He kicks the stand out of the way . . . switches on the ignition . . . jumps on the starter . . . doesn't start . . .

Alerted by something somewhere, several cops come pouring into sight, chasing him . . .

And on the ground the helmeted motorcycle cop clears his head and reaches for his sidearm . . .

One last kick . . . Radford finally gets the motorcycle started and roars away . . . The motorcycle cop snatches up his walkie-talkie and barks into it . . .

Skittering down the hairpin turns of the spiral garage ramp, Radford can see the point several floors below where two squad cars slither into place across the foot of the ramp, blocking it—a fly couldn't get through there, let alone a man on a bike . . .

To one side he sees double doors open and two cops on foot appear. They stop, amazed, with guns lifting to aim at Radford on the speeding bike . . . Nothing to lose now. He aims the screaming motorcycle straight at the open double door—and goes through it like a bullet, scattering the two cops . . . All the cops react—astonishment . . .

In a building hallway Radford on the motorcycle comes roaring through the hall. Several gaping civilians flatten themselves back against the side wall as the juggernaut roars by . . .

The motorcycle thunders through the law office bullpen, smashing glass doors, and roars down the aisle between rows of desks. Typists leap for safety.

Another hallway—and at its far end a solid closed door, and an armed cop lifting his revolver in both hands, as . . .

Radford on the speeding bike sees the obstacle and slithers to one side, crashing the bike through double glass doors that disintegrate to let him into—

A designer furniture showroom—and the man on the motorcycle wildly plows through the place, knocking over lamps and statuary, making a shambles of the place—

—Then he's descending one of the building stairwells— zooming downstairs, bumpety-bump . . .

Vickers bulls his way out of the unfurnished office in time to see a man on a motorcycle heading straight toward him. This is very fast. Vickers gets off two wild shots but then his nerve fails and he stumbles back into the doorway as the motorcycle roars past. Vickers pushes forward out of the doorway to take aim at the dwindling fugitive, ignoring several cops and civilians who are in the line of fire, but now Clay comes out in time to knock Vickers' shooting arm up. The bullet goes into the ceiling.

Clay is furious. "How many bystanders you want to kill?"

Vickers glares murderously at her . . .

In the multi-story garage the street floor is all quiet now. Two cops by the toll booths. The don't notice when a side door softly opens. They can't see into those shadows, and aren't looking for it, but then—

—SMASH of sound as the motorcycle lays down rubber, screams around the backside of the toll booths, up over curbs, through a narrow pedestrian walkway, out onto the street as the two cops belatedly open fire . . .

On the street Radford whips out of sight around a corner, the cops cease firing, squad cars roar out of the garage in pursuit . . .

That afternoon the boulevards are totally coagulated with multiple lanes of afternoon rush-hour traffic: nothing moving. Gridlock. Horns honking, angry commuters shouting "Assholes!"

Police cars come up against the tangle of traffic and are stymied, as—

Radford on the motorcycle threads a swift bold path through narrow openings—going the wrong way between a couple of stopped trucks—disappearing . . .

The stalled police get out of their cars, stand on tiptoe and climb on top of the cars to search for the fugitive. They can't find anything. They look at one another in baffled dismay . . .

Two joggers trot by in running suits. They look curiously at all the police activity—and they laugh . . .

Finally the rest of the motorcycle squad begins to arrive. There's a lot of pointing and shouting. Helicopters swoop above the buildings, searching.

And nobody knows which way he went.

The helicopter that lands on the City Hall helipad has no official markings.

Vickers climbs out, fuming, followed by two business-suited FBI agents. He's snarling to them: "I don't believe these fuck-ups."

Then, seeing the press approaching, Vickers composes his features into a semblance of a confident smile. The agents break trail for him through the crowd, in which Vickers is not happy to recognize newspaperman Steve Ainsworth. Cameras and microphones are shoved at Vickers. He hears a babble of ad-lib questions. He fires responses: "No, we haven't got him in some secret hiding place. That's ridiculous . . . Don't spread rumors, Christ's sake. We know of no conspiracy at this time. We've identified one suspect and we're looking for him."

He escapes into the building.

It's a busy hive. Ringing phones. Whizzing printers. Talk. Clay issuing terse orders to a group of cops, including Dickinson. Beside her is Dr. Trong, still in his medical corps uniform. Vickers enters with the two FBI agents, again talking to them: "Armed and dangerous. If necessary, shoot on sight."

Dickinson overhears this last. He swings toward Clay. "That mean we can shoot on sight?"

"No, you may not shoot on sight. You may not shoot at all unless it's to save a life . . . Any fool can shoot people. You'll get no answers out of him if he's dead." She's looking pointedly at Vickers. He reacts. She takes a pace toward him. "On notice, Colonel. Homicide investigation. My turf."

"You think this is a two-bit murder case? A very important international figure has been assassinated. We've got a world-class political flap—they've sent these gentlemen and a lot more like 'em from the FBI. We've got the State Department on our backs and the Joint Chiefs have their thumbs on the buttons . . . The President himself—"

"You'll have to wait on line. It's our jurisdiction." Clay isn't giving an inch.

Vickers glares. Then he decides to defuse things. He puts an arm confidentially across Dr. Trong's shoulders. "Look, doctor, the man snipes at VIPs . . . He seems to have a little attitude problem."

Dr. Trong politely moves away, out from under the Colonel's arm, showing distaste for Vickers' old-buddy nonsense.

Vickers continues to thrust: "This is the same clown that turned traitor and did a propaganda broadcast for Saddam's goons. Now obviously his elevator doesn't stop on all the floors. You were his shrink . . ."

Dr. Trong says, "That mean you want my freehand diagnosis? He was an unacknowledged POW in an Iraqi torture camp. They messed with his head. And he's got a bullet lodged in here." He points to his own head. "Poor son of a bitch is a mess. If he was a horse you'd have to shoot him."

"The man committed treason, Doctor. And now assassination on top of it."

"You trained him to be a killer, Colonel."

"I didn't train him to go on TV for the enemy."

"The man had a head wound. Indescribable pain. He had no resistance left. Sure he broke. Tell me you wouldn't have."

Clay tries to calm things. "Iraq's a few years ago. We're dealing with right here, right now."

Dr. Trong says, "For some people the blood still hasn't dried."

In an alley there's a trashing of cans, bottles, empty cartons. Under the mess lies a motorcycle, almost completely hidden. Radford huddles in darkness. His police uniform is dirty and mussed. He's far beyond exhaustion. He can hear an approaching police siren but it doesn't bestir him. The sound dopplers down and fades. Radford drags the two nightsticks into his lap and slowly his face changes—anger and the beginnings of resolve—as purposefully he weaves the nightstick lanyards together . . .

There's a loading bay behind a boarded-up store. Radford coasts the motorcycle to a stop, leaves it propped against the building and walks away, stumbling a bit, rubbing his head. He holds one nightstick, and the other swings from it. He's made himself a nutcracker.

Outside Anne's apartment court he waits, hidden by the wading pool. Nothing stirs.

Old instincts make him cautious. He moves forward like a soldier in a combat zone, from cover to cover . . . Finally he reaches Anne's apartment. He warily eases close to a window and looks in.

It's empty, silent. The furniture's still in there but the place has been cleared out. No personal belongings remain. There are no sheets on the bed.

It's puzzling; he tries to think it out. He isn't tracking too well. This was his last hope; now he doesn't know what to do. He stumbles with pain and exhaustion. Finally he moves away . . .

Across from the wading pool, in the opposite direction from Radford's earlier angle of approach, Harry and Gootch wait in hiding, armed. Gootch is complaining *sotto voce:* "How the hell'd he get away from that fat cop?"

Harry whispers, "Son of a bitch must be able to handle a dose that'd put an elephant into a coma. Maybe built up a resistance from those pain drugs he takes . . . Maybe we should've thought of that." Now he sees something; reacts;

stiffens. "We got him, Gootch!"

Because that's Radford across the court, cautiously poking his head out to search.

Harry lifts his gun to aim it.

But Radford is skittish and ducks back out of sight.

"Get the car," Harry whispers, and heads toward Radford's corner while Gootch wheels back toward the street.

Radford, passing under a half-open casement window, catches a reflection in it of Gootch running toward the parked car, the same car in which Harry drove Radford to the shooting range. Alerted, Radford fades from view.

Harry runs to the corner of the building and eases past it for a look.

It's a mess of back yard fences and narrow passageways. The guy could've disappeared down any of them.

Harry knows they've lost him for now. "Shit."

Fading with exhaustion Radford returns on foot to the loading bay behind somebody's shuttered store. The motorcycle's still here—well that's not much of a surprise; even a Neanderthal knows better than to steal a police bike. "Which makes me a little sub-Neanderthal," Radford thinks, not amused, as he gets the motorcycle started and gently pulls away into a street—down which is rolling Harry's car.

Harry and Gootch are in it. They spot Radford at the same moment he spots them.

Radford peels away—just inches ahead of Harry's car. The bike and the car squeal away as if welded together . . . Harry tries to run down the motorcycle. Radford zigzags just in time. The car fishtails after him . . . Gootch in the car is shooting at Radford . . . This is a terrific high-speed pursuit through alleys and sidewalks until—

The river. A deep wide concrete channel, bridged by a tubular pipe the diameter of an oil drum. Radford's cycle roars up onto the conduit and zooms across the span—a spectacular high-wire balancing act . . .

Harry's car slides to a stop. Gootch savagely keeps pulling the trigger of his pistol but it's empty . . .

The motorcyclist flies off the far end of the pipe, slams down on the frontage road beyond, nearly falls over but then rights himself . . .

The two men glare in frustration as, across the viaduct, the cyclist disappears . . .

At sunset Radford rides the motorcycle gently around behind a gas station and stops. The place is closed up—deserted—its pumps taped off from the street. Construction equipment stands around, parked for the night. Radford dismounts, his face weary with pain in the sunset glow. He sags back against the wall, nearly passing out with the pain. His head lolls back and his eyes roll up . . .

In sudden bright sunshine we're in the desert. Barbed wire and bomb-damaged huts.

Watched by Charlie and several Kurdish prisoners, all of them manacled hand and foot, a uniformed Iraqi aims his rifle at Radford, who sits on the ground shaking his head stubbornly "no." The Iraqi begins to squeeze the trigger. Charlie is horrified. The rifle fires . . . The bullet slashes a streak across Radford's temple. Blood spurts. Radford drops. Charlie turns his head away in anguish.

A small crowd of officials and techs is swarming around the inside of Radford's flophouse bedroom.

Dickinson is looking at the illuminated screen of his

handheld computer—scrolling down from Radford's photograph (a fairly old one) past fingerprint boxes and vital statistics. "What's 'C.W.' stand for?"

"Nothing," Vickers says. "Just initials."

"Kind of got shortchanged," Commander Clay observes.

Vickers is glaring at Dr. Trong, who's looking around the room with curious interest. Vickers says, "It doesn't fit. You claim the guy's practically catatonic but he went through that building full of officers like a chainsaw."

Dr. Trong says, "He was a natural athlete. Under pressure it must've come back. But that's the operative term— pressure. An assassin cares about something, even if it's only his own rage . . . That profile doesn't fit C.W. He barely exists. Barely feels. He doesn't want to hurt anybody. He just wants to be left alone."

Clay says, "Somebody's robot, maybe? Wind him up and put a gun in his hand." She's reading the label off a prescription sheet. "Pain meds. You prescribed this."

"I did," Dr. Trong agrees. "And he's about due for a refill. Look, Commander, this just doesn't fit his pattern. One thing he'd never tolerate is someone trying to use him again."

Vickers snorts. "The man's a traitor and a murderer. I'm going to nail him."

Clay says, "Yeah. Well good luck, Colonel." Then, to Dickinson, "Walk me out."

Outside in the night Clay and Dickinson walk toward a car. Clay hands the prescription slip to Dickinson; she says, "He forgot this. If he's run out, maybe he'll look for a street retailer."

Dickinson takes the slip of paper and turns back; Clay gets in her car and drives off. That's when the reporter,

Ainsworth, intercepts Dickinson. "What's really goin' down, you old hairbags?"

Dickinson waves the sheet of paper in front of the reporter's nose, then pockets it too fast for Ainsworth to make out what it is. "A clue," Dickinson says smugly.

Ainsworth muses: "The federal agent and the lady cop— I see a story in that. I mean aside from the story everybody's covering. I could use a sidebar byline."

"Get out of here, pest. No press."

Ainsworth poises a stylus over the screen of his palm computer. "Chief of Detectives, Commander Denise Clay is a legend. In some quarters she is regarded as incorruptible and virtually superhuman. And now, into her previously unchallenged realm, we see a potentially explosive conflict in the arrival of a new outside authority . . ."

Dickinson turns and, walking away, says cheerfully, "Blow it out your bottom, huh?"

In the cafe kitchen, Don the waiter prepares a tray. Charlie fries burgers. From outdoors, Radford enters in his mussed police uniform. He's exhausted—haunted—in great pain. He carries the tied-together nightsticks: the nutcracker.

Don sees him, is galvanized—reaches for a handgun hidden in an ankle holster. Radford reacts—at first sluggish, but he expertly tosses the nutcracker. It tangles in Don's ankles and trips him. Radford is on top of him at once—disarms Don, recovers the nutcracker, clamps it tight around Don's wrist and squeezes. He can see in Don's face the agonizing pain this device causes.

"Move one inch, you're dead meat."

Radford's voice is like a tumble of coal down a metal chute: the new authority in it is enough to convince any tough guy that he means what he says. Don sweats, and lies still . . .

Radford picks up Don's revolver—a compact hammer-less pocket .38. Radford says to Charlie, "What's he doing with a piece?"

"Beats shit out of me. Ask him."

Don says, faint with pain, "Police officer. Wallet . . ."

Radford yanks out Don's wallet and flips it open. Sure enough there's a police badge in it. "And you're undercover in Charlie's place here for—?"

"Uh—drug enforcement. Vice."

"Try again."

Don begins to regain his bravado. "That's my badge. You don't question me, Radford. I question you."

Radford gives the nutcracker a twitch. It sends beads of pain-sweat to Don's forehead. But he's tough enough. "You ain't on the need-to-know list, C.W. I can't tell you shit. Even if I did, where would you take it? They got a federal fugitive warrant out on you—know what that means? Dead or alive. Like John fucking Dillinger."

Radford doesn't have time to spar with him. He looks up at Charlie. "D'you know he was undercover?"

"No." Charlie is scowling at Radford as if he doesn't like what he sees.

Radford says to him, "Hey. I didn't shoot anybody. They put the rifle in my hands."

Don scoffs. "Sure. They. Who's 'they'?"

"Wish I knew. Some people—gun club in a building on Broadway . . ."

"Yeah," Don says. "I hear you sayin' it." He looks up at Charlie. "Son of a bitch told a bunch of lies before. On Eye-rakky TV."

Charlie leans over Don. "You'd have done the same

thing, Donny boy, and you'da done it a lot sooner than he did."

Radford drops the snub-revolver in his pocket and gets Charlie's eye. "You want to keep this character on ice a little bit? I've got to get some answers. Want to know why . . . Who did this? . . . Look, I got to hit you up for some moving-around money. A razor . . . Pair of scissors . . . And let me borrow your jacket."

Radford comes out the side door from Charlie's Cafe, wearing a leather jacket that hides the police uniform. He's clean-shaven and he's cut his hair shorter, but he stumbles a bit. He's disoriented and in pain—that headache: again, still . . . always.

Charlie looks both ways from just inside the door. "You belong in a fucking emergency ward."

"I could be putting you out of business here, Charlie. Undercover narc idiot could run you in, aiding and abetting."

"Maybe he knows me better'n to try that." Charlie's deadpan gives way to a wicked unamused grin.

"Yeah . . . If I'm still alive sometime I'll pay you back."

"When'd we start keeping books on you and me?"

Charlie shuts the door and Radford trudges away.

He reacts when he sees—

The redheaded dealer. Still wearing those camouflage combat fatigues. Radford asks, "What outfit were you with?"

"Huh?"

"In the service. What unit?"

The dealer frowns. "Man, you got a problem or what?"

"Never mind. I—uh—I just want to make a buy."

The dealer looks down at Radford's cuffs and shoes.

Police blue and black.

Radford continues, "I need a painkiller bad."

The dealer's gaze very dryly climbs back up from the police Oxfords and the blue slacks to Radford's face. "My man, I got nothin' for you."

"Come on. I really need . . ."

"Don't they tell you guys about entrapment?" He turns away laughing. "Next time try to remember—eighty-six the pig shoes."

Radford says, "Hey, you're wrong . . ."—and in his desperation he thinks about knocking the dealer over with the nutcracker—but now something stirs in the corner of his vision and he turns to see a cop coming in sight, a block away. The cop looks this way, and Radford shuffles away into alley shadows . . .

Later in the night the redheaded dealer crosses a silent downtown street and stops in a doorway to see if he's being followed. When no one appears, he walks on. Then, out of sight one turn behind him, Radford emerges from the shadows and dodges forward, cautiously following the dealer . . .

Inside Union Depot it's so late there's very little activity. The dealer stands at a magazine rack near the bank of lockers and pretends an interest in the magazines while he has a look around. He doesn't spot Radford, who watches him from a distance. The dealer turns, produces a round-headed key, opens one of the lockers and takes a package out.

Radford is about to move in when—

The baldheaded officer and two other cops converge from three different directions upon the dealer.

Radford fades back just in time; in harsh disappointment he watches it go down.

The dealer sees he's trapped. Knowing the routine, he sighs and turns to spread hands and feet and lean against the wall. A cop frisks him. A cop unwraps the package and finds a thick bankroll. The bald cop takes it. He shows a picture of Radford to the dealer. The dealer says, "I know only one thing. My lawyer's phone number."

"Okay, then." The bald cop takes out a cigarette lighter and sets fire to the bankroll. The dealer looks on in horror as his money burns up.

Radford lurches through the dark streets, hammered with pain.

Under a sudden, hard, white light, a younger blood-stained Radford lies on a table in a spartan prison hospital—primitive; rudimentary. Iraqi soldiers watch a doctor probe Radford's head wound, look up at the soldier who interrogated Radford, and shake his head "no." The doctor discards the probe, wraps a bandage carelessly around Radford's head and walks away . . .

Charlie moves forward and cradles Radford's bloody head in his hand. And now, to Charlie's amazement, Radford, horribly cut and bruised, opens his eyes to look at Charlie. He's alive on sheer will power, everything raw and bleeding. We see Charlie's tears as he reaches out gently to touch Radford's cheek.

Under a street lamp in the silent city Radford lurches on—afraid, confused, in pain—blindly into the night . . .

Conrad's parked van stands at the curb in front of a suburban house on an ordinary street. Inside the house, in the kitchen, Harry—clean-shaven now—takes two beers from the fridge and tosses one to Conrad. Anne is watching a TV newscast. She's worried. She glares at Conrad. She fidgets. "I want to talk to Damon."

"Grow up." Conrad pops the beer top.

Harry says, "We'll see Damon sooner or later . . . You're gonna stay here right now. Radford running loose, shit, God knows what may be going on in that messed-up brain of his."

Anne says, "The poor son of a bitch."

Conrad points a finger at her. "He's a trained sniper. A killer, and by now he's madder'n hell. He gets his hands on you, you won't feel so sorry for him . . . You just worry what happens if they get him alive and he talks. He ID's you—you're an accessory."

Anne shows a flash of heat. "So are you, Conrad baby."

"Yeah. Well you just sit here quiet till he's dead."

"Jesus," she says. "And I was once an honest-to-God fevered zealot." She points at the TV. "Wasn't supposed to be this way!"

"No, it wasn't," Conrad agrees. "Your buddy Radford was supposed to get dead."

Harry tries to embrace Anne possessively. She pushes him away. "We started as good people. What happened to us?"

Harry says, "Hell, honey, you can't make an omelet without—"

"Oh spare me. I hear that breaking-eggs shit enough from Damon."

Conrad says, "This country and the tree-hugger crazies were getting too close together. It had to be stopped." He heads for the door. "I've gotta go."

Anne won't let it go. "I bought the philosophy, Conrad—but I'm starting to think it's a hell of a way to preserve freedom and justice for all."

Before dawn in a scuzzy downtown park—place of business for felons; home for the homeless—a cop prowls, exploring. A few derelicts sit at trash campfires, eating scraps, drinking out of brown paper bags. Others sleep under trees or in makeshift shelters or on benches. The cop gently straightens an overcoat over a sleeping woman with a small child. He walks on, past a huddled shape under rumpled newspapers. It lifts a corner of paper stealthily to watch the cop depart—It's Radford, shaking with a fever of pain. When he moves, his head hurts so bad he can't stop the groan.

In the bright light of an interrogation hut the younger Radford—his face an ugly half-healed scar—peers up without interest into a TV camera. An Iraqi woman clumsily paints pancake make-up over his scabs while a soldier holds up cue-cards beside the camera. On a black-and-white monitor Radford can see himself, and on the TV screen the make-up doesn't show; he looks puffy but not seriously injured.

He speaks straight into the camera with what seems to be peaceful calm. His eye movements betray that he's reading from cue cards.

"I'm sorry that the leaders of my country have picked the wrong side this time. I've seen the terrible destruction that's been visited on this little country by American bombs, and I feel ashamed. Ashamed of my leaders, ashamed of the petroleum imperialists who're promoting this war on innocent civilians. I don't want to hurt anybody. I just want to come home. I'm asking my government to reconsider—and to get out of this place where they have no business being."

When he finishes talking, he simply stares unblinkingly

into the camera. He doesn't stir. The monitor's screen slowly goes to black.

In the city park Radford lies in the night, hopeless amid the homeless. Something draws his attention and he turns sluggishly to see several cars drawing up over at the edge of the park. A dozen men in suits get out of them. Most of them carry shotguns or rifles.

Vickers gets out of the back of one of the cars. Behind him are the two FBI men and reporter Ainsworth. Vickers makes rapid hand-signals. The dozen armed men fan out into the park.

Radford, moving with agony, crouching to stay out of sight, staggers across a street threading traffic . . . and takes cover by a parked truck, and looks back at the park where the dozen men brutally roust the homeless people, shining flashlights in their faces.

Vickers and Ainsworth watch the search.

"Colonel Vickers, you really think this is going to find him?"

"Only if they get real lucky. The idea's to give him no chance to rest. Keep him tired out. A tired man makes mistakes . . . He's up there all alone without a net. He only has to slip once, and I've got him."

Radford watches from behind the parked truck across the street. A government agent comes up behind him. Radford turns, looks at him. The agent deliberately takes a photo from his pocket and looks at it, comparing it with Radford's face.

That mug-shot of Radford shows him as he looked in a previous life. The agent isn't sure whether this is the man or not. "Mind if I see some identification?"

Across the street the dragnet is working its way toward them. In no time at all, somebody in that lot will be close enough to recognize Radford. Knowing that, he moves quickly as he takes out a wallet (cop's wallet) and flashes the badge at the agent, and feigns exasperation. "Move on, man, you're fucking up my stakeout."

Embarrassed, the agent moves on. Radford reacts to the near-miss, and fades back into the shadows just before Vickers comes across the street and collars the agent.

"Who was that?"

"Some cop on a stakeout."

"Shit. You idiot! Radford stole a cop's ID along with that uniform." Vickers looks in all directions, fuming with frustration.

A big illuminated sign emulates a green beret. Sure enough its lettering spells out "GREEN BERET BAR." On both sides of the door are glass-covered shadowboxes protecting posters of soldiers, guns, combat action. Radford looks up at the "bar" sign and hesitates, and goes in. His head is killing him.

Inside he walks past a hand-lettered sign thumbtacked to the wall: "WET PANTY COMBAT NIGHT!" He goes on to the bar. The place is crowded and very noisy—a lot of exuberant shouting. Several scantily-clad women seem to be dancing in some fashion on an elevated stage, and over the sound of heavy metal music he can hear men shouting:

"Commence firing!"

"Play guns! Come on, play guns, guys!"

"I said—Commence firing!"

At first Radford can't tell what's going on and doesn't care. He pays no attention to the raucous uproar. He gets a barmaid's attention and grits out the words in pain between his teeth: "Double vodka. Straight up."

Then he waits, enduring his pain until after an eternity

the barmaid sets the drink before him. Radford slugs it down fast and waits for a hint of surcease.

There's a tumult of enthusiastic yelling—finally he turns to see what's going on.

Up there on stage four women are dressed in tight T-shirts and skimpy bikini panties. They're wet. He sees bursts of water drops, and thin streams of water, coming at the women from the audience, soaking them. Not understanding, he shifts his gaze to the men in the audience—all ages; rough clothes mostly; blue collar guys. They're having a wild time shooting at the women on stage with water-guns that are look-alike models of real submachine guns and rifles and pistols. The guys aim and shoot—some with gleeful enjoyment, some in combat stance with deadly grimness.

"Shoot 'em in the crotch, guys—Right in there between the legs!"

Not believing what he's seeing, Radford squints.

On stage three of the women thrust themselves forward, pelvis first, grinning at the guys; streams of water soak them. The fourth woman—a little shy, scared—hangs back.

"I wanta see some wet pussy! Man, she's hot! You see that? I got her—and she likes it!"

Here and there in the audience Radford can see a few women, most of whom obviously have been dragged here by their men and would rather be anywhere else.

"Come on, Francine, you can't win prize money if you don't make like a good target!"

The fourth woman gives it a game try, pushing herself forward, but somebody's spray hits her in the face and she flinches.

The streams of water are zeroing in with increasing accuracy on the four women's crotches.

"All right! You guys shot like this in Vietnam, we

wouldn't of lost the war!"

Unable to take this, Radford shoves away from the bar and flees out of the place.

He stumbles outside and looks back at the Green Beret Bar. "Jesus H. Christ."

He disappears.

At some ungodly hour of the morning in the kitchen of Charlie's cafe, Denise Clay is interviewing Charlie while Dickinson examines Don the waiter's ID. Don is explaining, "I been working out of Vice . . ."

"Yeah," says Dickinson, "so what do you know about this Radford son of a bitch?"

Charlie is saying to Clay, "Said he didn't do it. Said they put the gun in his hand after the shooting. And I believe it. I know him. If C.W.'d killed the guy, he'd say so."

Don says to Dickinson, "He's a loony, man. Beat three guys damn near to death—right here in the dining room."

Charlie says to Clay, "Said something about a gun club in a building on Broadway."

Clay and Dickinson come out the side door of Charlie's Cafe and walk toward their car. Dickinson yawns, big. Clay tells him, "That waiter—talk to Vice, find out who sent him down here. Something funny there."

"Yeah. Gotta tell you I am whipped . . . If we don't nail this turkey fast—"

Commander Clay says, "What if he didn't do it?"

"Come on. You're not buyin'—"

She indicates the cafe. "That guy's his old Army buddy. Knows him better'n we do. And—why is it the murder weapon had his fingerprints all over it—but there's no prints on the ammunition?"

They get into the car . . .

The Army base is asleep, its drab military buildings and parked vehicles silent. On a company street a couple of enlisted soldiers walk by a sign that indicates the way to the dispensary. Radford, emerging from shadows, goes in that direction. At the dispensary door he looks all around, then tries to open it. It's locked; it won't budge. In a sweat, trembling, he fades back around the side of the building.

There's a high window at the back. Radford strips off his jacket, wraps it around his fist and punches in the window. He uses the jacket to sweep slivers of glass from the frame before he crawls in through the high opening. If he sees the small red light glowing on a keypad panel he disregards it; how's he to know the light was green until he smashed the window?

Dr. Trong and his wife are awakened by a strident buzzing noise. Dr. Trong fumbles for a switch, finds it and silences the alarm buzzer. He gets into his robe and slippers, and takes a revolver from a drawer. At the door he pauses and smiles at his wife. "Yes, dear, I'll be careful." When he goes out, his wife yawns and goes back to sleep.

In the back room of the dispensary Radford paws with increasing desperation through cabinets. He finds a bottle of tablets and tries to read the label—"Aspirin"—he stuffs it in his pocket and searches on . . .

Dr. Trong arrives on foot outside the place, in bathrobe and slippers, carrying his revolver. With absolute silence he unlocks the front door and enters, cocking the revolver.

In the back room Radford opens a cabinet door and discovers—a big steel safe, like a half-size bank vault. And a sign on it in great big printing: "In here, stupids. The narcotics. Don't break in. It's booby-trapped."

Radford reacts: hopelessness. He's trembling violently and soaked with sweat. He looks ghastly. And now he glances around and for the first time really notices the glowing red light on the alarm keypad. As he gapes at it he deflates even further. He seems paralyzed. Then—did he hear something or is it his imagination?

Dr. Trong moves cautiously through the corridor toward the door that leads into the back room. He moves through the dark without sound, and the cocked gun is ready in his hand.

He slowly enters the back room, silent, gun up. He flips the light switch. Lights come on. And just then—

Radford jumps him from on top of a steel filing cabinet.

Dr. Trong starts to struggle, then recognizes him and relaxes. It requires little effort—too little—for Radford to wrestle the revolver away from him.

Radford stands back, holding the cocked revolver, and gestures toward the safe. Dr. Trong obeys: twirls the combination dials. "You look god-awful, C.W."

When the vault door begins to open, Radford pushes the doctor back, pulls it wide and looks in. Vials, bottles, papers. He rummages among them.

Dr. Trong says conversationally, "Where's it hurt? Your head?"

"No. My big toe, you asshole."

Radford finds a syringe, loads it from the vial, rolls up a sleeve, prepares to inject himself—all this while keeping the revolver close at hand and one eye on Dr. Trong across the room.

"I didn't assassinate anybody."

"All right," Dr. Trong says. "Who did?"

"We didn't get formally introduced."

"You saw a face? Faces?"

Radford makes no answer; he's distracted, reading the label of a vial. He puts it back and tries another. This one satisfies him.

The doctor says, "Between them and the police, it must feel like Kurdistan all over again—you can't see them but you know they're coming back to nail you again, maybe now and maybe next week, and it's got you all bent out of shape."

Radford says, "I don't need your sympathy."

"My sympathy won't kill you."

"Don't mess with me. I don't want people messing with me any more."

He injects—and unexpectedly the injection hurts.

"Oww!!" He bends over with pain; rocks in agony, finally fumbles for the revolver. He points it accusingly. "What'd you put in this stuff?"

"What's it say on the label?"

Radford holds his arm in pain. "Don't lie to me!"

Dr. Trong shrugs. "Morphine . . . A little oil." He grins amiably. "Hurts like a son of a bitch, don't it."

"You bastard." Radford's just about mad enough to shoot him; he's doubled over—his arm is in agonizing pain.

The headline on the paper at the corner newsstand is a bold banner: "Assassin Escapes—A Loner? Or Part of Intricate Plot?"

Wojack, the shooter, buys a copy and while the news agent fishes for change Wojack remarks in a supercilious Yale drawl: "Every time some politician gets assassinated, people just can't settle for the simple obvious facts—not good enough to have some homicidal maniac out there—always got to be some far-fetched theory about a sinister conspiracy."

The news agent nods agreement. Wojack walks to the corner—just as Conrad's van pulls up. Wojack gets in, and the van pulls away, hardly having stopped at all.

At the wheel Conrad lights a cigarillo. Wojack fastens his shoulder harness. He hands the newspaper to Gootch, who sits in the plush custom room behind the seats.

Gootch glances at the headline and folds the paper; he's got more urgent things on his mind. He says to Wojack, "Timetable's moved up. It's today."

Wojack considers that, then nods with satisfaction. "While Radford's still on the loose. That's very bright of someone."

Gootch agrees. "He'll get blamed for this one too."

Conrad puffs smoke. "Doesn't matter. These things have to be done—if somebody doesn't exterminate these vermin, this world won't be fit to live in. I'd be proud to take the blame if I didn't have orders to stay covert."

Wojack says, "Your orders don't amuse me very much, old sport. Your money does. I want the next installment tonight."

"It's waiting. What else you need?"

"High-speed ammunition and a twelve-ex scope."

"You got it," Conrad says, and the van turns a corner, running for a green light.

Radford leans against a wall in Trong's dispensary as the painkilling narcotic takes effect. His arm still hurts. He holds the revolver and watches the doctor suspiciously.

Dr. Trong is saying, "—saved all this trouble if you

hadn't been too stubborn to die way back then."

Radford says gloomily, "I should've died."

"Oh for God's sake quit being so absurdly macho. Learn a little humility, C.W. Get rid of that thousand-yard stare . . . All right, you felt like the worst fink in history—you thought you were the only man who'd ever been tortured to the point where he broke the code of conduct . . . You know, we've found out a lot of them broke. You're not so special after all . . . Hey. Hear what I'm saying. The only thing you did wrong was you were there illegally in the first place and they had no right to send you in there. You didn't do anything."

Radford broods at him, absorbing it.

Dr. Trong sees he's got an opening. He leans forward. "Wars are fought by old men using young men's bodies. Now somebody's doing the same thing to you all over again. Somebody's used you."

"Shut up."

"Come on, then. Get mad. It's all right. Getting mad— it's the first step in getting even."

In the kind of shop where you can buy any weapon that's legal and—if you know the secret word, some that aren't— three men enter from the parked van out front: Wojack, Gootch and Conrad. A clean-shaven man unlocks the side door to let them in to the shop. The main thing that makes him recognizable is his bad tooth when he smiles: Harry Sinclair. Otherwise he's changed his appearance again—a regular Lon Chaney.

The gun shop is a motley cluttered arsenal. Harry locks the door. Gootch takes an immediate childlike interest in a tripod-mounted machine gun and plays with it—a kid with a toy. Conrad unlocks a steel drawer, takes out an envelope and hands it to Wojack, who leafs through the money inside it, rapidly counting. He says to Harry, "Let me have forty 308s with one-ten-grain soft-points."

Conrad asks, "Forty cartridges?"

It makes Gootch look up. "You fixin' to start a war or something?"

Wojack says, mock-gentle, "I'd like to burn up a few sighting it in—if you don't mind."

Harry digs out two boxes of rifle shells and hands them to Wojack. Conrad turns on a TV set, but gets only snow.

Harry says, "These'll give you a minus nine-point-three trajectory at three hundred yards. Or I can give you a boat-tail soft-point that'll give you eight-point-four . . ."

"These'll do." Wojack yawns. "They'll kill the man—dead enough."

Radford holds the revolver. He looks up through the smashed window at the dawn sky. Dr. Trong watches, unafraid. Radford rubs his arm, trying to think.

The doctor says, "Call the police. You haven't got a chance on your own."

"They'd put me in a hole. I can't take that any more." Radford examines the revolver.

Dr. Trong says mildly, "I don't think killing yourself is a sensible alternative."

"Not right away anyhow. It's not me I want to blow away."

"I see. But you do want to go after someone? That's progress, for you."

"Now you think it's progress to want to kill people?"

"It's progress for you to want something." Then Dr. Trong picks up a phone. Radford moves, as if to stop him—then stops, and after a long beat decides to trust him; he nods permission. Dr. Trong reacts—a profound moment—and then dials.

The doctor says into the phone, "Hi. Me . . . Any danger of us getting a bite of breakfast?"

On an outdoor shooting range at dawn, with a scrubby hillside for a backstop. Wojack sits at a bench-rest table and sights in his rifle on a long-range target. Conrad smokes. He and Gootch watch from nearby while Wojack fiddles with the weapon—the same kind of .308 rifle as before, with a 'scope mounted on it. He fires a shot and then studies the target through the 'scope. Through its lenses he can see one hole a bit wide of center. He adjusts a set-screw and aims again. When he squeezes it off he can see the image jerk a bit with recoil; it settles down—and the second bullet hole is dead-center in the bull's eye.

On the indoor shooting range—the target range where Radford first met Harry. Several men and women are shooting at targets. An elderly supervisor looks up as Clay and Dickinson enter. They show him their IDs. And ask him a question or two.

He's puzzled. "Sunday? Wasn't anybody here Sunday. I've been closed Sundays for eighteen years."

Dickinson asks, "How many people have keys?"

"Well gosh, I don't know for sure. Too many, I guess, after all these years. I keep meaning to change the locks, you know, but—" He gives them an apologetic look.

Dr. Trong and Radford sit at the dinette table, having toast and coffee. In the middle of the table is that same morphine vial, and a packet of disposable syringes. Mrs. Trong, in houserobe and slippers, absently kisses her husband's cheek and turns to go. Her husband touches her sleeve. "See if I've got any clothes big enough for C.W."

She flaps a hand in acknowledgement and exits.

Dr. Trong says, "She's used to my patients dropping in at weird hours . . . That injection still hurt your arm?"

"Stings like holy hell."

"Good." He indicates the vial and syringes. "Take 'em. I don't want you busting into any pharmacies. Your burglary technique, you'd getting caught for breaking-and-entering."

"Right. You got a cellular phone I can borrow?"

Trong looks at him. "You want to call her on the phone?"

Radford just watches until the doctor shrugs and hands him a flip-phone. It slides into Radford's pocket. Then he winces. "You put something in there. To make it hurt."

Dr. Trong gathers the dishes and begins to wash them. "It's harmless . . . Look, C.W., you just think you need drugs for the pain. You healed a long time ago. The headaches are psychosomatic. You don't need drugs."

Wojack studies the consulate through his rifle 'scope, sliding the view across the forbidding fences and walls and the imposing building behind them, then down past uniformed guards to a brass plaque on the gatepost—"consulate" but he can't see which country's—and he continues to shift his aim up past the wall to an upper-story window. Through it we see a man sitting up in bed with a pad in his lap, writing. Something foreign about him. He looks powerful; important. The man is smoking a cigarette, deep in thought. The 'scope's reticule centers on his chest. Wojack speaks softly: "Don't smoke in bed, you twit. Hazardous to your health." He squeezes it off and the image jerks with recoil; when it settles the man in bed is dead, his chest blown apart in blood, the cigarette falling from his limp hand.

Wojack runs, stooped over, to the back of the rooftop and swings himself out over the back of the building onto something that looks like a miniature window-washers' scaffold. It's supported on a system of pulleys and lines. It lowers him, swiftly and smoothly like a high-speed elevator, to an alley floor where Gootch matter-of-factly recovers the lift-lines and tosses the apparatus into the back of the van while Wojack and his rifle climb into the passenger seat; Conrad puts it in Drive as Gootch jumps into the back and pulls the rear door shut, and the van pulls away at a sedate speed, breaking no traffic regulations.

An Army Jeep pulls up opposite the vast lawn of a house that exudes solid establishment wealth, where a very attractive woman in her thirties, wearing shorts and T-shirt but very well groomed, is snipping roses, collecting flowers. This is Dorothy, depicted in the photograph that was in Radford's room; it was taken when they both were younger.

Dr. Trong, at the wheel of the Jeep, says, "She waited for you. Even after you cracked. When everybody else gave you up for a traitor, Dorothy waited. I think she may still be waiting."

Beside him Radford wears windbreaker, khakis—newly borrowed clothes. The engine idles and they continue to watch the estate across the street. Dr. Trong says, "She could accept it even when you couldn't. She had faith."

Radford says, "She should've married some guy."

Dorothy, cutting roses, is unaware she's being watched.

Dr. Trong says, "She understands why you ran away— why you dropped out. I think she's more understanding than I am. You were on your way, C.W. You'd have been a chairman of the board or maybe you'd have taken over her father's seat in the Senate."

"What're we doing here? Come on. Let's go."

"Dorothy loves you, you know. She's waiting, C.W."

"Yeah. Well your timing's terrific. I've got nothing to offer her but a death watch."

By a culvert along the edge of a country road Dr. Trong stops the Jeep. Radford gets out. The doctor says, "It may not be just a death watch. We may just get this thing turned around. If we do, what happens after? I don't want to see you washing dishes again."

"I'll give it some thought when I get the time."

"Promise?"

"Get the fuck out of here." Radford waves Dr. Trong away and watches the Jeep drive off. Then he climbs down to the overgrown culvert under the road. He uncovers the hidden motorcycle. And goddammit he's got a headache again.

In the culvert there's plenty of reading material. Graffiti, including: "To hell with tomorrow," printed with surprising neatness.

The headache is too much for Radford. He unwraps Dr. Trong's medicine and prepares an injection—hesitates but finally shoots up. At first there's blessed relief. He switches on the bike's police radio to listen to the calls and hears mostly scratchy dispatch broadcasts that he can't understand. Then there's a dreadful pain in his arm. He doubles over, clutches the arm, dances around.

"Holy shit. SON of a bitch!"

And then after a moment he is distracted by sound of the police radio; he crosses to the motorcycle to listen. It's a woman's voice, crackling with static: ". . . State police requested to assist. Subject C. W. Radford. New assassination seven a.m. this morning, same M.O., same kind of rifle. Cancel all leaves and passes. Off-duty personnel report in for overtime assignment."

Radford stares. He just doesn't *believe* this.

Police headquarters is crowded with intense activity—noise, arguments, cops and officials, everything moving busily. Commander Clay hurries toward her corner office. Reporter Ainsworth trails her. "Commander Clay . . ."

"Later."

Clay swings into her office and turns to slam the door in Ainsworth's face. Dickinson squeezes in past both of them.

Ainsworth pleads. "Hey, how about it?"

Dickinson slams the door, shutting Ainsworth out. "Shitfuck. No witnesses, no physical evidence except the 308 softpoint ammo—you can buy it anywhere."

The ringing phone interrupts him. Clay grabs it up. "Commander Clay. I trust it's important?" Then Dickinson sees her react. "You're kidding! Put him on—and trace it."

Radford stands by his motorcycle around the blind side of the boarded-up filling station. He's talking on the flipphone he borrowed from the doc. "I don't have to make this call. I'm taking a chance, right? So listen to me. I didn't even know about this new killing. I just heard about it on the radio. I'm not the one you want. I'm telling you because I want you to look for the real assassins."

Clay's voice reaches him as if from far away in the stars. "They out there with the real killers in the O.J. case? Well hell—describe for me the people you say you saw."

Radford gives a thumbnail description of Harry, the way Harry looked the last time Radford saw him. He adds, "He knew the club—he knew the range. And there was a woman. A blonde. Natural blonde." He describes Anne.

Clay says, "C.W., I want you to come in here. We can protect you. I give you my word, we'll look for them."

"Some other time, Commander. You find 'em first."

"You haven't got a chance."

"You can't always go by that. Anyway you've got rules. I haven't."

"Oh, we've all got rules, C.W. Even you . . . We've traced this call and I'm going to nail you."

Radford clicks the END button, gives the cell phone a quizzical look, then sets it down gently on the lid of a trash can and gets on the motorcycle and rides away, not in a hurry.

He arrives at the back-road culvert on the motorcycle, stops, looks all around, and when he knows he's unobserved, rides the bike down the embankment and hides it in the culvert under the road. He sits down in his hidey-hole, holding his aching head, talking to himself: "Okay, smart ass. Now what?"

This pain is unbearable in his head. He takes out the syringe kit and gets ready to inject himself. Then he looks at the painful needle—and finally puts it back in the case without using it. He puts the stuff away. Then he bends over—way over, nearly upside down, holding his throbbing head in his hands. And from that angle he's looking at the culvert wall and he sees, upside down, the graffiti "To hell with tomorrow." He reacts, because upside down, the "To hell" part looks like "7734 OL." He sits up, staring at the graffiti. He's remembering that cafe window reflection of the upside-down backward reflection of the van's license plate.

Aloud, he says, "To hell."

Slowly, relishing this discovery, he settles astride the motorcycle, starts her up, smiles, and—lets 'er rip.

At speed on the highway he thrusts his face into the wind and—he's enjoying this . . .

Sign on the counter: "Department of Motor Vehicles." Radford casually shows his badge to a clerk, who then brings out a book. Radford looks through it, searching for a number—and with sudden triumph he jabs his finger onto the page.

There it is—the 7734 OL license plate—on Conrad's van. It waits parked in front of a high-rise apartment house.

Radford rides his police motorcycle past it. His eyes study everything at once. He makes one pass, hangs a U-turn and comes back. Finally he parks the cycle. The van has just been washed; it sparkles.

Radford studies the polished van, then looks up at the apartment house above it. Balconies up there. Posh.

He takes a small object from the saddlebag and walks around, pretending to admire the sparkling van. Near the back he "accidentally" drops something in the street. He crouches to pick it up—it's an all-steel one-piece ice pick. While he's crouched by the rear bumper of the van he reaches out underneath and thrusts upward several times with great strength.

Fluid begins to drip from the punctured gas tank. It starts to form a pool. Without hurry Radford gets to his feet and, carrying his nutcracker nightsticks, strides purposefully around the side of the apartment house.

The service door is locked of course, but it's only a spring-lock. He pries his ice pick in against the face-plate, works it hard and finally gets the door open and wheels inside toting the nutcracker.

Conrad is in the front room of his apartment talking on the phone and smoking a cigarillo. An open pack, and a lighter, are on the glass coffee table by the phone. The flat is a modern well-appointed masculine place on an upper floor. Glass doors, leading out onto the balcony, stand open. He's saying into the phone, "Okay, we had an uptick; go ahead and execute the short sale." He's interrupted by the sound of the door buzzer. "That must be Gootch. Gotta go. I'll talk on you later." He hangs up and goes to the door.

When Conrad begins to open it, the door slams in against him, knocking him off balance, and a very angry Radford swarms in violently, kicking the door shut behind him, bashing Conrad to his knees and wrapping the nutcracker around Conrad's neck all in one smooth coordinated move.

"Okay, Mr. Conrad. You can talk to me, or you can die."

Conrad hacks, half choking, "Get this fucking thing off me."

One-handed, Radford frisks him. He takes a revolver out of Conrad's belt from where it was hidden under the shirt. Then he whips the nutcracker away from Conrad's throat. "Don't move a whisker."

Radford does a quick search to make sure no one else is in the apartment: keeping one eye and Conrad's own gun pointed at the motionless Conrad, he hurries from door to door, peering into rooms and closets. At one trophy cabinet he pauses to look at a couple of photos that are matted on the wall among various golf and fishing trophies. It includes a photograph of a group of rifle competitors at an outdoor meet. Mixed amid half a dozen strangers in shooting jackets and vests, he recognizes Harry (no beard), Conrad and Gootch. Harry, front and center, is holding a trophy and smiling. We see the bad front tooth.

"Hey Conrad. Tell me about your little shooting club."

Conrad is still hoarse from the nutcracker. "How the hell'd you find me?"

Radford happens to be looking at the adjacent photo—this one showing Conrad standing proudly by his shiny new van, and favoring a banner: "Custom Van Show—FIRST PRIZE." Radford returns to the photo of the shooters. He rips it down and stuffs it in his pocket. He looks at Conrad, then goes swiftly out to the balcony, looks around, looks down over the edge. From here he can see the street below and, straight below, the polished top of Conrad's van. He can see the glisten of the spreading puddle of fluid behind the van.

Radford re-enters the apartment. Still holding Conrad's revolver, he sits down by the phone, studies the photo of the shooting team and contemplates Conrad as if trying to figure out how to handle this. He reaches for the open pack of cigarillos; puts one in his mouth and lights it.

Conrad says, "Thought you didn't smoke."

"Why? What gave you that idea?"

"We've got a file on you—Look, I'd be sore too, in your shoes, but don't mix that cigarillo smoke with melodrama, old buddy. I'm just a sub-contractor. A voice on the phone, that's all I know. You can try bamboo under the fingernails but I still won't know anything that'd help you."

Radford goes out onto the balcony. He looks down, judges the wind against his moistened finger, then drops the lit cigarillo and steps back, looking deadpan at Conrad. A moment later they both hear the sound of a major explosion. The blast unsteadies Radford on his feet and as he rights them he sees Conrad's eyes go wide as Conrad, peering past him, sees recognizable pieces of the van soar up past the window in a graceful arc.

Conrad leaps to his feet, runs to the balcony, stares down. Disbelief—astonishment. "You son of a bitch!"

Radford glances down over the edge as what's left of the van is consumed in a conflagration.

Conrad is beside himself. Radford shoves him back inside. He shuts the glass doors and speaks:

"Now I'll ask. Just once."

Conrad walks away gathering his composure; he's trying to think. Radford readies the nutcracker and begins to walk forward. Half the length of the room separates them.

Conrad says, "I've studied you inside and out. I memorized that file. I know you."

He swings back in his pacing. Walks toward Radford—not hurrying, and not approaching too close. "You got brainwashed someplace between sniper school and coming back from Iraq. What happened, you get hypnotized by some Zen priest? You had a chance to kill those guys in the cafe the other night, but you wouldn't do it. You had 'em dead to rights, you let 'em go. So you're not going to kill me now—I've got no gun and anyhow I'm no use to you dead . . . You won't shoot me in the back."

And abruptly Conrad leaps to the door, yanks it open and dives through. Radford throws the nutcracker but it's a fraction of an instant too late; it clatters against the closing door. Radford races to the door, picks up the nutcracker, exits on the run . . .

He races along the hall, looking every which way . . . And sees—a door sighing shut on its springs. Red sign above it: "EXIT." Radford flings it open, plunges through . . .

He's on a landing. The stairs go down several stories and he can hear the clattering sound of racing footsteps down there, Conrad fleeing toward the bottom, and Radford leaps down the stairs, half a flight at a bound, pursuing . . .

On the avenue the racket of fire and police sirens approaches the burning debris of what used to be Conrad's van, as Conrad comes out of the building at the dead run, racing, reaches the bottom, crosses to an exterior door, exits . . .

Radford emerges from the back door just in time to see Conrad disappear around the far corner of the building. Radford gives chase, running full-tilt. Around two, then three sides of the building—and then just as Conrad runs out into the street, a police car and a fire engine arrive at the flaming wreckage of the van. Radford stops in cover—sees Conrad running across the street; sees two alert cops pile out of the police car . . . sees firemen start hosing the van fire . . . sees one of the cops look at the fleeing Conrad, and the other cop look straight this way, almost as if he's looking at Radford but actually he's just trying to see what Conrad's running away from.

Radford reluctantly gives it up and slips back into the alley.

In Commander Clay's office, Dr. Trong and his wife face Denise Clay. Dr. Trong is angry. Clay is impatient. "Doctor—Major—whatever, get to the bottom line. I'm busy here."

"Bottom line, Commander, he couldn't have done the second assassination because he was right in our kitchen eating breakfast."

Mrs. Trong gives her husband a dry look.

Clay is stony. "Who's going to believe that? They know you're on his side."

"I don't care what they believe. I'm telling you to believe it."

Clay nods. "I could buy him for the first one. But this second murder—it's political and it's organized . . . But he's our only lead, and we've got to get him . . . If you're telling the truth, you harbored a capital fugitive and you could do time as an accessory."

"Not if he's innocent, I won't. And some people will have a lot of egg on their faces."

Dickinson bursts in. "They spotted him . . ."

Dr. and Mrs. Trong hold their breath. Clay whips toward the door; Dickinson restrains her. "—And they lost him . . ."

Clay reacts—big exasperation—and Trong smiles at his wife, and she makes a face at him.

Outside a sporting goods store Radford parks his cycle and takes out the photo from Conrad's apartment—the group photo of shooters, emphasizing Harry and the trophy. He takes it into the store and shows the picture to a saleswoman, asks questions, gets an answer: "Sure, I know that guy. Lives out on Highland . . ."

In Harry's kitchen Anne talks on the phone with repressed fury. "It's too far, that's all. How many more wet operations are you people setting up? . . . I don't care. Don't talk to me like that. You find Damon. Find him right now and tell him either he calls me tonight or I go to the police."

She hangs it up violently and that's when she looks around and sees Radford, standing frighteningly near her.

" 'Wet operations'—I thought that one went out with the Iron Curtain."

Anne tries to shrink away. Radford moves in on her. "Or is it what you do under the covers with guys you're setting up for a frame?"

"C.W.—I didn't know. Oh God, how can I explain this? They just wanted your fingerprints on the rifle. They said they were going to give you a head start."

Radford whips the nutcracker around her throat.

"Head start to where? . . . Where's Harry?"

She doesn't comprehend. "Who?"

He whips out the now-crumpled photo of the gun-club group and shoves it in front of her, forcing her to look at it.

"Your husband."

Anne goes weak. "He's not my husband. And his name's not Harry."

"This is his house. You live here."

"I—I got a divorce. From my fourth husband. I had no place to go. I never really had any kind of a home—you know? He offered, and I moved in here with him—I never meant to stay."

"They sicced you on me. I was the perfect sucker, wasn't I?"

"C.W., I—" She's very scared. "What do you want?"

Radford taps the photograph. "For openers—him."

After nightfall behind his gun shop Harry is showing a sleek new limousine to a customer in a chauffeur's uniform who looks like a bodyguard for a crime boss. "Yes sir, state-of-the-art. Three eighths-inch Teflon armor plate." He moves around, pointing out features on the new luxury limo. Not far away is parked an older limo. "All bullet-proof glass. Not just the windows. Even the mirrors."

Radford watches this, from concealment in a doorway down the alley. He's got Anne, not gently; he holds one hand around her mouth.

Harry kicks a tire. "Bullet-proof steel cord in the side-walls and tread. I'm tellin' you it'll take an anti-tank ba-zooka to stop this mother."

The customer says, "Okay . . . When?"

"She's all gassed up. I'm just waiting on that upholstery. Be in tomorrow, for sure Friday."

"Well then you call me and I'll come pay the balance. Right?"

"Right. Sure. You got it, my man."

The customer goes to the older limo and drives away while Harry takes the keys out of the new limo's ignition and pockets them—Radford particularly notices this ac-tion—and then Harry goes into the shop's back door.

Radford, carrying the nutcracker, pulls Anne with him, approaching the same door.

Inside the gun shop Harry crosses to the front window. He pulls back a slat of the blind to peer suspiciously out into the night, cupping his hand around his eye to see better.

Out there a police patrol car slowly cruises forward.

Harry lets the blind fall back into place and turns, and that's when he sees—Radford, looming, moving silently for-ward—almost on top of Harry—nutcracker lifted . . . Harry reacts: recognition; dread . . .

Two cops are in the slow-moving patrol car. The cop in the passenger seat sees something, switches on the car's swivel spotlight and swings the beam around until it re-veals—a motorcycle parked in the deep shadows of the alley.

"Hey." Softly.

The car stops. The cops get out and approach the motorcycle, with flashlights. One whispers to the other with suppressed excitement: "We got it! Put in a squeal!"

Harry is backing up, flustered, with Radford pursuing him, not hurrying, keeping within arm's length, swinging the nutcracker at his side, holding it by the end of one stick, holding Anne's arm with his other hand. Harry nearly falls over the tripod-mounted machine gun. He's talking very fast:

"You get nothing out of me, hear? You spilled your guts out, but you don't get a thing out of me. Go ahead. Chickenshit bastard. Fucking traitor."

Radford swings the nutcracker underarm. Hinged on its lanyards, the nightstick flicks up into Harry's crotch . . . Harry's eyes bug out; he doubles over in shrieking agony . . . Falls down by the machine gun . . . Radford stands above him, swinging the nutcracker gently like a pendulum. Harry slowly focuses on it, his eyes hypnotically following it back and forth. When it begins to swing toward him he yells: "No! Hey!"

The pendulum stops. Radford waits, looking down—patient as a Buddha.

Harry licks his lips. After an interval Radford says quietly, "Okay. The hard way." The nutcracker begins its pendulum swings again.

"All right, all right. Wait. You want to know—the next assassination. Next target . . . It's Clay. Commander Clay."

Anne looks down at him, still able to be shocked. "Oh, Jesus Christ. You bastard."

Radford says, "Commander Clay. Sure. She's a real cop. She can't be bought, so she's in the way." Abruptly he crouches and gathers Harry toward him. Nose to nose.

Harry's glance breaks away.

But Radford isn't letting up. "Who are you people?"

"We're just trying to—"

"Give me a name. The head man. Who's on top of the shitpile?"

And the nutcracker whips around Harry's throat and begins to tighten. Harry tries to pry it away with his hands but the choking leverage continues to tighten . . .

Anne makes an abrupt decision. "Damon."

Radford looks up at her.

She says, "It's Damon Vickers."

Harry coughs. He's relieved now that it's out; he's got nothing to lose by going along. His whisper is hoarse. "Yeah. Colonel—Colonel Vickers."

It takes a minute for Radford to absorb this. "The White House?"

"He ain't the White House, Christ's sake. He just works there."

Radford looks at Anne, then at Harry. They both have the exhausted look of people who've given up their most dangerous secret; he's got to believe they're telling the truth. "Where does he live?"

Several police cars silently roll up and stop, forming a perimeter around the gun shop. Quietly, cops on foot steer pedestrian passers-by away. As cops barricade themselves, surrounding the gun shop, Commander Clay gets out of her car and meets Dickinson. They talk in hushed voices.

She says, "We've had trouble with him before. Automatic weapons, illegal sales."

"We think Radford's in there with him. They've got a real arsenal in there. Keep your heads down."

* * * * *

Harry is on his knees. Anne fidgets. Radford flexes the nutcracker. "Tell me about it. Tell me about your outfit."

Harry hesitates; Anne begins to speak; and they all stop, frozen by the sound of Commander Clay's voice amplified on a bullhorn outside: "This is the police. You in the gun shop—we have you surrounded. You've got one minute to come out with your hands in the air."

Radford's eyes dart from front to back. He settles back hard on his heels, his face bleak. Harry's grunt overlaps the bullhorn speech: "Holy shit!" Anne doesn't know which way to turn. Radford finally swings toward the front, where the bullhorn sound comes from, and in that instant while his back is turned, Harry swiftly feeds a belt of ammunition into the tripod-mounted machine gun.

Radford catches this corner-of-the-eye action just in time and dives to one side, knocking Anne protectively to the floor just as Harry begins to shoot—full-rate automatic fire—the bullets shattering the big levelor blind and the front plate-glass window . . .

Cops cover their heads and hunker down as machine gun bullets from the shop spray the street, ricocheting everywhere, smashing car windows, creating havoc . . .

Commander Clay is rock steady. "Tear gas—now!"

And Dickinson simultaneously shouts, "Open fire. Fire at will. Son of a bitch!"

Clay's angry "No!" and her sharp look are too late to stop the chaos. Cops open up with revolvers and shotguns. One of them fires a tear gas grenade from a flare pistol into the store.

Inside, the grenade explodes in a puff of evil smoke near the front of the shop. Harry is blazing away, having lunatic fun, overheating the machine gun. Police bullets return the fire, banging around inside the shop, and Radford shoves Anne toward the cover of the counter and scrambles to follow. Tear gas rolls back toward them. All three begin to cough. Radford growls at Harry: "You gun-happy son of a bitch!"

A blaze of police bullets shatters glass everywhere. Anne goes down, shot. Radford tries to protect her. "Give her a hand here!"

Harry ignores him—maybe doesn't even hear him; must have adrenalin pumping so loud he can't hear a thing. His machine gun swivels back and forth, raking the street. And runs empty.

Radford lowers Anne gently to the floor.

Harry with deranged glee yanks open a hidden floorboard compartment, heaves out a goddamn flame thrower, ignites the sumbitch and starts to shoot a long spout of deadly flame out through the smoke toward the street.

Under the smoke Radford is trying to rouse Anne but he sees that she's dead. Finally—coughing desperately—he's driven back, stumbling back into the fog of tear-gas and smoke.

The roaring blast of flame hoses out from the smoky smashed front of the shop. Cops fall back, desperately seeking cover. And the idiot's flamethrower has set half the shop on fire; it's blazing dreadfully.

Inside the thick smoke, coughing, Radford pounces on Harry and wrestles the flamethrower away from him and turns it off.

Harry shoves him away. Both men are coughing hard.

Harry yells like a spoiled child whose toy has been taken away. He jumps up and down, throwing a tantrum.

Radford yells at him. "Get down, you stupid—"

But the warning is too late. Harry goes down, cut to pieces in a fusillade of police gunfire.

Amid ragged aftervolleys of police gunfire the smoke billows from the smashed front of the shop. Finally Clay, very weary, stands up. "Cease fire, for God's sake."

Total stillness now. An expectant hush. Cops begin to peer out from behind cover . . .

Now several cars in convoy arrive—Vickers and his G-men get out of them; Vickers deploys his troops with hand motions. Vickers as usual is dressed like a suit mannequin in an expensive shop window.

Dickinson says dryly to Clay, "Cavalry to the rescue right in the nick of time, like always." As the feds approach, Dickinson gets up and greets them in some disgust, addressing his insult to Vickers: "Here's Ken. Where's Barbie?"

"Don't fart around with me, cop."

Clay ignores him; she says to Dickinson, "Put another tear-gas round in there. I want to be sure."

Another tear-gas grenade lobs into the smoke. There's the muffled puff of its explosion inside the inferno.

Vickers stands with his hands in his pockets, looking dubious. "You sure he's in there?"

Clay says, "Let's wait and see."

Dickinson says, "Nothing alive in there by now but maybe a few cockroaches."

Vickers thinks a moment, visibly. Then he pulls a riot shotgun out of the nearest cop car and, carrying it, circles around toward the back of the shop. The smoke thickens. Flames appear; the building is a goner. Everyone waits . . .

Behind the gun shop the armored limousine stands near the back door and Vickers sees cops farther back, in a rough perimeter around the back of the shop, watching nervously. Vickers moves in closer to the building, shotgun in hand, working from cover to cover. Smoke pours from the building, beginning to obscure it, but Vickers can make out the back door. It stands wide open.

Radford comes out on his belly, holding a wet towel across his mouth and nose, snaking under the smoke. Billows envelop the armored limo, hiding it, and he slides through it into the driver's seat of the limo.

Vickers is squinting against the smoke and flames, trying to see the back of the shop. He peers intensely, then suddenly reacts as, like a monster from hell, the armored limo comes roaring out of the smoke straight at him.

Vickers blasts it with the shotgun.

It has no effect.

He drops the shotgun and now stands with feet spread, revolver lifted in both hands, fearlessly shooting at the windshield as the limo roars straight at him.

The limo roars forward. Bullets bounce off the glass.

It veers at the last minute and slithers past Vickers, fishtailing into an alley. Vickers swivels and pulls the trigger again but his revolver is empty . . .

Around him, cops are blazing away at the fleeing car. Hit but unscathed, the limo skids away, bullets ricocheting off its armored body.

All around the burning shop, police cars and government cars begin to peel out in pursuit. Vickers leaps into one of them, and it nearly collides with arriving fire engines . . .

Radford flees in the armored limo, pursued by an army whose bullets bounce off the armored metal and glass and rubber.

★ ★ ★ ★ ★

Into a six-point intersection, late at night, police cars converge from every street and alley until they create a tangled gridlock. Everyone stops. Cops and feds emerge from cars—some furious, some simply bewildered.

Clay and Vickers get out of adjacent cars. Clay on her cellular phone. She's looking up at a helicopter that swoops overhead; she's talking to its pilot. "Which one?" She gets an answer, glances at Vickers and points to a parking garage.

Solid buildings all around the intersection. No way out except the streets, which are clogged with cop cars. Various stores (closed for the night), office buildings, restaurants, a theatre with surprised patrons at the front door watching the Keystone Kop activity.

Vickers and Clay walk slowly toward the garage, ushering cops in with arm signals. Heavily armed, the detachment deploys into the building.

In the garage, on a second-level ramp by the Disabled parking slot, crouches the limo. A sad, silent, bullet-smeared mess, but nonetheless intact.

Dickinson walks over to it, uses a gloved hand to open its door—he's ready to shoot if somebody's in there but he doubts it and he's right; it's empty. He raises his voice in weary summons: "Over here."

From the hallway of a restaurant-bar on the top floor of a high-rise, Radford has a splendid view of the city. He's on a pay phone by the rest-room doors. "Like to leave a message for Commander Clay . . . I know she's not in her office right now—"

Down through the plate glass he can just make out Commander Clay as she emerges on foot with Dickinson from the ramp-entrance of the garage. Radford says into the phone, "This is C. W. Radford. So take this down and get it straight." He sees Clay and Dickinson cross to a police car; Clay takes out its radio mike and begins to broadcast.

Into the phone Radford is saying, "Tell Denise Clay she's the next target for assassination. Tell her the boss honcho behind the assassinations is Colonel Vickers. That's not a mistake. I don't give a shit if *you* believe me. Colonel Damon Vickers. Tell her I said it."

Down below, he sees Vickers join Clay; Vickers says something—probably sarcastic—and Vickers and Dickinson get into an angry shoving match, with Clay trying to calm them down.

Radford walks away from the phone.

The Vickers house at dawn is secluded to the point of isolation, manicured, exurban, surrounded by flowing meadows. From a hedgerow of trees Radford studies the place. It's just past dawn. Nothing stirs.

While the sun rises, Radford waits with infinite patience, moving a few inches around the bole of his tree each time the sun begins to reach around to him. He's not doing anything at all—just watching the house.

And an End . . .

In the open maw of a high barn somewhere in back hills a camouflage-painted Humvee stands squat and forbidding, like a sentry across the opening. Vickers walks in past it and sizes up the six men assembled: Conrad, Gootch, Wojack, Curly, Moe and Larry. They're assembling automatic weapons that they've just cleaned and triple-checked. Moe's is an Uzi submachine gun. Wojack, in neat Ivy League duds, sits on a crate, wiping down his 308 with the studied care of a perfectionist.

Vickers says without preamble, "They have a few questions for me."

Wojack says, "Well they came to the right place. You're the one with all the answers."

Ignoring him, Vickers says to Conrad, "Seems they got a phone call from Radford . . . We have to assume those two talked their heads off in the gun shop."

Conrad says, "I told Harry that blonde would get him done in."

Gootch says, "So where's Radford?"

For some reason this all amuses Wojack. "He was all used up. Didn't care if he lived or died. It never occurred to you that you back him into a corner, he'd turn and fight. Poor bastard. They all think he's a deranged homicidal maniac—some animal that needs to be exterminated. And here he's the only innocent son of a bitch in a hun-

286

dred thousand square miles."

Vickers gives him a look, decides it isn't worth the trouble, and turns to Conrad. "We have to assume Radford knows where I live. So that's where he's going to be. You're all coming with me to wait for him."

Gootch says, "What if the cops are there too?"

"Then he'll die while resisting arrest."

Wojack, thumbing cartridges into his rifle one at a time, inspecting each one with practiced care before it slides into the magazine, talks half to himself, with a soft note of derision. "Patriots. Heroes. How do you tell a freedom-fighter from a terrorist without a scorecard?"

Vickers snaps, "I'm paying you for your marksmanship, not your lip."

Wojack shakes his head. "You people amaze me. Don't you ever think of yourselves as the bad guys?"

Vickers answers civilly because he wants a convert. "We've tried working within the system. Hell, I practically am the system, but when you're surrounded by idiots it's no good. The world gets more dangerous every day and those morons just keep playing pork-barrel politics as if . . . Well we're dealing with monsters who don't play by rules. Assassination's the only way to get at them. You cut off the head of the menace. And you keep cutting off each new head as it emerges, until they learn to change."

Wojack slams the rifle's bolt shut on the final cartridge. "Sure. I mean, you're not trying to steal the deed to the ranch or anything. Bad guys never see themselves as bad guys."

Conrad says, "And who the hell are you? Some hired two-bit hit-man!"

"It's my trade. I'm a craftsman . . . At least I know what I am."

★ ★ ★ ★ ★

The room is an office-library. Lots of high-polished woodwork. Radford stands just inside a kicked-open set of French doors. He's looking at the display case beside him and the framed photographs on the leather-topped desk. Photos of Vickers in uniform getting medals pinned on his chest; Vickers in front of the White House; Vickers at a podium, flanked by American flags, addressing a crowd, with a big caption "Col. Damon Vickers," and a big banner above his head that reads: "America Now!"

Radford has the nutcracker in one hand, a revolver in the other. He looks all around, ready for anything. Nothing stirs. He rams forward out of the room.

His charge takes him through a hallway into a big kitchen; all the mod cons. The stove is a gas range. There's a center-island counter. Nobody in the room until Radford reels in from the hall. He looks around, picks a direction arbitrarily, plunges through a door . . .

Conrad drives a luxury sedan down the blacktop highway; Vickers and Wojack are in it with him. The other guys—Gootch, Curly, Larry, Moe—are in the Humvee four-by-four behind them. And there's something ominous simply in the way the two-vehicle convoy rolls relentlessly forward, not speeding at all but somehow implacable, as if they'd run right over any innocent pedestrian who happed to be in their way and then they'd just keep right on going without even glancing back.

Radford prowls into a dining room. He hears a sound of approaching vehicles so he goes to a window and looks out and sees the two vehicles approach, crunching their way up the driveway, in no hurry. From this angle he can see the

smashed-open French doors of the house, so he's not surprised when the car and the Humvee stop some distance
short of the place and seven guys get out. Radford recognizes Vickers, who examines the place with field glasses,
then makes hand signals and leads the other six in a
spreading-wide skirmish line, converging toward the house
on foot, most of them carrying automatic weapons except
for one Ivy League–looking man who hangs back, holding a
308 rifle at the ready but not joining in the war-game ma-
neuvering. That one watches the troops with a pose that
conveys sardonic bemusement.

Radford fades back into the house.

Vickers sends Conrad around one end of the house.
Conrad goes, walking straight up as if invulnerable to
enemy bullets—he knows Radford's not going to shoot him
without warning.

Vickers looks back, sees Wojack ambling forward with
his rifle ready, and angrily waves Wojack toward the opposite end of the house. Wojack shrugs and turns that way,
watchful but not enjoying this part of the game.

Radford squeezes himself into a narrow space so con-
fining and so completely dark that he can hardly breathe.
He begins to sweat—claustrophobia . . .

Without making a sound Gootch appears in the den, gun
first, framed in the smashed-open French doors, and comes
in, watching everything at once. Behind him the others curl
into the room and fan out fast—Larry, Moe, Curly. Then
Vickers enters behind them. Vickers signals with his automatic weapon toward the far door, and Gootch sidles out
through it . . .

★ ★ ★ ★ ★

In the kitchen Gootch and Curly and Moe poke under counters and table, nobody making a sound.

In his narrow dark enclosure Radford is really starting to come unglued, but with a tremendous effort of will he remains absolutely motionless.

At one end of the house Conrad eases up to a window and looks in. He doesn't see anything exciting.

At the opposite end of the building Wojack hangs back in the shade of a tree, studying the turf. He's a sniper, not a close-quarters brawler; far as he's concerned, snooping in closed quarters where you could get ambushed is not included in the price of his ticket. He stays by the tree.

Moe is stooping to pull a door open and look in the cabinet space under the kitchen sink when behind him a broom-cabinet pops open and Radford plunges out, gasping for air. Radford whacks Moe's wrist with his nutcracker.
"Hey—!"
The nutcracker loosens Moe's hold on the Uzi and whips the weapon away before Moe can figure out what's happening.
Gootch and Curly wheel—Curly opens fire with his automatic weapon before he's had time to see who he's shooting at, and his bullets cut Moe in half.
Radford levels the Uzi; Curly ducks down behind the island counter . . . Gootch, facing the muzzle of Radford's Uzzi, backs out into the hallway . . . Radford pulls the fridge door open and uses it for armor-plate while Curly shoots at him from behind the counter. Radford returns the

fire. Bullets chatter and scream.

In the dining room Gootch comes windmilling back. Larry and Conrad run forward to join him. Vickers comes in from a hall door, seeing it all, understanding it instantly. Gootch yells desperately, "He's a banana truck!" while in the kitchen Curly, on his knees, dodges around the end of the island counter, looking for a shot—and suddenly Radford comes vaulting over the counter, kicks the submachine gun out of Curly's hand and slams Curly upside the head with the free-swinging end of his nutcracker. It lays Curly out cold.

. . . Gootch returns into the kitchen, followed by Conrad and Larry; and now suddenly Radford from behind the door is all over them—uses his nutcracker as a flail, holding one stick and swirling the other, bashing Gootch and Larry, not wanting to use the submachine gun that's in his other hand; but Conrad is very fast—deflects the nutcracker by parrying with his gun, then (as Radford lifts the Uzi, ready to use it) wheels back outside with Gootch and Larry.

From the dining room side, Conrad slams the door. Immediately he and Larry and Gootch start firing bursts through the closed door. In no time at all their bullets splinter it, turning it into kindling.

Radford crouches behind the counter. Bullets come in through the closed door, busting the kitchen all to hell. Curly, dazed on the kitchen floor, groans and stirs; bullets are busting him all to pieces. The bullets also tear up Moe's body.

Vickers yanks open a window—shouts outside: "Wojack—get your ass in here."

Outside Vickers' house several police cars arrive fast. Wojack, seeing them, dodges away from the tree with his

308 rifle and hurries into the house.

As Clay, Dickinson and cops spill out of the cars, they hear a brutal racket of automatic fire from inside the house. Dickinson says, "The hell?"

Vickers, having seen the approaching cops, shouts at the three guys but Gootch and Larry are still blazing away through the shattered door and Conrad is reloading and they don't hear him. Behind them, Vickers slips quickly out of the room.

Gootch and Larry stop to refill their weapons. That's when—in the abrupt silence—Conrad glimpses Radford—a faint movement beyond the barrier of the island counter—and Conrad opens fire viciously and—the bullets bust up the gas range.

The range explodes—and the fire rapidly begins to spread.

Radford, trapped behind cover against the counter, looks up and around, seeking a way out.

Wojack comes into the den through the busted French doors and stops to consider his options.

Through a kitchen window Radford comes hurtling out of the fire, falls to the ground, lands rolling, picks himself up, runs for cover. He's still got the nutcracker but not the Uzi.

Behind him, inside the kitchen, Conrad kicks down what's left of the door and bursts in, crouching, spraying bullets in an arc. The place is on fire. Gootch and Larry are right behind him. And they see there's nobody here except the bodies of Curly and Moe. Conrad wheels to the busted-out window—and sees several cops running toward the house, led by Denise Clay.

Behind Commander Clay runs Don the waiter—now wearing a police uniform—lifting his revolver to aim at Clay's back . . .

Dickinson, behind them both, sees what Don's doing. In a flash—from the hip—he shoots. Don is hit; falls . . . Dickinson and a cop, running past, slow briefly to make sure Don is no longer a danger. Don is dead. They run on.

From inside the den, aiming out through the broken-open French doors, Wojack coolly draws a bead on the approaching Clay.

Clay sees the rifle aimed at her—hasn't got a prayer . . .

Suddenly in a single startling motion Radford looms up through the French doors and slams Wojack to one side with the nutcracker.

Wojack falls back; the rifle shoots harmlessly into the air. Wojack works the bolt to load a new shell into the chamber but Radford kicks the rifle out of his hands . . . Slams Wojack again with the nutcracker. It dazes Wojack; he falls back against the wall.

Radford growls, "They're gonna want you alive."

And then he wheels to run into the house, as Clay approaches the window, having seen it all. "Radford—wait!" But he's gone.

Dickinson rushes in ahead of her and picks up the discarded 308 rifle and claps handcuffs on Wojack.

Larry, Gootch and Conrad are backing away from the kitchen's rapidly spreading fire, into the dining room. Larry shouts, "Where's my brother?"

Conrad shoves him. "He bought it. Haul ass outa here." He steers Larry quickly toward the exit—as Clay and Dickinson come slamming in. Conrad lifts his gun but

Dickinson (with the 308 rifle) shoots first . . . Conrad goes down . . . Larry, moving like an automaton, lifts his automatic weapon and aims it at Clay—and Clay, regretting it, shoots Larry down . . . Dickinson shakes his head. "Jesus H. Christ."

Radford spills out the front door, toting the nutcracker. He's searching for Vickers; he runs along the burning side of the house. Two cops hold the stunned Wojack, handcuffed, in custody . . . Radford wheels around a corner, to find himself face-to-face with Clay and Dickinson.

And just then, behind the two cops, appears Vickers.

He comes up alongside Clay, every inch the federal man. Running a colossal bluff. He trains his gun triumphantly on Radford. "All right, scumbag. War's over."

But Denise Clay pushes Vickers' gun aside. "Not him. You. Damon Vickers, you are under arrest . . ."

And suddenly the muzzle of Vickers' gun is lodged against Clay's throat and he's making her drop her gun and he's dragging her away, using her as a shield . . .

They freeze: Radford, Dickinson and the other cops—as Vickers backs away with his hostage . . . The house burns high . . .

Vickers drags Clay into the nearest car and turns the key in its ignition, all the while holding his revolver hard against Clay's throat.

Dickinson lifts his gun. He's going to open fire

Radford says, "Nobody shoots that good. What if you miss?"

Dickinson lowers the gun. Cops hold their fire; they watch helpless frustration as the car begins to back away.

Radford speaks very calmly—icy. "But he'll kill her anyway! Only chance to save her is now." And he plucks the

308 rifle from Dickinson's grasp and in the same smooth synchronous motion drops to one knee and takes careful aim at the retreating car while it swirls backward, turning nose-out, ready for getaway. Dickinson thinks about making a move, decides against it, doesn't know what the hell to do, and Radford, silhouetted against the flames of the burning house, steadies his aim. Like a rock.

The car slithers for purchase. It's a very tricky moving target.

In the car Vickers removes the revolver from Clay's neck long enough to whip the shift lever from reverse to drive, and that is when Radford squeezes off his shot—quick but steady and careful.

It hits square on the skull. Vickers' head snaps to one side; he is instantly unconscious.

Clay grabs the revolver out of Vickers' limp hand, and switches off the car's ignition.

The car stops. Clay closes her eyes and breathes in, very deep, and out, all the way.

Dickinson follows Radford to the car, as Clay gets out and comes around—and looks Radford in the eye. Radford looks right back. In back of them the house burns.

Vickers is flopped back limp against the headrest, his head lolling, bleeding from the head wound. Clay opens the door and picks up Vickers' wrist, feeling for a pulse.

Dickinson gently takes the 308 and the nutcracker from Radford. Radford doesn't resist.

A couple of cops bring Wojack along, handcuffed.

Clay says, in surprise, about Vickers, "He's alive."

Radford says, "Yeah. I want to hear him explain all this."

Wojack murmurs, "And a fascinating tale it'll be."

Dickinson yaps at a cop: "Call paramedics."

Wojack looks up at Clay. "Tell you what. I'll swap you the whole story for immunity from prosecution. What do you say?"

Radford and Clay meet each other's gaze—now slowly they both begin to smile. She takes his hand in both of hers. A warm bond.

Vickers' house colors the sky red with its leaping flames . . .

Dr. Trong parks his Jeep in that same spot across the street from the big lawn leading up to the Senator's house—gardens, tranquility, solid establishment, wealth.

In the passenger seat Radford looks neat and refreshed in a new suit. The two men exchange glances. Dr. Trong nods, indicating the house.

Radford hesitates, then gets out of the Jeep and, with visible misgivings, walks toward the house, then looks back.

Dr. Trong just watches him.

Radford turns to face the door, and rings the bell.

It opens. Dr. Trong sees Dorothy there. At first she's shocked. Then with a wonderful smile of disbelieving happiness she invites him in. He goes inside, and the door closes.

Dr. Trong smiles, and drives away.